Praise for

A *Washington Post* Nota

'Lewis is major' – **Max** *a*
The Road to Perdition

'*GBH* is a novel as direct as it is stunning... I reckon he knew a good deal of what he was writing about from very close – perhaps dangerously so. That leaps out of the work immediately' – **Derek Raymond, author of the *Factory* novels**

'A pulp-fiction triumph worthy of Jim Thompson or James Ellroy. I can't remember the last time I turned pages so eagerly... his work cuts to the bone, both literally *and* metaphysically' – **John Powers, NPR's *Fresh Air***

'One of the most coldly brilliant crime novels you will ever read... a mesmerizing story of power, love, hubris and betrayal – but, above all, the portrait of what one might call a tragic villain... Complicated in plot, propulsive in its narrative pace, beautifully structured, it is a book you'll want to read'
– **Michael Dirda, *The Washington Post***

'*GBH* shows Lewis stayed true to his unnerving vision and voice to the end, even while pushing it into farther-out places. This hitherto-obscure book's resurrection should further enhance the Lewis legend' – **Tom Nolan, *The Wall Street Journal***

'Ted Lewis wrote brilliantly about ruthless men clinging to their humanity with mordant wit and misguided but powerful senses of honor. That these quintessentially British novels are finally available in the US is real cause for celebration'
– **Scott Phillips, *New York Times* bestselling author of *The Ice Harvest***

'A must-read for all noir fans'
– ***The Strand Magazine***

'His final novel and masterpiece... you won't find many nice guys upon these pages' – *Dayton Daily News*

'Aristotle when he defined tragedy mandated that a tragic hero must fall from a great height... but he never imagined the kind of roadside motels of James M. Cain or saw the smokestacks rise in the Northern English industrial hell of Ted Lewis's *Get Carter*' – **Denis Lehane**

'Lewis remains a sharp social anatomist of the hopelessness and soul-sucking dinginess of his era. Starting with [*Get Carter*], Lewis sketched the horror of a Britain where home was the kitchen sink, the sodden bar towel, the decrepit industrial landscape' – **Barnes & Noble Review**

'Lewis gives new meaning to suspense with this masterly tale of a man's downfall and the bloody trail he leaves behind' – *Publishers Weekly*, **Starred Review**

'That bleak tale [*Get Carter*] of revenge became an influential crime-fiction classic, and deservedly so – but for some fans, his swan song [*GBH*] was an even bigger literary achievement' – *Booklist*, **Starred Review**

'The dark storyline is punctuated by Lewis's bleak narrative and crackling dialogue, the plot full of foreboding, the climax an orgy of violence. And when you finally put the book down, you'll need a breather. They simply don't get any better than that' – **Jim Napier, *Reviewing the Evidence***

'While [*Get Carter*] will likely always be the most noted of Ted Lewis's nine novels, *GBH*, the final book Lewis published, is his masterwork' – *The Life Sentence*

'It is like a sip of absinthe on a three-day empty stomach, a book that will chill you and ricochet your thought process at least temporarily, if not permanently' – **Bookreporter.com**

BOOKS BY TED LEWIS

Get Carter (first published as *Jack's Return Home*)
Jack Carter's Law
Jack Carter and the Mafia Pigeon
Plender
Billy Rags
Boldt
All the Way Home and All the Night Through
The Rabbit
GBH

PLENDER

TED LEWIS

NO EXIT PRESS

This edition published in 2020
by No Exit Press,
an imprint of Oldcastle Books Ltd,
Harpenden, UK
noexit.co.uk
@noexitpress

A catalogue record for this book is available from the British Library

ISBN 978 978-0-85730-281-6 (Print)
ISBN 978-0-85730-282-3 (epub)

Typeset in 11.3pt Minion Pro
by Avocet Typeset, Bideford, Devon, EX39 2BP
Printed in Great Britain by Severn, Gloucester

For more information about Crime Fiction go to crimetime.co.uk /
@crimetimeuk

PLENDER

INTRODUCTION
by Nick Triplow

An unnamed hitman takes aim. Squeezes the trigger. A rifle shot echoes across the black sand. '*He lies on the beach. The waves lap around his head. A small trickle of blood pours out of the hole in his temple. He's dead.*'

So ends *Get Carter*, the landmark British gangster film adapted and directed by Mike Hodges from Ted Lewis's 1970 crime debut, *Jack's Return Home*.

Lewis's post-Carter novel, *Plender*, published in November 1971, is a story of murder, pornography, blackmail and retribution set in the dockside streets of Hull and suburban Humberside. Lewis twists autobiography into fiction, scratching the surface of respectability, breaking apart the cosy expectations of conventional crime fiction. In the process, he enhanced his reputation as a writer who wrote graphically and believably about characters at society's squalid margins.

Mike Hodges remembers receiving an early proof of *Plender* with a view to a second adaptation. He turned it down, rejecting provincial grime for the clean air and blue skies of Malta to shoot the black comedy, *Pulp*. (French director Eric Barbier would film a largely faithful version of *Plender* as *Le Serpent* in 2007.)

In five further books between 1973 and 1977, including two Carter prequels – the claustrophobic *Jack Carter's Law* and the disappointing *Jack Carter and the Mafia Pigeon* – Lewis continued his pursuit of the Black Novel. He wrote for the long-running BBC police drama, *Z-Cars*, which led to a commission to write for *Doctor Who*. But his scripts were rejected, considered too dark for the programme's early evening audience. Unable to repeat the commercial success of *Get Carter* and with his personal life descending into chaos, Lewis turned increasingly to drink.

In failing health and seemingly with little left to lose, Lewis exploited his own deepening sense of dislocation and alcoholic paranoia for what would be his final novel, *GBH*, in 1980. A fractured narrative reflects the psyche of porn trade gangster, George Fowler, on the run, hiding out in isolation on the Lincolnshire coast. In a brutal climax, Fowler comes to represent that part of Lewis which, in the decade since *Jack's Return Home*, had been personally and professionally driven to the brink. *GBH* shows him staring into the abyss. It is Ted Lewis's masterpiece.

For too long it seemed Lewis had been denied a place in the roll of influential British crime writers. *Get Carter* aside, his books were out of print. Yet these novels redefined the possibilities of British noir fiction. Unflinching violence, evocative connections with landscape, and the reek of the authentically domestic; the brutal and banal trading with the dark, sexual, weak-minded and obsessive.

To have *Plender* and *GBH* back in print in his home country feels like justice served. As Lewis's literary hero Raymond Chandler wrote, 'The test of a writer is whether you want to read him again years after he should by the rules be dated.' Alongside *Get Carter*, *Plender* and *GBH* provide the definitive answer.

Nick Triplow is the author of *Getting Carter: Ted Lewis and the Birth of Brit Noir*.

PLENDER

The double glazing shuddered.

A grey wet wind screamed up the estuary and into the city centre, rocked trolley buses and swept old cabbage leaves along the cobbled docksides. Dirty barges shifted surlily on the greasy swell. Windows of workmen's cafés were blank with inside steam. Raindrops flicked spitefully into the faces of the Saturday afternoon shoppers. Icy neon exaggerated the chilly faces of the shuffling crowds in the teatime indigo.

But where I was, behind the double-glazing, twelve storeys up, it was warm and cosy and nice. I stood in front of the plate-glass and looked down at the crowds and thought how nice it was to be twelve storeys up, in the warm, out of the wet.

I turned away from the window and walked over to my beautifully plain, beautifully Swedish desk and took a cigarette out of the rosewood box and lit it with the table lighter. I smiled as I clicked the mechanism; the trick was that down one side it was wooden, carved in the shape of a woman, except for the tits, they were in silver and you pressed them to operate the lighter and the flame would spurt out from between the figure's legs. I smiled out of habit, the habit of smiling along with people who reacted to the gadget for the first time.

I put the lighter back and sat down behind my desk and carried on staring out of the big window. Speckled with rain the window twinkled darkly with the city's afternoon lights and the wet warped images of cranes flowed down the glass. Beyond the cranes I could see the broad river the colour of stone and across on the other, rural, bank three miles away, sparse lights winked fitfully, delineating the flatness of the neighbouring county. Through the blue gloom I could just make out the faint lights of the opposite pier; and at the end of the pier a concentrated cluster of lights that began to move very slowly out into the river. I stared at the moving lights as they grew in size, as the ferry got closer to the northern bank. Any moment, I thought, he'll ring. He always does. Too soon, every time.

Rain rattled and wind gusted and the phone rang. I let it ring twelve times before I picked up the receiver.

'Plender speaking,' I said.

'Is she there yet?' said the voice at the other end.

'Not yet, Mr Froy,' I said. 'The ferry'll be docking in about ten minutes and then it'll take them –'

'Yes, yes, all right. How did it go at the other end?'

'Fine.'

'No press?'

'No press.'

'How did she behave?'

'I'll put it in my report. But you needn't worry. It was in our favour that she was in love with the herbert. She won't say a dicky bird.'

'Let us hope not.' Froy's cold fishy voice seemed to recede down the phone. 'Phone me the minute they arrive.'

'Yes, Mr Froy,' I said.

The line went dead. I put the phone back on its cradle. You old fart, Froy. You terrible old fart. You think you can trust me. If you only knew.

I looked at my watch. There was plenty of time yet. So I opened a drawer in my desk and took out a large stiff backed notebook. I flipped through the pages of names and numbers. Some of the names had ticks by them, some of them were underlined in red. I ran my finger down a column of names until I came to one which was underlined in red. Then I reached for the phone and dialled the number that went with the name and waited until the receiver was lifted at the other end.

'Hopper speaking,' a voice said; a voice short, sharp, and to the point.

'It's Saturday,' I said.

The voice at the other end altered its tone.

'You said you wouldn't call me here. You promised.'

'We did say Friday, and then when I didn't hear from you, well, I thought, what's a day. I can wait a *day*, but then...'

'It's been difficult. I can't explain now. But I can let you have it on Monday.'

'I'm sorry,' I said. 'I'm afraid that won't do. I'd like it tomorrow. Tomorrow morning.'

'That's out of the question. I've...'

I sighed. It was quite incredible how exactly alike they all sounded. I said:

'The usual place, Mr Hopper. Between ten and five past.'

There was a silence, then a sound that told me he'd be there. Then the line went dead.

I dialled another number. The receiver was lifted.

'Yes?'

'Plender here.'

'*Mr* Plender. What a time to ring. I was just watching me rugby.'

'Never mind that.'

'Never mind that, he says. Gawd, a girl's got to have some little pleasures in life!'

'I need you tonight.'

'What for?'

'Don't come that. You know what for.'

'Yes, but what *for*?'

'A new one. I'm meeting him at nine in Peggy's bar.'

'So?'

'So I'll be introducing him to you, won't I.'

'Oh, no. No. Not tonight you won't. I've got this date.'

'That's right. In Peggy's bar. About nine-thirty.'

'Now look. I'm telling you –'

'Don't be silly, Derek, eh? It just gets a little bit tedious, you know?'

'Camille, Mr Plender. Please. It's Camille.'

'All right, all right. So you've got the time?'

'Yes.'

'And the place?'

'Where else?'

'Good.'

'It's just that I don't like being called… the other.'

'Gurney'll be round your place at eight to set the gear up. Right?'

'Gurney! That pig!'

'And you'd better not get saucy with him, either. I'd get him to break your back for you. Tonight, at any rate.'

'You're horrible.'

'And no drag.'

'We're going to Peggy's, aren't we?'

'No drag.'

'Not even when we get home?'

'That's for you to decide. Personally, I think he's relatively straight. By your standards, that is.'

I put the phone down before I could hear his inevitable whining. I pulled a face. They made me want to vomit, those.

The yellow light on my desk began to flash on and off. I pressed a button and the flashing stopped. A minute or so later another light flashed on and off above the door opposite my desk. I pressed another button. The door opened. A man and a girl came into the room.

'Hello, Colin,' I said. 'How was the journey?'

'The journey was fine, Mr Plender. We got snarled up just below Doncaster but apart from that it was fine.'

Colin Gurney was six feet three inches tall and thirty-four years old. He was going thin on top and the sheepskin and the twills he was wearing had seen better days, but his public-school manner was in just as good nick as ever. Nothing would ever fade that, and he knew it. He also knew how I felt about him, but he had to put up with that. And he knew I enjoyed his putting up with it. I relaxed in my chair. I enjoyed playing out this kind of scene: the indulgent employer, patting the head of the faithful servant in acknowledgement of a job well done. Expansively patronising. Gurney hated it because in his book, it was all the wrong way round. Well, he was right. And that made it all the sweeter.

'Good,' I said. 'I'm glad the journey was fine.'

I looked at the girl. She was dressed exactly the way a first year university student taking liberal studies should be dressed. Apart from that she wasn't bad at all.

'Sit down, Miss Gorton,' I said.

The girl didn't move. I ignored the gesture and lit a cigarette.

'Now then,' I said. 'Let me tell you what will happen if you ever try and get in touch with Mr Nboro again.' I looked into her face. 'A file compiled by this office will be sent to the Police Drugs' Squad. The file contains tapes and photographs made during the course of a party given by Mr Nboro for students and staff of the university. Mr Nboro is heavily featured. Smoking, offering, and talking about pot. Plus airing certain views about student revolution and student participation in the university's administration that would, to say the least, rather unsettle his superiors, not to mention a few of our more crusading national

15

dailies. And it's no good warning him so that he'll keep himself clean just in case I send the lads the file: they'd hate to balls up a chance like this. They wouldn't go empty handed. If you understand me.'

Gurney smiled.

'So there it is. You write to him, phone him, send a go-between, that's it. The file goes and if you think you could get in touch with him without us knowing, ask yourself a question. How did we get the tapes and the pictures?'

The girl just stayed stock still, where she was, just looking at me. I leant back in my chair.

'He might get away with a fine,' I said, 'but then he's not Mick Jagger. He's a Black Power militant in charge of a load of kids. The main thing would be that his career would be busted. And that would damage his ability to function usefully for his party. Which is his principal concern. Above anything else.'

Even that didn't get a reaction.

'Does Nboro know what's happened?' I asked Gurney.

'No, he doesn't know, Mr Plender,' said Gurney, careful to let the irony drip through the surface of necessary politeness. 'I was particularly careful to observe your instructions in that regard.'

'As I hope you were in every regard,' I said.

Gurney reddened slightly.

'Yes, Mr Plender.'

'Did she write the letter herself?'

'Yes.'

'Exactly as instructed?'

'Yes.'

I looked at the girl again.

'So that's that,' I said. 'Now it's home to Daddy.'

'You bastards,' said the girl. 'You bloody bloody bastards.'

Her voice carried the soft accents of school fees but they

hadn't been heavy enough. The Yorkshire was still in her voice. She wasn't the real thing, not like Gurney.

'Don't blame us, blame Daddy,' I said. 'We're just businessmen. You're just cargo to us.'

Very quickly the girl stretched forward and scrabbled the table-lighter off the top of my desk and threw it at me. It hit me on the edge of my jawbone, just below my ear. I didn't move. I just sat there and gritted my teeth and felt the aching pain flow into my face and continued to stare at the girl who had been prevented from flying at me by Gurney. At first she tried to struggle against Gurney, but Gurney had gripped her by the muscles in her upper arm and the numb pain very quickly became too much for her.

Eventually she burst into tears.

I got up and walked round the desk and stood in front of her. I lifted her chin with my forefinger and looked into her eyes. Little grammar school girl, I thought. Daddy's little grammar school girl. Never had to worry about anything. Gets her O levels and her A levels with no trouble because she hasn't the imagination to do otherwise. Then she falls in love with her second Black Beauty and bingo! Suddenly she's committed. The first stiff prick that comes along and she not only screws it, she votes for it. She made me sick, this daddy's little whore. But I had to leave it at that. There were bigger things at stake. Perhaps I'd have the pleasure later, when her old man was no longer of any political value to Froy and his mob.

'Lucky girl,' I said. 'Lucky little girl.'

I sank back on to the edge of my desk. Gurney released his grip on her arms.

'Take her home to Daddy,' I said to Gurney.

'Yes, Mr Plender.'

'And Gurney.'

'Yes, Mr Plender?'

'That shirt. Is it clean on today?'

That threw him. He even had to clear his throat.

'No, Mr Plender. You see –'

'It's all right,' I said. 'Don't explain.'

Gurney and the girl stood frozen in the middle of the room like two people playing statues while I walked round the back of my desk and sat down again. I looked at them both. Then Gurney jerked back to life and opened the door and ushered the girl out.

'I want you back here in an hour,' I said to Gurney just as he was going through the door. 'Something else has come up.'

Gurney managed to nod and then the door closed behind him. I put my hand to the telephone receiver and squeezed it, hard. With my other hand I stroked my cheek. Bloody bitch. Bloody clever little whore. If it wasn't for daddy's shady money she'd be behind the counter at Littlewood's instead of pissing her time away at university. I expect she thought we fancied her, Gurney and me. (Why should we? Only daddy's money makes her any different from the rest. And that isn't a big enough difference.) Still, it's back to reality now. Daddy's money turns out to be double-edged. She won't be straying too far from home for a while.

I picked up the phone and dialled. The receiver at the other end was lifted almost at once.

'Yes?' said Froy.

'She's on her way home now,' I said.

'Have you seen her?'

Jesus Christ.

'Yes, I've seen her.'

'And?'

'Everything perfect. No problems.'

'The press?'

'I told you.'

18

There was a slight pause.

'Good. I'll be in touch.'

'Mr Froy?'

'Yes?'

'I was right.'

'Right? About what?'

'He is a power militant. One we didn't have on file. Gurney sniffed it.'

'Interesting,' said Froy. 'At that level, I mean.'

'There's not much of it, but most of what there is we have. Except for the occasional surprise. I'll send you the breakdown we did if you like.'

'Yes, I'd like to read it, but don't send it. I'll pick it up when next I see you.'

'Actually, it's a bit of a pity really. If she hadn't been Gorton's daughter, I mean. We could have used the situation to benefit the Movement far better.'

'I realise that.'

'I mean, it was tailor made. If she'd been somebody else's brat, one of our titled opponents, say, we could have tipped the Drugs' Squad and made sure the Power stuff came out as well. A nice bit of negative PR: PEER'S DAUGHTER IN DRUGS SWOOP ON BLACK POWER PARTY; AFRICAN LECTURER CHARGED. And etcetera and etcetera.'

'No situation ever remains constant. If Gorton were ever to slip, we might reconsider what we have along the lines you mention.'

'I can't see that happening,' I said. 'Gorton's a dedicated man. There are no blemishes on his record as far as the press are concerned.'

'And you should know,' said Froy.

Now what did *that* mean? I let it pass.

'Still,' I said, 'the by-election should run smoothly enough now. Thanks to us there's still flesh on the skeleton in Gorton's cupboard.'

'Yes. By the way, what do you propose should Nboro try and contact the girl? If he doesn't accept her departure as it stands?'

'Luckily for us she was more interested in him than he was in her. Basically, he was just screwing Whitey. In any case, we have some more letters prepared.'

Froy didn't say anything to that.

'I'll be in touch,' said Froy.

The line went dead.

I put the receiver back and stared at it. I wondered what Froy's silence had meant. Probably nothing. Just his usual gamesmanship to keep his minions toeing the line. But I wasn't a minion. I was his Number One and he knew it. But he didn't like it. I was almost too good. I hadn't slipped up yet. I hadn't made even the smallest error. That was the kind of performance the Movement wanted, therefore so did Froy. But it irritated him to think that someone else could provide it besides himself. But it would irritate him even more to know that I'd got recordings of every conversation he'd made over the last twelve months; that I had a complete history of his fifty-one-year-old life; that I knew every movement he was going to make during the next twenty-four hours, and the twenty-four hours after that and so on and so on; that I knew his brother was in deep trouble with a certain finance company; that the dog Froy's neighbour had been looking for all over their neighbourhood during the last four days had a bullet in its forehead and was buried behind Norman Froy's tomato plants; that Froy had a frogman's rubber suit hung up in his wardrobe; in fact everything. Which gave me a great deal of pleasure. Especially as Froy didn't suspect a dicky bird.

But you had to give the old sod his due. He was bloody careful, whether he suspected anything or not. He kept himself well-covered. His superior had no worries on that score. He'd not been an easy man to tag. He never went direct from A to B. He never used names on the phone. He never sent or received mail to do with the Movement. He never met with any of the superiors, only with people at his own level, or beneath it. All of which meant that my efforts to find out the *real* power behind the Movement had so far come to nothing. But I would find out and when I did I'd have them over a barrel. The lot of them. They wouldn't know which arse to disappear up first and I'd have a nice little organisation all of my own, instead of just maintaining the set-up for their benefit.

Not that the set-up wasn't sweet. It was. I was provided with this office, half-a-dozen full time men in this city alone, (plus the funds to call on as much muscle as I needed), all the latest equipment to run the business, agents under my direct control in every major city in England, plus permanent offices in Manchester and Birmingham, besides the one in London and the one here. No, it was fine and I'd access to a small private army. A lot to thank the Movement for.

The day Froy had first turned up at my London office pretending he wanted to hire my services to recover a missing wife had been a very lucky day indeed. But that had been two years ago and I didn't have to be grateful any more. I had been given the power and I wanted to know where it came from. And when I had that knowledge I would be able to use it. To bargain. Their secrecy was their strength and their weakness. They'd have no choice when I presented them with what I was going to find out. They'd have to give me what I wanted: a seat on the executive. Whatever and wherever the executive was. With Froy working for me. A bigger army. More power. More independence. More political involvement. But in the meantime what I had would do. It really was very nice. The Movement had supplied me with the facilities to expand my previous operation in a way which wouldn't have been possible before. As a Private Investigator I'd managed to build up extensive files on individuals who could afford to pay for discretion. But with the Movement employing me among other things to dig up the muck, my little bit of private enterprise had expanded into big business. I could afford to be clever. Whereas most blackmailers were greedy and demanded too much too often, I had so many clients that individually their payments must have seemed to them to be quite reasonable, like, say, additional HP commitments. Of course if Froy ever found out about it I'd be finished. But he wasn't likely to find out. Not in the near future, at any rate. And later, when I'd found out who I was working for, then it would be difficult for Froy to say anything at all without finding himself out on his ear.

Wind buffeted the window and slapped rain against the glass. I looked at my watch. Quarter to six. Mrs Fourness was expecting me back for supper. I'd give her a ring: there was hardly time to get there and back into town again. Besides, it was too nice here, where I was, cosy and snug behind the double glazing.

KNOTT

The car jerked to a halt. Rain raced across the car park and rattled on the roof.

'We'll have to make a dash for it,' I said.

'Can I borrow your scarf?' said Eileen. 'I don't want me hair getting all ruined.'

'Yes, sure,' I said.

I handed her the scarf.

'Cost me two pound ten this little lot did,' she said, weaving the rayon round the rinse. 'Shocking, they are, these days.'

I nodded. Come on, come on.

'If they get any dearer I may as well start going to Madame Gretas'. It'd still cost more but not enough to make any difference. And at least there they don't behave as if they were in a race.'

She tied the scarf in a bow beneath her chin. Her head looked like a wrapped cabbage.

She squeezed my leg and grinned up into my face.

'I expect your wife goes there, doesn't she?'

I smiled a sort of smile and nodded.

'Funny if we were ever sitting next to each other under the driers.'

'Hilarious,' I said. 'Look, I think the rain's easing off a bit. Let's go now.'

We got out of the Mercedes and rushed across the car park

and into the alley that led into Jackson Street. I swore. The neon that said Peggy's Bar was unlit. That meant that the alley entrance was locked. I tried it just in case.

'Aren't they open yet?' said Eileen.

'They're open,' I said. 'But it means we'll have to go in via the hotel lobby.'

'So?'

The silly cow. That was one of the reasons I'd chosen Peggy's Bar, because of where the entrance was.

'Come on then,' I said.

We walked through to Jackson Street and into the lobby of the Royal Hotel. I ushered Eileen quickly over to the winding staircase that led down to the basement and into the soft lights of Peggy's bar.

The bar was empty. Except for Peggy himself, setting up his bar with his usual fussy, meticulous care.

I sat Eileen in one of the booths. The waiter service didn't begin this early so I went over to the bar.

'So what's all this then?' said Peggy, coming the arch bit. 'Bringing Auntie Peggy some competition, are we?'

'Give over,' I said. 'You know you love it. Gives you a chance to show off.'

'Well, I hope she's broadminded, that's all I can say.'

'So do I or else I'm on a wasted evening,' I said.

'You married men,' said Peggy. 'You're the worst of the lot.'

'Anyway,' I said, 'I'll have a gin and bitter lemon for the lady and a large Scotch for myself, and what are you going to have?'

'Well, if you don't mind,' he said, 'I'll have the same as the lady's having.'

'You won't, you know,' I said. 'You'll have a gin and bitter lemon and like it.'

'Well,' he said coyly, 'it was worth a try.'

Peggy turned away to make the drinks and I took out a

cigarette and thought about the evening ahead. This was the best part, really. The thinking about it, the excitement generated by the expectation, the mind's-eye two-way mirror, clear as crystal, the clarity of the mental images blurring the physical reality which could never be so good. But even knowing that whatever happened, knowing that the let-down would come, the excitement was still real, undeniable, unmanageable, whatever the rationalisation before or after the fact. It didn't make any difference. I always jumped in feet first and ended up hoping for better luck next time.

But this girl seemed the best better-luck-next-time for ages. The type. The looks told me. A real Top of the Popper. She should know. But would she want? Would she even if what I wanted didn't turn her on? Some girls were insulted. A frontal attack on their pre-conditioned sexual patterns usually evoked the source; memories of mum beating out her great respectability riff squashing and squeezing the imagination of the kiddies' games, preventing me from acting out my own stifled pre-adolescent frustrated fantasies. Not that they didn't want to; they did. They'd probably seen the games, heard the hot-flushing little stories in the cloakrooms and even if they hadn't they'd occurred in their minds, like it or not, admitted or otherwise. 'But that wasn't the same,' they'd say, 'that was at school. You couldn't behave like that now.' 'Why not?' 'Well, you couldn't, if you did you'd feel...' 'Guilty?' 'Well, yes. Ashamed.' 'Precisely. Couldn't have put it better myself.' Shame. Guilt. The Protestant ethic. Hand in hand with hard work and self-restraint and self-respect and well-kept-up appearances goes the wrongness of semi-detached enjoyment, the antidote of repression.

But this girl might be the one. She'd got the right kind of potential.

I'd met her over at the agency. She'd been the switchboard

girl but, as the switchboard was in reception, that made her the receptionist as well.

The minute I'd seen her I'd thought how right she was. I'd known what she was going to sound like before she opened her mouth, trying to disguise the Yorkshire in her voice by affecting the accent according to the new aristocracy; the classless aristocracy with not only the vowels but the emotions flattened, the way the telly told them. A face without a trace of make-up proved it. And there she'd been before me, no make-up, that was true, but her hair was dyed and the way it was dyed gave everything away. She had the right functional clothes, the right non-functional detached look but the dyed hair gleefully spoiled the lot: she didn't come off. And the beauty of it was, she thought she did; and the whole set-up, the exciting I'm-a-receptionist-in-an-advertising-agency thing would help her to pretend. And so would I.

But I'd played it very carefully at first. I hadn't given her too much of a rush. I'd just phoned her a few days later.

'Priestley and Squires. Good morning?' she'd said.

'Hello,' I'd said in my best nervous voice. 'Am I speaking to the receptionist?'

'Priestley and Squires, Advertising Agents. Can I help you?'

'Look, I'm sorry, but are you the receptionist? The one with the blonde hair?'

Her manner had changed.

'That's right. Why?'

'Oh, good. Well, it's –'

'Who's that calling?'

'…it's a bit difficult, actually…'

'Is that you, Eric?'

'…but the thing is…'

'If that's you Eric I shan't half be mad. I've told you about…'

'…I was wondering if I could use you.'

'I beg your pardon?'

'For my catalogue.'

'Who *is* that?'

I gave a laugh.

'Look, I'm sorry,' I said, 'I seem to have made a complete hash-up of this. Let me start again.'

'Who *are* you?'

'I'm Peter Knott. I was in the agency the other day. I'm a photographer. If you remember at all, I was the chap with Mr Farlcrest. I'm taking the pictures for the Premier Boilers' Account.'

Her manner had changed again.

'Oh, yes,' she said. 'I think I *do* remember you.'

Oh, good, I'd thought.

'Oh, good,' I'd said. 'At least that proves I'm not some kind of telephone nut.'

'Well?' she'd said, in a voice that was meant to be charmingly coy.

'Well, the thing is, when I saw you the other day, it struck me how right you were for shots I have to do.'

'Shots? You mean photos?'

'Yes, that's right. Do you know Saxby and Hassell's?'

'Oh yes, you mean the mail order people.'

'That's right. Well, I do their catalogue; I mean, I take all the pictures, the whole lot. So, the point is, as you know, they do an enormous fashion range, all ages, and when I saw you I thought you'd be just right for their teenage range, the Junior Miss.'

'Junior Miss?'

'Of course, I realise you'd have to make yourself look a bit younger, but I'd make the main adjustment photographically.'

I'd known she was only seventeen anyway but I'd had to use the flannel a little bit.

'What made you think *I'd* be right?' she said.

'Oh I don't really know. You can't really put your finger on it, it's just something you sort of automatically know. I suppose it's my job to know,' I'd said, wincing, 'otherwise, I suppose, I wouldn't be any good if I didn't know just like that.'

There'd been a silence at her end, so I'd gone on:

'Anyway, the point is, would you be interested? I mean, you'd be paid obviously, the proper rates. And it wouldn't interfere with your job: you could work evenings. A lot of girls do, the professionals, they have to if they've got other work on that involves daytime shooting.'

'Well, I don't know whether I *could*...' she'd said, and that had been that. Except for one thing.

'There's only one thing,' I'd said. 'I do quite a bit of work for your agency, and the point is, I don't think Mr Farlcrest would like it if he knew I'd been offering what he'd consider to be another job to one of his staff, so I wonder if you'd mind not mentioning it to anyone at Priestley and Squires. Word could get back to him.'

Her name was Eileen Yarwood.

We'd arranged to meet at lunchtime the next day. She'd been all done up in gear appropriate to her new rôle as a famous model. She'd been full of excitement which she'd done her best to try and hide.

I discovered that she was from Leeds. She'd left school a year ago and home three months previously. Her father had died the day after she'd left school. Since then the dislike she and her mother had always felt for each other had come out into the open; her mother was only thirty-six and she'd liked the gay life but she hadn't liked the looks the fellers she'd brought home had given Eileen. So Eileen had packed up and come here. Here because a girl friend of hers from school had moved to the district a couple of years ago; but when Eileen'd turned up on the doorstep her friend's parents hadn't been too pleased to see her, so she'd spent the following day flat-hunting. She'd got what she'd called a nice place on Hebden Road where she'd lived on her own ever since. I'd asked her if she didn't find it lonely. She'd given me a look and said that after living with her mother's routine she'd never feel lonely again. And besides, the agency had a thriving social life. She'd implied she was never short of boyfriends.

I'd let her know just enough; that business was good, that I'd lived in London before coming back up north, that I'd been brought up in a small town on the other side of the river and gone to Art School here, that I wasn't short of a few bob, and that I was happily married. And I'd done right to tell her judging by the flicker on her face and the friendly relaxing after I'd mentioned it; another little girl with a conquest complex excited by the prospect of scoring by seducing a married man. And by laying it on about my house and the things I had in it it made the contemplation of her victory even sweeter. After all, I had so much to lose.

And, of course, she'd thought she'd known what was on from the start. Her reasoning must have gone like this: he finds me attractive enough to photograph for his catalogue, so if he finds me attractive he must want to make a pass at me and if he makes a pass at me he must want to carry on with me but he might pretend he doesn't because he's married so I'll do my best to make it easy for him or difficult which ever way you care to look at it.

Which was exactly the way I wanted her to behave. Let her think she was steering things along her way. So that she'd behave with the kind of confidence she'd got tonight, feeling sure that she knew the way things were going to go. So that when they didn't she'd be confused. And her confusion would lead her where I wanted her led.

I walked over to the booth and put the drinks down on the

table. I spilt a little of her tonic as I set the bottle down.

'I always like a drink before I work,' I said, sitting down. 'It relaxes me. Makes the ideas flow easier.'

I poured the tonic into the gin and rattled the bottle on the edge of her glass.

'Looks as though you need it,' she said.

'I beg your pardon?' I said.

'Relaxing,' she said. 'You seem all tensed up.'

PLENDER

I plugged in the percolator and walked over to the filing system and took out the file that contained the latest correspondence to the magazine. I'd had a busy week. I hadn't had time to sort through the letters. It'd give me something to do until Gurney got back.

It didn't take long to discard the male and female pro' stuff, or the stuff from the nutters. Just as long as it took for the percolator to boil. I got up and switched it off and poured myself a cup and sat down again and began to sift the mail for answers to the ads I'd put in myself. There'd been two of them: ATTRACTIVE YORKSHIRE MISS (20) WOULD LIKE TO HEAR FROM MATURE MALE DISCIPLINARIAN FOR THE FUN OF IT: ALL GEAR NEEDED FOR BIZARRE FUN. MY PLACE OR YOURS. GENUINE FIRST AD. NON-PROFESSIONAL. NO REMUNERATION REQUIRED; DISCIPLINE HAS ITS OWN REWARD.

The other one was: GOOD LOOKING BLONDE YOUNG MAN (23) NEEDS OLDER GENTLEMAN TO DISCIPLINE HIM. CORRECTION WILL BE NEEDED AS I AM COMPLETELY INEXPERIENCED. MY SUBMISSIVE NATURE, SHYNESS, ETC., CAN BE YOURS FOR CORRECTING. YORKS. ANON.

There were twenty-four replies for the first ad and seven for the second. Of these six were from Leeds, six from Doncaster, three from Halifax, two from Barnsley, two from Scunthorpe, two from Grimsby, one from Scarborough, and one from

Harrogate. The remainder were from towns or small villages, mainly places I'd never heard of. I made a list of the names and addresses which they'd so trustingly supplied and put them in my secretary's in-tray for her to begin on when she came in on Monday.

Her job was to find out who they were by checking electoral roles, credit files, company lists, business directories, street directories, etc. All she thought she was doing was finding out their credit-worthiness for HP companies. Well, in a sense, she was. Except that the HP company was me. When she'd told me what I wanted to know, the few names that remained from the original list would go on file and a few days later these select correspondents would receive replies to their letters suggesting dates and times and places. Then I would sit back and wait for the braver of the remaining correspondents to commit themselves to action.

After I'd made out the list of names I went through the remaining unsolicited letters, the ones I hadn't slung out, the ones containing drafts of ads to be placed in the magazine. There was one that might bear checking out: WEALTHY EDUCATED EXECUTIVE, 50, UNDERSTANDING, EASY MANNER, SENSE OF HUMOUR, SEEKS INVITATION TO VIEW ENTHUSIASTIC AMATEUR FRIENDLY COUPLE/S. HIS VISIT WOULD COMBINE DISCRETION WITH CHAMPAGNE AND COULD MEAN USEFUL WEEKLY INCOME. PHOTO WITH DETAILS APPRECIATED. DISTANCE UP TO TWO HUNDRED MILES ROTHERHAM. (YORKS).

I read it again. Sounded as though it might be right up Andrea's street. Her and Les would be ideal to follow that one up. I filed the letter and got up and walked over to the window again. The rain was still belting down but the sparse lights across the river were still visible. I turned my head slightly and looked farther down the river, farther inland, my eyes searching the blackness for the small collection of lights that mapped out my home town. They were so far away and so faint that at first I couldn't see them: it was always the same when the weather was bad. Then I saw them and I couldn't understand why I hadn't been able to see them before. I wondered what was going on over there right at this minute, what it was like right now. I hadn't been back in ten years. I hadn't wanted to. But just occasionally I wondered. Sometimes I thought I'd like to go back there and splash the cash and let them all see how well I'd done, give them something to chew on, something that they wouldn't like swallowing, the fact that Brian Plender, against all prediction, had made it.

I saw the reflection of the light on my desk wink on in the black window before me so I stopped thinking about all that and went back to my desk and pressed the button. Eventually the green light above the door came on and I pressed the other button and Gurney came into the room.

'Well, that's that,' he said.

'What happened?'

'Nothing. I dropped her off and that was it.'

'Did you see her into the house?'

'I saw her to the door. Nice place Gorton has.'

'Ought to be. The money came from his percentage for the Rotham by-pass contract. Did you see Gorton?'

'Briefly. He fluttered about a bit at the door. He couldn't wait to get inside.'

I lit a cigarette.

'Anyway,' I said, 'I know you've had a busy week, but I'm afraid there's something come up.'

'What?'

'Camille has a client. I want you to supervise the cine and the rest of the gear.'

Gurney's face twitched a little bit which was his way of throwing a tantrum.

'Oh, I mean to say, sir – ' he began, but I didn't let him get any farther.

'I'd do it myself only Mr Froy wants me to do something special for him. And Froy is keen to get the goodies on Camille's Playmate of the Month. He doesn't want any slip-ups.'

That shut him up. Gurney was Froy's man. He was the only person who worked for me who knew about Froy and the Movement. Apart from the muscle and the informers and the queers and the brasses and the conmen the other politically motivated gentlemen who worked for me were from such scramble-headed groups as the NF or the Union with Europe mob. The two things my little helpers had in common was their dedication to the job and the fact that they all had records. They knew I had political links with something they could only guess at and that was good enough for them. They were well pleased to find themselves so gainfully employed. But Gurney was different. Gurney had been Froy's man from way back. He'd been a condition of my employment. Not that I didn't want him: I did. But he hated my guts. He felt he should be sitting where I was. But Froy hadn't thought him good enough. So he had to put up with the ride I gave him. The only satisfaction he got was his reporting back to Froy, letting Froy know what I was up to, because that was a part of his duties, too. But so far he'd had nothing of any consequence to report. He knew nothing of my extra-curricular activities; he knew nothing of my file on Froy. So he was just waiting his time out, waiting for me to slip. But he'd have a long wait. I'd no intentions of getting my feet wet.

'So there you are, Gurney, old boy,' I said. 'Looks like another working weekend.'

Gurney smiled one of his smiles.

'Looks like it, Mr Plender,' he said.

KNOTT

I looked at my watch.

'Here, look at the time,' I said. 'It's twenty-to-eight.'

Eileen knocked back the dregs of her fourth gin and bitter lemon.

'Time flies when you're enjoying yourself,' she said, giving me the knowing look she'd given me at least fifty times in the last hour. 'Still, we've got plenty of time. The night's young.'

'Well, we'd better get a move on. It'll take an hour or two to get through.'

I got up and gave Eileen a hand and she levered herself out of her seat.

'I hope I can stand up straight,' she said. 'I'd hate to make a muck of your pictures.'

PLENDER

I hated Peggy's Bar. It made my skin crawl. All that perfume and shrieking and prancing about. But I'd thought I'd better wander over just to check on Camille. Make sure he turned up. It would've been typical of him not to: he even behaved like a woman in that department, too.

I walked into the bar. Thank God. It was almost deserted. The rain must have kept most of them in.

I sat down on a stool at the bar.

'Good *evening*, Mr Plender,' Peggy said. 'To what do we owe this rare pleasure?'

Peggy was the exception to the rule. Peggy I could stand. I don't know, but he was the only one that didn't make me feel creepy. Perhaps because he was getting on a bit and he was a bit cynical about the whole scene.

'Thirst,' I said.

Peggy smiled.

'I was afraid so,' he said. He poured me a vodka with ice and a twist of lemon. 'On me.'

'Thanks,' I said. I took a sip. 'Business good?'

'You must be joking. It's wicked.'

'That bad eh?'

'Use your eyes. It's been like this since Wednesday. Appalling.'

'I thought it was tonight. The weather, like.'

'I wish it was. I wish it was.' Peggy looked at me. 'And just as a matter of interest, what brings you in here on a night like this? It must be business or else you wouldn't be in here in the first place.'

'Well, in a way, yes.'

'In a way,' said Peggy. 'Anyway I don't want to know what it is. You keep it to yourself. The less Auntie Peggy knows about what *you* get up to the better it is for Auntie Peggy.'

'Don't worry, Peggy,' I said. 'I'd never shit in your bar.'

'I know damn well you wouldn't,' said Peggy. 'Otherwise you'd never get past that doorway.'

I smiled.

'Give me another drink,' I said. 'And have one yourself.'

'Ta,' said Peggy. 'I'll have a gin and bitter lemon, if you don't mind.'

Peggy made the drinks and I gave him the money.

'And if you don't mind,' I said, 'I'm going to sit in one of your cosy little booths.'

'Get a better view that way, do you?'

I smiled and said nothing.

'Sometimes, Mr Plender,' said Peggy, 'you really give me the fucking creeps.'

I smiled and turned and walked away from the bar. Peggy knew I used the place from time to time to put the drop on clients but he didn't care so long as none of his regulars were involved or one of the clients brought the law back with him. Well, there was no danger of that. Not with the people I arranged to visit Peggy's with.

I sat down in one of the booths and looked round the bar. It was a depressing place at the best of times, all faded plush and lime green paintwork, but it was worse when it was deserted because you could see all of the décor, all of the lime, in spite of the almost non-existent lighting.

There were only four other people in the bar; an early evening creeper in clerical grey with his fawn trilby set at its weekend angle; a blank looking Greek sailor obviously in port for the first time; and in the booth opposite the one I was in a man and a girl drinking themselves into an early bed. It wasn't an uncommon sight in Peggy's, that. Some blokes thought it turned a bird on, bringing them in to mingle with the gingers. Maybe it did. Maybe underneath all the giggling and the staring the birds cottoned on to the fact that maybe their blokes weren't so straight after all to want to bring them to Peggy's; maybe the reasons went deeper. And maybe some sick bitches liked that. It wouldn't have surprised me.

I watched the couple for a while. The bird was very young, and she was well away. Not reeling or glazed or anything like that, just giggly in the knowledge that she was all set for the evening's later coming events. The bloke was sitting with his back to me but even from that angle he was so obviously putting on the Mr Sincere bit it was painful. There was no need. He'd been home and dry yards back. All I could think, though, was how hard up he must be. Christ, she couldn't have been more than sixteen or seventeen. What was the point? He may as well have stayed in bed and had a J. Arthur. Because she wouldn't be worth much more, that was certain. And from what I could see of him it wasn't that he was a bad looking bloke. He had the gear and the hair. He could have done all right for himself a bit farther up the market. Maybe he was kinky for kids. But he seemed too young to fancy the young stuff. Anyway what was certain was that he was ready for the all off. He'd been drunk up and shuffling ever since I'd come in. Couldn't wait to get down to it. But she was stretching it out a bit. The cat with the mouse. Playing the sophisticated flirt, or thought she was. She'd decided he was going to get it but she wanted to keep him guessing. It was pathetic, it really was. I went back to my drinking before I threw up.

I made motions to Peggy. He brought me another large one and I took my time with the first mouthful. I made it last long enough for it to make my eyes water and my chest burn. I didn't drink a lot but I drank regularly so I made sure that what I drank was clean and relatively harmless. That's why I stuck to vodka: no hangovers to stop me wanting to get out of bed and do my daily workout. And that was something I never missed. Christ, at school the only athletics I'd ever concentrated on was keeping one step in front of the teachers. I'd thought physical fitness was for thick idiots. But it was like a lot of attitudes you had at school; they were the other way round once you'd left. Like in this case. I'd started doing judo classes when I was seventeen. And funnily enough the classes had been in the gym at my old school, the same place I'd skived off everything that had been shoved at me for the previous five years. And nowadays it wasn't just judo, thanks to the Palestine police, it was armed hand-to-hand combat as well, plus the daily workouts, twice a day, in the evenings and in the mornings. The difference being of course, that nowadays, there was a reason for everything. A purpose. A purpose that had come with the respect for myself that I'd discovered, the discovery of the *importance* of respect for self, the power it engendered through the discipline of self. Since I'd discovered I'd become someone new. Whole. Everything worked, instead of just bits of me. And because I functioned properly, my success was effortless, like my body. I couldn't fail because my mind and my body were tuned to succeed. It was simple. Literally, the healthy mind in the healthy body. The disciplined mind in the disciplined body. I smiled. If the PT master could see me now.

A movement across the other side of the bar caught my eye. It was the couple getting up to leave. The man stood to let the girl get out of the booth. I looked into his face and immediately I was aware that I knew him. But I didn't know who he was. In fact the face was so familiar the recognition had jolted me. It was like seeing a TV star in the street: the initial reaction was surprise that you remembered someone you didn't actually know, and then when you realised who they were, that explained everything and you felt stupidly embarrassed. But in this case it was a matter of recognising someone without knowing who the hell they were.

The girl continued to drift over to the exit. The man went over to the bar to get some cigarettes. The girl waited in the doorway and looked at the man while he opened the packet, took out a cigarette and lit up. Then he threw the match into an ashtray on the bar and began to walk towards the girl. Head forward, shoulders bowed, walking on the balls of his feet. The walk. The walk was even more recognisable than the features. The last time I'd seen that walk was seventeen years ago. Marching out of assembly on the last day of school, three boys away. With his usual mates tagging on. The handsome hair flowing off the clever confident face. Striding out to meet the future his parents were going to pay for. I wondered what he'd made of it.

Peter Knott.

I hadn't seen him since that day.

I wondered what he'd made of it.

Had he done as well as me? He should have. He'd had the start.

I looked at my watch. There was time.

I drank my drink and got up to leave.

KNOTT

The wipers whirred and I wondered for the hundredth time what I was doing, driving this silly cow to my studio to weave her into my web. And yet I always wondered and the wondering never did any good. It was like masturbation! Each time you finished you told yourself that that was it, that was the last time, it's never as good as you imagine it's going to be so why bother? But the next time you got a hard on it was always straight to the toilet for a quick one off the wrist. Sometimes it was just to stave off depression but the joke was it always made you more depressed. The same with birds like Eileen; female masturbation machines that were obsolete and boring the minute you came. And like masturbation the more Eileens I had the less they satisfied. The initial excitement was always the same, always as good, the thinking, mind's-eye wanking, but when it came to the moment of too-real truth, after the ball play was over, then the fall, then the let-down, then the desperation and the unnamed (unmanned?) fear.

So devices had had to be manufactured, introduced into my seductions for the purposes of enhancing the excitement and shielding me from the depressions and the realities of hard flesh. Gauzes and veils and wisps of fantasy had to drift between my eyes and my mind in order to keep my activities enjoyable. The sex act itself was the final necessary stopper to an ever increasing bag of tricks, all equally exciting and, like masturbation, self-defeating, evolving without any direction except perhaps towards some kind of madness.

I was like an addict. Girls were a habit I couldn't shake. It was as if there was an empty space in my make-up that needed filling with some sexual experience. It wasn't as if I was loveless. My wife and I didn't get on but that was my fault, not hers: she still loved me, whatever I felt for her, whatever I got up to. And even if she stopped loving me past experience told me I wouldn't exactly have a job finding someone to take over where she left off. I'd always been someone who'd got their own way with people, male or female, although these days I no longer considered the fact with pleasure. These days it was just a fact. It had ceased to have meaning since I'd recognised it and admitted it to myself. I'd always wanted to be liked and I'd schemed and plotted in the subtlest of ways to achieve popularity but I'd only recently realised it and to think of it made me feel sick.

Neither was it night-starvation, my hang-up. My wife was good in that department too. (In fact, she was the best screw I'd ever had. And she went along with my games and embellishments, not just for my sake but because she enjoyed them too, that is after she'd been persuaded that what we did was neither debasing nor purely carnal or indicative of any feelings I might have – or not have – for her personally.) And, wife apart, there were plenty of Eileens, a species of female that under normal circumstances I disliked intensely: shallow, coy, *faux-naif*, deliberately petulant, the complete suburban, ushered into puberty to the strains of Telstar, sprung into a background where the myth-figures of Bernie the Bolt and Robin Richmond entered the common consciousness and steered it along the paths of rightfulness. But it was the very awfulness of their environment that attracted me to girls like Eileen. It gave my intrigues an extra dimension; the thought that I was disturbing the bland subconscious of the great catalogue market, the audience I touched with the gloss of my own photographs.

But, as usual, no answer, no reply. I wondered if the knowledge would solve the problem, remove the addiction. I knew plenty of people with big sexual appetites who considered themselves perfectly healthy; why did I suspect my own? Was it the refinement of the appetite that caused me to be suspicious?

I turned the car into the White Lion car park. It was early yet and I could pick my spot. Not that the White Lion had much of a carriage track. The trawlermen that did the real spending moved from spot to spot in taxis, so as not to let anything like a fatal accident interfere with their drinking.

I pulled on the hand brake and Eileen said, 'What, are we going for another drink?'

'No,' I said. 'At least, not here. We may have one in the studio. This is where I park the car. I have an arrangement with the pub.'

We got out of the Mercedes and splashed our way across the car park's reflected neon. We rounded the pub corner into the spitting rain. Facing the pub was a sheer eyeless row of old warehouses. Rain sidled across their faces in great drifting sheets. Beyond the warehouses, further down the road to our right, was a level crossing. The gates were closed and a sluggish goods train, black-wet, trailed across the cobbled road. Eileen shivered and I took her arm and led her across the road towards the warehouses. I stopped at one of the warehouse doors and unlocked the padlock on the smaller door inset in the woodwork. Next to the padlock, on the brickwork, there was a sign that said, PETER KNOTT, INDUSTRIAL PHOTOGRAPHY.

I pushed the door inwards and leant in and found the light switch. Inside the loading bay and the string sacks of bananas were flooded with neon. I stepped back.

'After you,' I said to Eileen.

Eileen pulled a mock-nervous face.

'Bit creepy, isn't it?' she said, tentatively lifting a nyloned knee to step into the ghastly light.

'The only thing that's creepy in there,' I said, 'is spiders.'

She withdrew her leg quickly causing her coat to fall open and her skirt to ride up and reveal even more thigh than was usual.

The dryness arrived in my throat and Eileen said: 'Christ, I hate spiders, I really do. Can't stand them. They make my skin crawl.'

'Shall I go first?' I said. 'Then I can squash all such spiders that dare to cross your path as I go along.'

'Ugh,' said Eileen.

I stepped through the opening. The damp decaying vegetable smell immediately hit me and the cold of the stone floor seemed to chill my feet and my ankles.

I turned round and held out my hand and helped Eileen through the doorway.

'God,' she said, shivering, 'isn't it *cold*.'

I could see she was beginning to have her doubts. I smiled to myself. The surprise when she saw my studio would be more unbalancing than usual.

'Up the stairs,' I said, indicating the tall stairwell. The stairs themselves were rough planks put together in an open fashion that led without invitation up into the rank gloom of the upper storeys of the warehouse.

Eileen looked at the stairs.

'You've probably guessed,' I said. 'It's right at the top.'

PLENDER

The White Lion didn't have any ice. They managed a piece of lemon that was all peel. I supposed that that was something. I took a sip from my glass. Fluff from the drying-up towel lined the dry part.

'Do you have a pay phone?' I said to the Mick.

'Yes, sir,' he said. 'Between the two bars. Next to the snug door.'

I went through a door with ornate opaque glass panes that carried flowery versions of the brewery's name. I was in luck. The telephone directory had some pages in it. I found the Ks and then I found the Knotts. There were twenty or so of them. But only one P. A. Knott. Only one Peter Arthur.

I looked at the address: The Cottage, Corella. Corella was a river village that lay in the lee of the wolds, about twelve miles farther inland. A haven for the well-heeled businessman who considered the city's richer suburbs suburban. A very nice little spot indeed, if you had the cash. The few locals that were left there must have been the greediest. The prices were fantastic by the standards of other places in the area. I knew that for a fact, because I knew someone who'd bought a place there and I knew how much they'd paid.

Froy had lived there for nearly two years now. I closed the book and went back into the bar. I drained my drink and ordered another. While it was coming I looked at my watch. It was nearly nine o'clock. The meeting at Peggy's should have been getting under way by now but it didn't look as though I was going to make it back there to keep an eye on things. Not now. Now that I was about to renew my acquaintance with my long lost mate, Peter Arthur Knott.

It was funny, but I could remember the day, the precise kind of day, the day we first met. Sunshine. Golden August sunshine. No clouds in the sky, the dust in the streets of the small rural town warm and static in the drowsy morning. The smell of the engine of the big green removal van outside number forty, the wet shirts of the removal men, the newness of the three piece suite. And the car. The shiny maroon car. An Austin – with a sparkling chrome grille. The first car in the street, at least as far as my short memory had gone back. A lot of people hadn't liked that, I remember. Particularly my mother's mate, Mrs Parker, our next door neighbour.

'Oh, yes,' said Mrs Parker, arms folded. 'You can tell. Consider themselves a peg or two up from us.'

My mother filled the kettle again and sat down at the kitchen table and lit up. I wondered how Mrs Parker knew, how she could tell. But my mother always agreed with Mrs Parker, and so that meant Mrs Parker was never wrong.

I wandered over to the side window and looked out at the shimmering road beyond the green corrugated shed. The omnibus edition of Dick Barton was droning out of the wireless in the dining room but this morning I was too interested in what was going on across the road.

A minute or two ago a boy of my age had come out of number forty with a bat and ball and had began to play on the path that ran down the side of the house, bouncing the ball off the wall with the bat. Once he'd got started he bounced and returned the ball without making a mistake, not even the smallest slip. The regular sound was hot and hollow in the still of midday.

Then a different movement caught my eye on my side of the street. Robert Rankin appeared in his garden, bouncing a tennis ball on the iron-hard ground, pretending not to notice the activity over the road. Robert Rankin was second in command in my gang. He was a pretty good fighter, the best I'd got, and he'd found us our hideout in the fields at the back of the crescent as well. Obviously he'd come out to draw the interest of the boy across the road so that he could find out what he was like and report back to me all that there was to know about him. Then I'd decide whether he was fit to join our gang, whether he was going to be friend or foe, and if he was friend, what rôle he was to play in the gang's structure. I hoped he was a good fighter; we needed some. The Butts' Road gang had raided our hideout a few days ago and we were bound to strike back. We would use the new kid if he was any good. And if he wasn't then we could have some fun with him. You could always find some kind of a game to play with cissies.

So I watched and waited to see what happened. The sounds of the different bouncing made a drowsy pattern in my ears. The new boy made no attempt to speak to Robert, but it was obvious he'd seen him because once the ball had bounced wrong and run loose and to pick it up the boy had had to walk in Robert's direction, facing him, but it was as if Robert wasn't there. The boy just went back to his bouncing. So eventually Robert left his garden and went into the road and kicked the ball against the kerb so that he had to rush up and down in the road to collect it every time.

The new boy stopped his game and walked over to the fence and watched Robert for a while. Now Robert just carried on with his game. Eventually the new boy said:

'Are you all mad-heads round here?'

The sound of his voice echoed round the empty crescent. His accent was different to ours. Robert trapped the ball and looked at the new boy.

'You what?' Robert said.

'I said are they all mad-heads round here?'

'No,' said Robert. 'Why?'

'Don't you know it's cricket season?' said the new boy. 'You can't play footog this time of year.'

'Yes you can,' said Robert. 'You can play it when you like.'

There was a silence while the two of them looked at each other. Go on, Robert, I thought, ask him if he can fight. Ask him.

The new boy said: 'Do you like Dinkys?'

Robert stared at him.

'Do you?' said the new boy.

'Some of 'em,' said Robert.

'Do you want to see mine?' said the new boy. 'I've got thousands.'

'Where are they?' asked Robert.

'In the house.'

Liar, I thought. That's why he's said they're in the house. That way he can't prove it: kids didn't often go in each other's houses round here. Parents didn't like it.

'Bet you haven't got thousands,' Robert said.

'Bet I have,' said the new boy, and turned away from the fence and walked towards his house. He stopped in the open doorway and turned back to look at Robert.

'Are you coming in, then?' he said.

I drained my glass again. I smiled to myself as I saw in my mind's eye the exact movement of Knott's head as he'd beckoned Robert into number forty. That had been the beginning of it all, that little inclination. The beginning of his take-over. By the end of the summer the gang that had been mine was his. So I'd had no choice but to become his best friend but it wasn't until the grammar school that I'd really begun to hate him.

KNOTT

Click.

'Right, if you can just move your arm a little, yes, lower, that's it, more to the left, *that's* better...'

Click.

She's loving it. You can tell. Brought the roses to her cheeks. She's being a somebody. This is a real event.

Click.

'Now, if you lean forward a bit, put your arm back up again as if you're looking out for someone, someone in the distance, that's it...'

Click.

I expect she's wondering when the pass is coming. Any minute, I expect. The next time I get in close. I can see her tremble a bit when she thinks I might be moving in.

But she's got the wrong idea.

'Fine,' I said, putting the Yashica down. 'Okay. Have a break. I want to set up the Rollei and change the background.'

Eileen relaxed and leant against the plaster sundial while I slid the photo-mural of the thatched cottage out and replaced it with a kitchen interior.

'Drink?' I said, dusting off my hands.

'Well...' said Eileen.

'Drink,' I said and poured two more.

As I poured I watched Eileen. She was still taking in the place, her eyes flicking from object to object. The initial impression hadn't left her. She hadn't had enough time to get over her surprise at finding a layout like this on the top of a smelly old warehouse.

'Have... have you had this place long?' she said as I passed her her drink. She was trying to sound as if she was in this kind of place every other day.

'No, not long,' I said. 'A year or so.'

Since Kate and I had moved back up North. Since Kate's old man had given me his catalogue contract. Since I'd understood what the word affluence really meant. And I always took a perverse pleasure in showing the place off; it always made me feel more guilty when I saw how it impressed the girls I brought up here. Reminded me that I was cheating on the person who'd made it possible: God knows I'd never have got what I'd got without her. Or rather without her old man. But as my mother said, I couldn't have wished for a nicer father-in-law. As far as she was concerned he was the ultimate in family planning. Still, thanks to him, my mother could look on me as the success she'd always insisted I should become. Which suited me fine because it meant I appeared to be successful without actually having had to do anything about it, while at the same time I could indulge my guilt complex on the different aspects of the situation: not realising the potential my mother had encouraged myself and everyone else to see in me, marrying for reasons of class and money as a means to a successful end, and cheating on the reasons for my false success. But so long as appearances were kept up it didn't matter how deceptive they were, as far as my mother was concerned. But then it had always been that way. Like that time when I'd been eight or nine...

Early evening, after tea. The high blue sky was still and quiet. The only sound was of Mr Morris putting his motor bike and sidecar away in his creosoted shed, scraping his heavy studded boots on the rough cast concrete. I stood in the front garden and looked across the road towards the sound. Beyond the privet I could see the big black-coated figure of Mr Morris move stolidly across the threshold of his shed. I waited until he'd closed the door behind him. Then I opened the gate, trying not to let the latch click so that my mother might not come out and ask me where I was going. If that happened I'd have to lie, say I was over to Brian's or Robert's or Stewart's, and if I said that that was what I was going to do, then I'd have to do it, while she waited and watched to make sure I did. Because she'd suspect me the minute I answered. She always knew when I was lying. And if I acted out the lie then I wouldn't be able to meet Linda and, as she was already at the place we'd arranged, then not to go was unthinkable. I knew she wouldn't agree to meet again if I didn't turn up. She was that kind of girl. She behaved to suit herself and no one else.

I'd seen her cycle past our house five minutes before, slowly, lazily, not sitting on the saddle. That had been part of the arrangement, too. I was to look out of my bedroom window at six o'clock and if she cycled past I was to follow her on foot to Johnson's Field.

I'd gone up to my room on time, full of dread, because to go upstairs except at bedtime was in itself worth suspicion, even more frightened in case Linda looked towards the house and my parents might see in her face what we were planning to get up to. But she'd sidled by without the flicker of a glance and so I'd gone downstairs again and let myself out of the front door which was also risky because to go out via the front door implied secrecy.

Once out of the garden and walking along the warm dusty pavement my fear was even worse. I had to push myself forward because I knew, I just knew, that if I met Linda my mother would find out. It was a terrible certainty but it was as if I were dreaming: I couldn't turn back.

I rounded the corner of the crescent and turned into the lane that ran behind the high board fencing at the back of the gardens in my row. Johnson's Field was on the other side of the lane.

I jumped through the gap in the hedge and cut diagonally across the field to the adjacent hedge where the three tall oak trees were, where the hedge was densest and lent itself to the transforming of bowers into dens. It was in one of these dens that Linda waited for me.

I crackled my way through the thick twiggy entrance and then suddenly found myself face to face with Linda in the still cool space of the den.

Linda was two years older than me, the only girl in the gang. She was as good at fighting as any of us boys but in the games we played she usually had to be content to pretend to bandage the wounded, whether she was being a cow-girl or a knight's lady. And as I loved her I always allowed myself to be wounded early on so that I could lay my head in her lap the way she insisted it was done, just like they did on the Saturday pictures.

But of course as leader of the gang I had no choice but to keep my feelings to myself. So when, one day on the way home from school, she'd ridden her bike along the kerb next to me and suggested what she'd suggested then I'd been flooded with a mixture of dread and happiness. Linda loved me, that was obvious, otherwise she wouldn't want to meet me alone. We could be hero and heroine together, unobserved; I would be able to be loving her without anyone laughing.

But the minute I stepped into the den fear fluttered at the bottom of my stomach. The expression on Linda's face explained the real reason for our meeting.

'Hello, darling,' she said.

Darling. The way she said the word was smug, self-conscious, triumphant. The sound of the word made me feel sick. It was a horrible word, a word that brought laughter and derision whenever it was spoken on the Saturday morning screen. A word that shouldn't be spoken to a boy. My parents never said it, never even acted what it meant, to me or to each other. It was a sissy word. I'd seen my parents exchange disgusted satisfied smiles whenever it was used on the radio. Their glances told me the word was nearly as dirty as swearing.

I didn't answer Linda.

'First,' she said, 'we'll have a kiss.'

She reached for me and pulled me to her and we kissed, flat mouthed and awkward. The warmth of her face made me shudder. She stepped back.

'There,' she said, 'now it's as if we were married.'

I found my voice.

'Good,' I said. 'I'll pretend to be Jungle Jim and you can be my wife and prepare me a meal while I...'

It was no use.

'Oh, no,' she said. 'That's just a game. We can play at that any time.'

Very quickly she pulled her dress over her head. I stared at the stark whiteness of her vest and knickers.

She draped her dress over a thin low branch and then took the rest of her clothes off.

'Look,' she said.

I looked, amazed at the lack of anything to really look at. This was it. This was what boys and girls weren't supposed to do together. It seemed so stupid. Now I'd seen what Linda was like, all the fuss didn't seem to matter. The fear I'd been feeling disappeared. But only for a second because Linda said:

'You can touch me if you like.'

I stared at her, horrified. How could I? I couldn't, not there. Besides, how? What did you do?

'Come on,' she said. 'Look, like this.'

I looked away, but at the same time the overwhelming feeling grew in me that I wanted her to touch me.

'What's the matter?' she said. 'You're not frightened are you?'

I shook my head.

'Well then?'

I said, 'Don't you want to see me?'

'Not now,' she said. 'We'll deal with you tomorrow.'

Tomorrow? How could she imagine I dare come back tomorrow.

'But look,' I said, 'it'll only take a minute. Then I'll touch you.'

She rolled her eyes and tut-tutted.

'Oh, all right,' she said. 'But hurry up.'

Trembling, I unclasped the snake belt and let my trousers down. I put my thumbs in the waistband of my underpants… and then I heard my mother's voice from the top of the field.

'Peter! Come here this minute. This minute, do you hear?'

My stomach turned to jelly. She'd found out. She knew. It was the end of the world. Tears sprang to my eyes. Linda grabbed her dress and furiously struggled it on.

'It's your fault,' she said, glaring at me. 'You let her know where you were coming.'

She finished fastening her buttons while I trembled the clasp of my belt together.

'Peter! Do you hear me? Come here this minute!' and then another voice joined in.

'Peter, Peter, your mum wants you. Quick.'

Then I heard: 'Now you go home, Brian. It must be nearly your bedtime.'

'It isn't,' said Brian Plender. 'Honest. It's ages yet, Mrs Knott.'

'Well, you go on home, anyway.'

Brian. He'd told her. He'd told my mother where I'd gone.

'Go on, then,' said Linda. 'Get going.'

I stared at her.

'You don't think I'm coming with you, do you? I'm staying here till she's gone.'

'But you have to come with me,' I said. 'If you don't me mam'll know what we've been doing. She'll think you're frightened and that's why you won't go.'

Linda just looked at me, saying nothing.

'Peter!' came my mother's voice.

I couldn't stay there any longer; if I did I knew she'd come for me. So I stumbled through the hedge into the evening brightness of the field and saw my mother in the gateway black against the dying sun.

I meandered up the field, occasionally thrashing the hedge with a twig I'd picked up, trying to look as casual as possible so that my casualness would convince her of my innocence. But when I got closer I knew nothing I could do or say would be of any use.

Before I reached her she turned and began to march away from me, back towards the house. That was the thing that made me go to pieces.

'Mam,' I cried, tears coming as I scrambled after her. 'Mam!'

She didn't turn and she didn't answer. We rounded the corner into the crescent. Brian was backing away down the pavement on his side of the road, hands in pockets, whistling and dragging his feet.

My mother went through our gate and into the house by the front door. This was to prevent my father, who was eating his tea in the kitchen, becoming involved and therefore embarrassed. My mother opened the door of the front room and stood back to let me pass. I walked through into the cold unaccustomed tidiness of the front room. The only time there was a fire lit in that room was on Christmas day. Even though the evening sun was streaming in through the bay window the room felt chilly and still and depressing.

My mother closed the door behind her.

'Now then,' she said. 'I want to know what you've been up to.'

'Nothing,' I said.

'You've been with that Linda, haven't you?'

I just nodded.

'What did you do?'

'Nothing. We were just playing.'

'Don't tell lies. You were doing something you're ashamed of, weren't you?'

I didn't answer.

'It doesn't matter whether you tell me or not,' said my mother. 'I shall find out anyway.'

And I knew she would, she always did, so I confessed. When I'd finished my mother knelt down and dried away my tears and then she took me by the shoulders and looked me in the face, her own face softening a little bit and she said:

'Listen to me, Peter, because this is for your own good: you want to stay away from girls like her. They'll only do you harm. They're nothing but trouble. They could do you a lot of damage. You stick to your pals like Brian and Robert. Do you hear?'

I nodded, dumbly. Her vehemence terrified me.

'And listen, let me tell you something else: girls can sometimes be worse than boys. You know what I mean? When a girl's bad she's really bad and don't you forget it.'

The next day when I saw Brian I asked him why he'd told my mother that I'd been down the fields with Linda.

'I couldn't help it,' he said, all careless and casual. 'Your mam saw me playing out and shouted across asking me where you were so I just told her you'd gone down the fields. Then she asked me who with so I told her. I mean, you can't lie, can you?'

'I would have,' I said. 'For you.'
Brian smiled an odd smile and said: 'I bet.'

I poured us another drink.

'Thanks,' she said, giggling. 'I really shouldn't have any more.'

'Why not?'

She gave me the look from under the eyelashes.

'Well, you never know...'

I smiled back the way she wanted me to. Then I let the cloud cross my face.

'What's up?' she said.

'Oh, nothing,' I said. 'Just business.'

Her eyes changed expression.

'Oh, don't get me wrong,' I said. 'Don't be offended. It's just that this problem I've got, well, it just crossed my mind. Just flashed in, you know.'

She changed back, moving her shoulder a bit closer to me, almost touching my shirt, cradling her drink to her breasts.

'What is it?' she said. 'Are you in trouble?'

'Well, I'm in a bit of a spot.'

'Is it money? Is business bad?'

I laughed.

'No, business is fine. It's nothing like that. No, I'm just in a spot as far as a couple of my regular models are concerned.'

'I see.'

'And it's not like *that*, either. No, the girls who usually do my lingerie stuff, you'd never believe it, but they're *both* ill at the same time. Both got this 'flu that's going around. So I'm stuck. I have to get the transparencies to the blockmakers by Tuesday morning but I've nothing to shoot. Well, I've something to shoot but nobody to shoot in them, if you see what I mean.'

'Can't you get somebody else. I mean, another model?'

'I've tried. Believe me, I've tried. But it's funny. You can get everybody to do bikini shots, draped towel shots, even back-nude shots. But there's something about bra and pants' shots. You can only get the occasional model who'll do it. I don't know, I suppose it makes it more personal. Or something like that.'

'I don't see why,' Eileen said, seeing very well why. 'I can't see that one's any different to the other.'

'I wish some of my models felt the same way,' I said, pouring more drinks. 'Then I'd be back in business.'

There was a short silence.

'I wouldn't mind helping out,' said Eileen. 'The only thing would be, I wouldn't want anybody I knew seeing it was me, like.'

'Well, they wouldn't, actually. The stuff I've got left is just pantie shots. Waist to knee.' I took a drink. 'But in any case, it's very sweet of you to offer, but I couldn't let you.'

'Well, if nobody's going to know it's me, and if I don't mind, why not?'

She was having the same difficulty as I was in keeping the excitement out of her voice. (Mother was right: girls *were* worse than boys, at least as bad, they always wanted to *show* you.)

I took another drink.

'Well, if you're sure, and *only* if... well, all right, but please... if you find you don't want to, after the first shot, say, then you must feel you can tell me, you know, if...'

'I will,' she said. 'I feel I could say *anything* to you, Peter.'

And so saying she squeezed my arm and pushed herself a little closer into me. Not yet, for Christ's sake, not yet, you stupid bitch. Do you want to spoil things? We've all night to do that.

I pulled away, pretending enthusiastically to get the camera ready. On a purely professional basis, of course.

'Well,' I said. 'This is marvellous. I really didn't think I'd make the deadline with what's left of this lingerie stuff. Now then, where are the packs? They should be under this lot somewhere. Ah, yes. Let's make sure I get the right numbers...'

'Peter,' said Eileen.

'Yes?' I said.

'What do you want me to do?'

'Sorry?'

'I mean, about posing?'

'How do you mean?'

'Well... my clothes. My other ones. Shall I take them off?'

'Well, you can hardly wear two pairs of panties, can you,' I said, making it seem a joke and inwardly delighted when she began to blush, even more so when she had to explain even further.

'No, I mean gym slip and things. What shall I change into?'

'I shouldn't bother,' I said. 'Just hoist up the gym slip round your waist and tuck it in. It'll be out of shot.' I handed her some of the underwear. 'Look, these are the ones we'll do first.'

'All right,' she said, taking them off me. She paused before she said: 'Don't think there's much point in using the changing room, do you? I mean I'd be going backwards and forwards all night, wouldn't I?'

I nodded pretending to be preoccupied with adjusting the camera tripod.

'Shall I stand where I was before?'

'Er... yes. Yes, that'll be fine.'

I looked through the viewfinder.

Eileen pulled her skirt up and tucked it in around her waist. She glanced towards me while she tried to make it stay up, looking to see what my reaction was but my expression was screwed up and hidden behind the camera. My open eye stared through the lens at her underwear. This was the best moment of the evening. After this everything went downhill, became ordinary. Once the underwear was gone, it was finished. But the charade had to be played out to the end. I had to appear as though I liked the girl. As though I wanted her.

PLENDER

I opened the inset warehouse door and pushed inwards very slowly. There was light beyond the door. I waited a moment or two then stepped through. There was a neon-lit loading bay and some old vegetables and nothing else except a staircase and stairwell and on the wall next to the staircase there was a sign that said STUDIO with an arrow pointing upstairs. I walked across the paved floor to the loading bay and eased myself up and sat down on the edge of the platform, out of the neon. Outside a car swished by, its sound faint and muffled. I took out a cigarette and put it in my mouth without lighting it. I looked at my watch. The luminous figures told me I'd been hanging about for over an hour and a half. I'd phoned Gurney and told him I wouldn't be back at Peggy's and I'd made another phone call and given instructions for the tape of Froy's phone calls over the last forty-eight hours to be dropped through the letter box at my digs instead of the night safe at the office. I didn't want any accidents with Gurney.

I sucked on the cigarette. The excitement of seeing Knott was making me feel slightly queasy and I realised I hadn't eaten since breakfast.

I'd been off sick for a few days. It was one of the few times I'd managed to put one over on my mam. I'd just kept going out to the lav and sticking my fingers down my throat so that she'd think there was something really wrong.

The reason I wanted to stay off school was that the end of term exam results were due and, being the end of our first year, I was terrified that I hadn't done well enough to go up into the A stream with Peter and his mates. And Peter was sure to go up. He'd been joint first with Ann Colman in the half-year exams. I'd been twenty-second. I knew I'd done better this time but I just didn't know how much better and the worry of it was making me feel almost sick enough not to have to put my fingers down my throat to convince my mam. But I had to go back sometime and find out. Just staying home and thinking about it was making things worse.

It was evening and I was standing in the front room looking out at the crescent. Although the weather was warm, great motionless banks of dark grey cloud soared like granite cliffs above the houses. The street was empty and the air in the front room was close and sticky. Then I saw Peter come out of his house and begin to walk away down the road. He hadn't been over once since I'd been off school. I knew where he was going now, only one place he could be going: pictures. Suddenly I felt a great need to get out of the house, have the freedom of the street outside, stroll down to the pictures with as careless a mind as Peter's.

I went into the kitchen. Mam was reading the paper and smoking.

'Mam,' I said.

'What?' she said. She didn't look up from her paper.

'You know I'm off to school tomorrow?'

'Well?'

'Well, as I'm all right now, maybe it'd be okay for me to go to the pictures.'

'No,' she said.

'Aw, Mam, why?'

'Cause I say, that's why.'

'I'm all right, honest.'

'I don't care. You're off poorly.'

'But I'm off to school tomorrow.'

'You can go tomorrow night, then.'

'But Mam, Peter's off tonight. I've just seen him.'

'I don't care.'

'Aw, Mam.'

I kept on and on at her like this until there was nothing left for her but to do one of two things: she would either fly into a rage and knock me flying, or she would fly into a rage and tell me to bugger off out of it with my moaning and give her some bloody peace. My heart began to sing when she chose the latter. I hadn't spent my pocket money, not having gone out for a few days, and so I didn't have to ask mam for the money; if that had been the case the evening would have been over before it started.

I rushed out of the house and down the road but I didn't catch up Peter. In fact I only just got to the pictures as the lights were going down, but I could see where Peter and his mates from school were sitting, all together, filling up an entire row. So I made my way down to the row behind them and waited for the lights to go up after the shorts had finished.

When the lights came up I tapped Peter on the shoulder. Peter turned around and so did some of the others. He didn't smile or anything but he said:

'I thought you were supposed to be badly.'

'I'm off back tomorrow.'

'I thought you'd wangle it till end of term.'

'Naw,' I said. 'I'm all right now. Mam says I have to go back.'

'What was up with you?' Dreevo asked. 'Wankers' cramp?'

'Naw,' I said. 'Bum boils'

Nobody laughed and they all began to turn back, but I said:

'Eh, up, Pete. Have we had any results yet?' I said the words as though I couldn't have cared less.

'Yes,' he said. 'Final results last Wednesday.'

'What happened?' I said, as though it were a big joke. 'I bet I'm off down to B stream.'

Peter shrugged.

'I dunno,' he said.

'Haven't they told you yet, then?'

He shook his head.

'What position was I in class, then?'

'Fifteenth.'

Fifteenth! That meant I was going up into the A stream. The two first forms had thirty children each; fifteen from each went into the A stream and fifteen from each form went into the B stream. I was safe.

'Hey, that means I'll go up with you, then,' I said.

'Should do,' said Peter.

I asked him what position he'd been.

'Top,' he said.

The big picture came on. I sank back into my seat. Wait till I told Mam! I was off up into the A stream. I sat back and enjoyed the picture more than any other picture I'd ever seen in my life.

But next day at school I found out Peter hadn't quite told me the truth. I'd come fifteenth in class all right, but the marks weren't up to the standard of someone going up into the A stream. In fact all the marks after the first thirteen in our class had been the worst they'd had for years, the headmaster said. Two girls were being kept down to do the first year all over again. So only thirteen children were going up from our class, and the two girls who were too bad to go up made room for two more in the B stream: Harry Clark and me.

The headmaster had told the class this the day I'd sat behind Peter in the pictures.

I struck a match and almost lit the cigarette before I remembered where I was. I shook the match out and turned over in my mind what I was going to do. I was certain he was married. I would have staked my life on it. Old Knottsy was the type that needed some kind of constant female company, even if it meant getting himself spliced. So if he was married what was going on upstairs in the studio was probably a big secret between him and the kid. In which case he probably cared for his missus. Or for the set-up she provided. That was more like Peter Knott. He'd hate to lose the architect responsible for his gracious living. And he'd be living graciously, no doubt about it. All that I had to do was to find out who the girl was. And I could find that out by following him to where he dropped her off and take it from there.

I slid off the loading bay. I had to get back to the car so that I'd be ready for them.

As my feet touched the floor I heard way above me the sound of a door opening and the voices of Knott and the girl as they came out of the studio.

KNOTT

I was the way I always was, afterwards. I could hardly speak with the feeling of sickness I had. All I wanted to do was to get rid of this girl and rush back to my wife and sit with her in front of the telly and afterwards kiss the soft cheeks of my two kids as they lay in bed asleep. I wanted to climb into the luxury of a hot bath, the door locked behind me, and lie there and think about absolutely nothing. I wanted to wake up the next morning and lie between the cosy sheets and listen to the church bells and have my kids fall all over me and let them make me forget what an evil bastard I was.

Eileen couldn't understand what had happened to me now that it was all over. Not that she was in a fit state to understand very much at all. She'd had more to drink than she'd thought she'd had and her brain was trying to take in what had happened after the formality of the catalogue shots. Not that she'd minded very much but some of the shots I'd taken once we'd stopped pretending and started doing just that must have struck her as being at least original. But now my present coldness was causing her to have second thoughts about her willingness. Dumbly she pulled her coat round her shoulders as I opened the studio door to get us out and I remembered that earlier I'd helped her off with it as proof that I was a gentleman. Oh, for Christ's sake, I thought as she went by me, just let me get her home and that'll be an end of it. Except for the pictures. But then when I developed them they wouldn't seem real. That wouldn't be a real girl in the prints, somebody I'd known and made love to. She'd be someone I'd dreamed up, unreal, a fantasy for masturbation.

I closed the door behind me and looked at Eileen. She was standing near the single rail of wood that acted as a banister, her foot on the top step, her back to the staircase. She was looking down at her toes, her face all still, silent and regretful. I wanted to say something to make her feel better but to do that would have required more effort than I was capable of so I said nothing at all and began to turn back towards the door so that I could lock it. But as I moved, Eileen moved at exactly the same moment, reaching out for me, for some kind of comfort. And seeing what was coming I completed my turn more abruptly than I'd intended, to avoid her gesture by pretending not to have seen it. But in her hurry to touch me before I turned, her foot slipped off the top step and she lurched towards me, falling against me just as I reached the end of my turn, as I pushed the key into the lock. The thrusting movement of my shoulder caught her in the chest. She spun round and was forced to begin trotting down the top few steps as the momentum carried her downwards.

She would have been quite all right if she hadn't reached out and tried to stop herself by hanging on to the banister rail with both hands. But when she did that her upper body was jerked to an abrupt halt while her legs shot out in front of her and instead of landing on the stairs they swung out into the space of the stairwell so that she was left dangling in the blackness of the stairwell, her fingers locked together round the banister. For a moment I couldn't move. Then, slowly, as if any speed might cause her fingers to slip apart, I began to walk down the stairs to help her.

Her coat miraculously was still clinging to her shoulders. As I drew close to her it slipped off her and half of it lay on the edge of the staircase, the other hanging in the empty space. I stared, fascinated, at the slow movement as the weight of the lower half dragged all of the coat over the edge and away out of sight. A moment later there was a soft slap as the coat hit the paved floor below. It was then, exactly as the coat made the sound, that Eileen's fingers parted and slipped from round the banister. She didn't make a sound. One second she was there, the next she was on her way down to her death.

I heard her hit and I screamed.

Then I sat down abruptly and still with my mouth open but now unable to scream I stared at the space where Eileen had been. My brain seemed to be paralysed. It refused to put any thoughts in motion, as if by freezing, it denied what had happened. If I sat there long enough, just staring, perhaps forever, then everything would be all right. Everything would become normal again. I would take Eileen home and drive back to my wife and kids and tomorrow would be Sunday and everything would be fine.

I sat there a long time trying to pretend it hadn't happened but it was no use. At the bottom of the stairs there was a dead seventeen-year-old girl and I'd been taking pornographic pictures of her and when the police came they'd know and my wife and my kids would know and my parents and Kate's old man would know and it would be the end of everything. And all because of an accident. That's all it had been. She'd tripped and she'd fallen. Misadventure, didn't they call it? Death by misadventure. And her misadventure had been coming out with me. I was responsible for her accident. Above all, I couldn't stand anybody to know that. That I was responsible for stopping someone living out the rest of their life.

I had to put Eileen somewhere else. Nobody would connect her with me. They couldn't. Nobody knew I'd even spoken to her.

Except Peggy.

Sickness welled up inside me. If her picture was ever in the paper, would he remember her? She hadn't even stood at the bar. I'd taken her straight to the booth. And Peggy, being the way he was, had perhaps refused to look into her face. Or maybe he'd looked too closely. God, oh my God. Perhaps I ought to go to the police right now and tell them exactly what had happened. It had been an accident. They'd probably believe me. There was no reason they shouldn't. No, it wasn't the police I was afraid of: it was the people I knew that terrified me. They'd hold me far more responsible than any unbelieving judge could. My life would be changed just as effectively as if I were charged for manslaughter. So I had to alter what had happened. Take a chance on Peggy. But dare I do it. Supposing... I pressed my hands against my face.

What was I going to do? A dead girl, alive two minutes ago. Dead because of a phone call from me. Seventeen years old. Lying there still warm and full of drink. What would she look like, dead? How had she landed? Would I be able to look at her? Would I be able to touch her?

I forced myself to stand up and made for the banister rail. I gripped the rail as tightly as she had done and leant forward and looked over into the blackness. The pale neon washed over the warehouse floor casting long shadows from the body of Eileen. Seeing her lying there made me close my eyes and jerk back from the edge. Seeing her lying there finalised the reality in my brain. Eileen was now a dead girl, dead because of me.

PLENDER

I waited out of sight in the shadows.

There wasn't a sound from above for at least five minutes. Then I heard the footsteps, distant and slow at first, but as they got closer to the bottom of the stairs they became quicker.

Peter Knott stepped on to the warehouse floor and looked at the girl's body. He only looked at it briefly. Then he wiped his mouth with the back of his hand and hurried over to the door that opened on to the street and climbed through and disappeared.

The silly sod, I thought. He's panicked. What a bastard. But I stayed where I was for a few minutes more, just in case. Which was just as well because a little later I heard the Mercedes draw up outside the warehouse. Knott stepped back into the light and walked over to the body and then straight past it, towards me.

I stopped breathing.

He came to a halt about three feet away from where I was. He seemed to be looking straight at me. I waited for him to speak. Instead he bent down and began to rummage about in the darkness, sorting through something which in the gloom I couldn't make out. Then I noticed the smell of dust in the air, rising into my nostrils from where Knott was rummaging. Sacking. The smell was unmistakable. Dusty sacking. I smiled to myself. Peter Knott had made a decision.

KNOTT

I let one of the sacks drop to the floor and stood by the body holding the other one in both hands, as though I was waiting to do the gentlemanly thing and slip a coat over a lady's shoulders. I looked down at Eileen's body and tried to forget that it had any connection whatsoever with myself or with death.

But her eyes were open and shiny and the lipstick she'd put on before we'd left fought with the redness that crept from her tongue. (Perhaps if she hadn't put the lipstick on then this wouldn't have happened: we would have come out of the studio at a different time and in a different way and by now I would be turning the car into her street and saying goodnight to her, probably arranging to see her again next week.)

I tried to stop thinking and bent down near her head and lay the sack with its open end near her hair. I tried to slip my hand under the back of her head in order to lift her up slightly so that I could lay her head on the lower lip of the mouth of the sack. But my fingertips discovered that the back of her head didn't exist any more.

I tried very hard not to be sick.

The only thing I could do to separate her head from the flagstones was to take hold of some bunches of her hair and pull. There was a sound that made me shudder. Then I let go of her with one of my hands and slid the sacking beneath her head and neck. I tugged the sacking under her shoulders then I covered her head with the top lip of the sack and I didn't have to look at her face any more.

PLENDER

I watched Knott drag the sack over to the warehouse door and wondered how the bloody hell I was going to get out. I should have chanced it when he went to get his car from the car park. Now it looked as though I was going to get myself locked in. What a bloody idiot I was. Not that I wouldn't be able to get out; a place like this was kids' stuff. No, it would mean missing out on Knott's plan of action, which was something I didn't really want to do. I cursed again.

When Knott reached the warehouse door he let go of the sack and stood there sizing up the best way of getting the bundle through the doorway. A thought must have struck him because he left the bundle where it was and walked back past me and past the loading bay right to the other end of the warehouse and began to trundle one of those porter's handcarts, the kind you see on railway stations, over to the doorway. He lifted the trolley through the doorway then, after he'd checked there was no one about, he manhandled the sack out into the night. Which gave me my chance. The minute Knott and the sack disappeared through the opening I shot over to the warehouse door and pressed myself behind a jutting brick return that flanked the doorway.

I could hear the iron wheels of the trolley on the pavement outside. The sound stopped and there was silence for a while until I heard the car boot slam. Then the trolley was trundled back to the doorway. Peter Knott lifted it through and pushed it back to exactly where he'd found it. And while he was doing that I nipped through the doorway and raced across the road to the car park.

KNOTT

As I drew away from the warehouse the gates at the level crossing began to close. There was nothing I could do without risking an accident so I slowed down and stopped the car and waited.

I sat with both hands gripping the steering wheel and stared straight ahead beyond the crossing gates, up into the night sky where the low cloud was breaking up and turning into rags that raced across the new moon, its face as pale as death. I felt nothing. There were no emotions churning about in my stomach. It was as if I'd locked off any feelings by closing some kind of air-tight door somewhere in my chest: my guts were no longer affecting my brain. Anything I thought now about what had happened was initiated only in my mind: I couldn't afford for the rest of my body to affect me. Not now, at any rate. Now I had to find somewhere to leave Eileen's body, a place where it wouldn't be found for a long time, at least until any trail had had time to go cold. Also a place where no one would remember seeing a brand new Mercedes SL. A place where I would leave no tyre tracks. A place I had to find within the next hour or two, so that my wife wouldn't suspect me of being unfaithful again because I'd got home late: any questioning that was directed at me tonight might activate the perverse in me and cause me to confess.

There was only one place I could think of. On the way home, off the main road, there was a track that led down to the river.

At one point it forked. If you went right, you got to the sailing club. The clubhouse was built on the edge of a vast, disused brick pit. I was a member of the sailing club: I went there quite often, but more for the drinking than the sailing.

But if you went left at the fork, the track led to the remains of the attendant brick works. One of the buildings was still in fairly good shape, a kiln house. In the kiln house there were ovens. One of them still had its cast iron door attached to it.

That was where it had to be. If I passed another car driving down there I'd just make for the sailing club. If I didn't, then I'd switch off my lights and turn left for the brick works. On my way back I'd still keep my lights off and watch for any approaching headlights: that way I'd know when it was safe for me to pull out of the brick works road.

It was the only thing for me to do.

There was no sign yet of the approaching train. Come on, I thought. For Christ's sake.

A movement in the driving mirror caught my eye. The white jet of headlights swung out of the car park then flared up in the glass in front of my eyes. A silver grey Cortina rolled to a halt behind me. I began to sweat. It was as if the boot were wide open and whoever was driving the Cortina could see the bleeding body of Eileen frozen in the car's headlights.

I pulled myself together. Nobody in the world except myself knew what was in the boot of my car. Nobody else *would* know. The only way I would be discovered would be if I panicked. And a silver grey Cortina parked innocently behind me was no reason for me to panic.

The train appeared. A two coach diesel. Then the gates staggered open and I rumbled the car across the rails. I looked in my driving mirror. The Cortina paused for a moment before pulling away.

PLENDER

I kept a good fifty feet between us all the way. He really began to get worried when he found I was still with him on the river road. He tried to shake me by putting on a burst of speed. In that car he could have lost me any day of the week, but he wasn't going to risk anything by letting his motor do its stuff. So I stayed with him when he accelerated away and slowed down when he slowed down, still keeping the same difference between us.

I smiled to myself. What he must be thinking. A body in his boot and a Cortina up his arse.

I wondered where he thought he was going to get rid of it. Not down on the river, surely. He may as well have dumped it on top of Queen Victoria's statue in Princes Square. Five minutes. That's how long it would take before somebody fell over it. He must have seen too many British pictures.

KNOTT

I'd be at the turning in five minutes. What the Christ was I going to do? The Cortina had stayed behind me all the way. It couldn't be the police. Didn't all police cars have to be marked? But supposing it was? Supposing I'd been seen putting Eileen in the boot. Supposing the driver was just following me and waiting to see what I was going to do? Didn't they sometimes just follow you in order to throw a scare into you? That had happened to Kate once, one time when she'd driven down to London. She'd been over the limit and a patrol car had stayed right behind for a good ten miles. She'd thought she'd had it until they suddenly pulled out and overtook her and went haring off in front of her.

But even if there was nothing more to it than the fact that the Cortina's driver just happened to be taking the same route as me, I couldn't chance going through with my earlier plan. The Cortina's driver would be bound to remember my car when Eileen's body was discovered, when the news went out on television, when Peggy the barman remembered seeing the two of us together – Christ, what a bloody fool I was. Why didn't I turn round and take Eileen's body back and go to the police and tell them exactly what had happened? And then the thought of losing everything I'd got because of a bloody stupid accident flooded back into my mind. Could I risk that happening? I thought of the body lying all twisted up in the boot. No one should have to lie like that, alone. I shouldn't have to feel responsible for someone lying there like that. If only I'd never phoned her. God, what was I going to do?

PLENDER

I thought it was time I gave old Knottsy a bit of a hand.

We were only a couple of miles from where he lived, if he hadn't moved since he'd had his address put in the phone book. The road we were on was at its closest point to the river. There were a number of narrow access roads running down to the bank. He *must* have decided to dump her down there. Christ, if he went any further he may as well leave her out on his front lawn.

No, he really did need the fairy godmother bit at the moment. So I went ahead and gave it to him.

KNOTT

I dipped my headlights as a car rounded the bend in front of me, coming from the opposite direction. But the minute I dipped the Cortina behind me began to pull out. The fool was going to try and overtake. There wasn't the time or the room. He must be able to see that. Any fool could see *that*. But he kept coming, accelerating all the time. He drew level with me. The other car was almost up to us. Then at the last minute the Cortina dropped back and tried to tuck in behind me again, but he misjudged my speed and his own speed and the length of our cars and just about every bloody thing else because he swung his wheel to the left too soon and clanged into the back of my Mercedes.

I don't know how I managed to keep the car on the road. The back end swung towards the kerb. I whipped the steering wheel from side to side until I thought I was out of trouble but the fool didn't even attempt to slow down after he'd swiped me and, as I tried to hold the Mercedes steady, the Cortina hit me again, ramming hard into the boot. I knew by the sound he'd done a lot of damage. Supposing he'd caused the boot to snap open. I had a mental picture of the body flying out into the road, sliding out of the sack, illuminated by the Cortina's headlights. I jerked the steering wheel hard over and bumped the Mercedes on to the grass verge and stood on the brakes.

I fully expected the Cortina to keep going; I imagined he'd be only too pleased to get as far away as possible without exchanging insurance companies. But that wasn't the case. The Cortina came to a halt a little way up the road.

I watched, fascinated, as the driver's door opened and a man got out and walked round to the front of his car. I wanted to run. A little while later he reappeared and began to walk towards me. I managed to open the door and get out before he reached the car: after all, I was the injured party. To be passive would be suspicious. I walked round to the back of the car. The boot, thank God, was still closed. I heard the man approach. I pretended to inspect the damage. The footsteps stopped behind me.

The man said: 'Bloody hell, I'm sorry. I don't know how it happened. I must have had a blank moment.'

I straightened up and turned to face him.

'It's done now,' I said. 'It doesn't matter whose fault it is.'

'Oh but it does,' he said. 'I mean, it was my fault. It was all my fault.'

'It doesn't matter,' I said, walking past him, back towards the open door.

The man followed me. He couldn't believe his ears.

'Doesn't matter?' he said. 'What do you mean? You're not intending to pay for the damage yourself?'

I eased myself into the driver's seat and looked up at the man. The interior light illuminated his face.

I stared at him. I could have sworn...

'Hey,' said the man. 'Hang on. Wait a minute.' A great grin broke over his face. 'I don't believe it. It can't be. I just don't believe it. Peter. Peter Knott.'

Now I knew I was in hell. Staring into the car was a face I hadn't seen for fifteen years. The face of Brian Plender.

A car swept past us, it's headlights turning Plender's face chalk white, blurring the features, and then bringing them back into focus.

Brian Plender. My Christ.

'Christ,' he said. 'Peter. Peter Knott.'

He stepped back. I was expected to get out of the car. Somehow, I managed to do what was expected of me. We shook hands and I found it in me to say his name out loud and smile and gabble a few meaningless phrases.

'I don't believe it,' he said again. 'I really don't. Here. What're you doing on this side of the river, anyway? You don't live over here, do you?'

'Well, actually, yes...'

'What a coincidence. Me and you. Neighbours for years and now we're neighbours again. In a manner of speaking.'

He punched me lightly on the upper arm.

'Do you live near here?' he said.

'Yes. Yes, I do.'

'Whereabouts?'

I told him. He whistled.

'You must be doing all right. I live in Henderson Street. Do you know it? It's off Carr Road.'

I shook my head.

'Not surprising,' he said, as though it was a joke. Then his face became serious. 'Anyway, look, about your car: I'm sorry. I really am. But, I know someone in the trade. He owes me a favour. Let me have it now and I can have it back to you by Monday.'

I opened my mouth but I was sure I wasn't going to be able to speak.

'No, that's all right,' I heard myself say. 'Don't worry about it. I'll get it seen to myself.'

'You sure? Look, honestly, let me...'

'No. My own garage'll do it.' I said. I managed a smile. 'They specialise in Mercedes.'

'Well, have it your way,' he said. 'I say, if you live in Ingham, you must know the Ferry Boat.'

I nodded. I knew what he was going to suggest. Sickness

welled up in my chest. I had to get away from him. My previous plan was useless now. I had to be on my own and think of something else instead of standing in the flicking rain acting out this bloody farce. But I daren't be too abrupt in case at a later date my abruptness was remembered.

'Yes, I do,' I said. 'I...'

'Well then, this calls for a drink.' He looked at his watch. 'We've over half an hour. Hell, we've fifteen years to fill in. What about it?'

'Look, Brian, I'd love to,' I said. 'But I told the wife...'

'The wife? You married?' He punched me on the arm again. 'You old son of a gun. You're the last of the old gang I'd expect to be married. Still, knowing you, she's worth the ball and chain, eh?'

I forced my mouth to work again and managed to nod my head at the same time.

'The thing is,' I said, 'I've been working all day and she's been expecting me since six...'

'Phone her up,' he said. 'This kind of thing doesn't happen every day. She's bound to understand. Better still, why don't we go straight round there? I'm dying to meet the lass that put a dog collar on old Peter Knott. How about it?'

There was no way out of it. I had to go and have a drink with him. Anything rather than take him home with me. That was unthinkable. Once home I'd never get out of the house again: there'd be nothing plausible enough I could tell Kate. A couple of drinks now and I'd be able to get rid of him at closing time.

'Well, we'd better not do that,' I said. 'But I suppose I've got time for a quick jar.' I forced a smile. 'As you say, it's not every day of the week this kind of thing happens.'

PLENDER

The Ferry Boat was full of Hoo-ray Henrys. It always was and it always would be. The kind of local the Hoo-rays referred to as Their Little Pub on the River. As we pushed our way through the mass in the saloon to get to the snug it appeared that quite a few of the Hoo-rays were on terms with Knott. It didn't surprise me. Knott was the type to aspire to that kind of jolly group.

There was a bloke and his bird in the snug which meant there was just enough room for both of us to get in.

I was lucky enough to get a barman straightaway.

'Well,' I said, 'what's it going to be, Peter?'

His face was the colour of a perch's belly.

'Er... do you mind if I have a Scotch?' he said.

'Have what you like,' I said. 'Why not make it a large one as time's getting on?'

'Actually, I wouldn't mind,' he said.

No, I bet you bloody wouldn't, I thought.

I ordered the drinks and turned back to face him.

'Peter Knott,' I said, looking him up and down. 'So come on... give. What've you been up to the last fifteen years?'

'I beg your pardon?'

He'd been looking at something somewhere in the middle-distance of his mind, something that had caused him to turn even greyer. I could imagine how he must be feeling; the reality of what had happened to him must have been washing over him like waves of nausea. I smiled to myself but outwardly the smile appeared as though I was trying to chivvy up his memory.

'Come on, the life story. How I made my first million and all that.'

He took a drink.

'Oh,' he said. 'Well, nothing much really. Art College after school...'

'Yes, I heard that was what you'd done. My mam sometimes saw yours down the town. When was it you moved house? Fifty-four?'

'About that.'

'That made the difference, of course.'

'What?'

'To keeping in contact: that's how we lost touch.'

'Oh. Yes.'

He took another drink.

'And?' I said.

He swallowed, hard, and it wasn't just because of the drink.

'I took photography at College. After that I went down to London for a few years.'

'So what made you come back up here? Weren't the bright lights bright enough?'

'I got offered this contract that was too good to turn down – Sid?' He snatched at the barman's arm. 'Sid, two more large ones, please.'

'Coming up, Mr Knott.'

'What contract was this?' I asked.

'What? The contract. Yes. The contract.' He was beginning to fray really badly. 'Well, my father-in-law, he gave me this contract to do his catalogue. Comes out twice a year.'

'Catalogue?'

'For his business. He's in the mail order business. He sends out a catalogue twice a year.'

'And you take the pictures?'

'Yes.'

'What, all of them?'

'Yes, nearly all of them.'

'This catalogue,' I said. 'It's one of those big thick ones with everything from household goods through to fashions and that.'

He nodded.

'And you take *all* the pictures?'

He nodded again.

'What, of all the birds and that as well?'

He tried hard to smile and nod this time.

'You lucky old sod. What a job. Photographing bird after bird, day after day.'

He grasped the fresh drinks and just remembered to pass me mine before he began to go to work on his whisky.

'Actually,' I said, 'I must tell you. Quite funny really: Mam used to get one of those catalogues when I was a lad, still does for all I know but anyway, I used to think it was the most incredible thing out because it had all these pictures of birds in their brassiéres and their corsets and that. I used to think it was great. Spent hours on the can with it until Mam got wise and belted me round the garden. Funny. Still, I expect you see so much of it you just don't notice. It must be –'

'You haven't told me about yourself,' he said, his face sagging and desperate. 'What's happened to you?'

'Oh, nothing much,' I said. 'I bought myself out in fifty-nine. Took some doing, getting the money together. Luckily there was some compensation for me mam's accident so I used that.'

'I heard about that. I'm sorry.'

'Long time ago.'

'What are you doing now?'

'I'm a detective,' I said.

He nearly fell apart.

'A detective?'

'Private Investigator. Just like on the pictures. It's a laugh, isn't it?'

'What? I mean –'

'I know what you're going to say: either how do you get to be a detective, or what does a detective do. It's always one or the other.'

'No, it's just that it's so unexpected. You, of all people.'

I shrugged.

'You pick up the chips wherever they fall,' I said.

The barman began calling time.

'I'll see if I can get us another quick one,' I said.

'No,' he said. 'I can't. I must be on my way. Kate'll really be worried by now.'

'Come on,' I said. 'You've time for a quick one. Tell you what, if you want an alibi, why don't I pop home with you now. Corroborate the evidence, so to speak? And meet the missus into the bargain.'

'Well, I really think it's a bit too late,' he said. 'Under the circumstances...'

'Okay,' I said. 'Fine. So what shall I do? Pop round and see you one night next week?'

'Er... yes. Fine. One night next week.'

'Which one?'

'Oh. Any night. It doesn't matter.'

'It might to your missus. Better set a date.'

'All right. Friday. Friday night.'

'Great. What time?'

'Time?'

'Yeah, you know. What they're calling now.'

He looked at the barman, a blank wildness in his eyes. Then the penny dropped but it didn't really make any difference to his expression.

'About eight,' he said, his voice dipped in madness.

'About eight would be fine.'

Then Knott turned away from me and began to walk out of the snug. He moved like a sleepwalker. I followed close behind. When we were out on the car park I said:

'Is your place far from here?'

He shook his head. The broad river swirled and smacked against the bank away to our right.

'Well, I'll tag on behind you if that's all right with you. Just so's I don't have to waste half Friday night digging you up. I'll know which is your place on account of which drive you turn into. Unless you're on particularly friendly terms with the neighbours.'

All he did was to stare at me. He opened his mouth to say something but the words wouldn't come. I smiled at him as though he had said something and walked over to my car and got in. I saw him shoot a glance at the boot of his car. No one else would have noticed it, even less the kind of glance it was. I wondered what the glance would be like if he knew what I knew.

KNOTT

I could feel my face setting into a new permanent expression; glazed eyes, slight mad frown, twisted mouth, slack jaw. I was beginning to lose control.

We drove away from the Ferry Boat; a mini-cortège. That was what we were. A funeral procession without a graveyard to go to.

I turned the Mercedes into the road where my house was. It was very quiet but that's what you paid for. My headlights stroked the street sign. Corella Way. It should have said Street of Dreams. The kind of place I'd always aspired to. Residential. My mother loved it.

I looked in the mirror. The Cortina was turning the corner behind me. There was nothing else for it: I had to turn into my driveway. I revved the engine as little as possible and turned the headlamps off so that they wouldn't sweep the house. If the TV was on there was just a chance my wife wouldn't hear me. Then I'd be able to slip the handbrake off and slide out again and with a little piece of God's own luck she'd never know.

But as I made the turn Plender accelerated the Cortina, blaring the horn as he went past, making a klaxon rat-a-tat, a siren Colonel Bogey. I snapped off my engine. Inside the house, a child had started to cry. Nicola. The bastard had woken her up. The Mercedes was facing the hallway. The outside wall of the hallway was made completely of glass. My wife would have to cross it to go to Nicola if the crying persisted. And if Kate came into the hallway there was no way that she could possibly avoid seeing me.

The crying persisted.

A shaft of light cut into the darkness of the hallway and washed over the Mercedes. Kate appeared, black as the mood her movements described. When she saw me she stopped in her tracks. I jumped to some kind of life and opened the door of the car and got out and walked towards the house. Kate turned away and carried on towards the stairs but that didn't create an alternative for me; I had to go into the house, for the time being, at least. And besides I needed to behave rationally in front of my wife to help stop me going mad.

I opened the glass door and click-clacked across the parquet floor. The soft light from the lounge tickled the delicate jets of the fish fountain. I walked into the lounge and stood in the middle of it, not sitting down, just staring at the night blackness of the picture window. I was beyond any kind of thought.

Eventually I heard Kate cross the hall and come into the lounge. I didn't turn to look at her. She didn't sit down either. I could imagine how she would be standing, one arm pressed into her side, the other bent, crossing her breasts, her fingers massaging the muscles of her rigid arm.

She waited for me to speak.

'What was all that about?' I said, still not facing her.

'Nicola,' she said. 'Some bloody fool blaring his hooter. You must have heard him.'

'Yes,' I said. I turned round. 'Actually, it was someone I know.'

'Oh? Who?'

I had to tell her sometime.

'Quite funny really. Quite a coincidence, I mean.'

'Coincidence?'

I told her what had happened. When I'd finished she said, 'And we're to expect him next week?'

'Yes.'

'What for?'

'What?'

'Drinks, dinner, what?'

'Oh… I don't know. Whatever you like.'

'Well, he's *your* friend. Do you want to give him dinner?'

'He's not a friend, exactly. I mean, really it'll be just a one-off thing. Get it out of the way.'

'Well, we'd better give him dinner, then. He's not likely to reciprocate, is he?'

I shook my head and sat down on the leather settee. Images from the evening slotted into my mind like slides in a projector: Eileen drinking, Eileen in her underwear, Eileen straddled across me, an alcoholic sweat teeming down her face, Eileen staring into my eyes, her own eyes dead, her mouth wet and bloody. I wanted to be sick again.

'I hope his table manners aren't as bad as his driving manners,' said Kate.

I didn't say anything. I searched about in my pockets for my cigarettes.

'There's some in the box,' said Kate, sitting down on the white pouffe, still scratching her arm.

She pushed the box across the glass-topped coffee table. I took a cigarette and lit up and sneaked a glance at my watch. It was almost eleven-thirty.

'What's he like?' she said.

I inhaled, looking everywhere round the room, anywhere except into Kate's eyes.

'What's he like?' I said, playing for time, hoping my

concentration would somehow miraculously return. 'I don't know, really. I mean, it's been so long.'

'Yes, but what was he like then?'

For Christ's sake, I thought, just leave it alone.

'Then? Well, we were only kids. What he was like then and what he's like now are bound to be two different things.'

'Oh all right. If you don't want to tell me.'

I couldn't afford for her to lose her temper with me so I said:

'It's not that. It's just difficult. Fifteen years is a long time.' I massaged my forehead as though I was trying to think. 'Let me see; well, really, he was a bit pathetic. Always on the outside. Of our group, I mean. Of any group. Always on the outside trying to get in. Trying too hard to get in.'

'And consequently no one would let him in.'

'Well, he was *in* the group, if you see what I mean, but *not* in it. He was suffered.'

'The group fool?'

'In a way. The butt of all the jokes. He took it all, though.'

'Just in the hope he'd be accepted.'

'I suppose he pretended the jokes were meant differently.'

'Affectionately.'

'Yes.'

'How bloody awful,' she said flatly.

I nodded and tried to focus my mind on a reason, any reason at all, to get me out of the room.

'What bastards kids can be,' she said.

Something back at the studio. Supposing I said I'd left the printer on. The heat would...

Kate stood up.

'How did the session go?' she said.

'The session? Oh, fine.'

'What were you doing?'

'Handbags. The new range.'

'Exciting.'

I stood up, about to tell Kate about the printer.

'How bad is the car?' she said.

'Not too bad,' I said. 'They'll be able to beat it out.'

'I must go and see,' she said and turned to go out of the room.

I tried to call after her, but what could I say? Don't, whatever you do, open the boot? Instead I found myself following her out into the night. She walked to the back of the car and bent forward and examined the car with that same clinical intensity that women have when they examine a spot or a rash or a cut.

Eventually she pulled a face.

'Nasty,' she said, and tried to open the boot.

I had locked it, hadn't I? I had locked it?

'Is it jammed?'

'No,' I said. 'It's locked.'

She straightened up and gave a last look at the car, a look faintly touched with a certain amused satisfaction.

'Well,' she said. 'They'll have their work cut out.'

She began to walk back towards the house.

I stayed where I was, not able to do anything at all.

Kate stopped and turned.

'Aren't you going to put it away?'

I stared at her.

'Hurry up,' she said. 'I've got something to show you.'

She turned again and carried on into the house.

I got into the car and nudged it into the garage. I had reached a decision by default: it would have to be done in the morning. I'd use Kate's Hillman. I'd tell Kate I was going down to the sailing club to take the dinghy out before the Sunday crowd got there. I'd get up early, before Kate, and I'd move the... I'd put Eileen in the boot of the Hillman and drive down to the brickyards and

I'd do what I'd decided earlier to do. After all, I'd be quite safe. Nobody would know she was here.

All I had to do was to go into the house and get into bed and try and pretend that there wasn't an unalterably dead girl in the boot of my car. I should be able to do that. Provided I didn't go mad before daylight came. Unless, of course, I was mad already.

I went into the house and up the stairs and into the children's bedroom.

Kevin, the youngest, was lying face down, the sheets pulled almost completely over his head. All I could see of him was a tuft of fair hair. It was the same every night. We called him the Sprout because of it.

Tears sprang to my eyes and my face twisted and I wanted to shudder and shake and fall to my knees and let it all surge out of me, let it rush out until I was empty and let the emptiness make the evening void.

But Kate came in and stood by me and looked down at the children.

'Aren't we lucky,' she said, taking my hand in hers.

I nodded, which was all I could trust myself to do. Kate looked at the children for a little longer, then she said:

'Come on. I want to show you something.'

She led me into our bedroom. While I'd been downstairs she'd changed into her dressing gown.

'Sit down,' she said. There was an odd look on her face, a mixture of expectation and shy triumph.

I sat down on the edge of the bed. She hooked her thumbs into the belt of her dressing gown and pushed. The dressing gown fell open. She wasn't wearing her nightdress. Instead she was wearing underwear, new underwear, but the thing was, part of the set was a suspender belt and attached to the suspender belt was a pair of black silk stockings.

I stared at her body showing pink through the soft whiteness of the new things.

'Well?' she said, half embarrassed, half expectant.

I didn't say anything. She must have taken my silence as meaning what she wanted it to mean.

'I finally managed it,' she said, pushing the dressing gown out behind her and twisting her torso round and arching her back so that she could look at the back of her legs. 'It was a devil of a job to find some. It's hard enough these days to get ordinary stockings, but these are as rare as moondust. And as for the suspender belt... I must tell you, in the shops they really thought I was someone out of the ark.'

I said nothing. It was just dawning on me. What she wanted. Now. My own fault. I'd always been on at her about getting stockings, how they turned me on. Today of all days she'd done something about it. She must have been feeling particularly uneasy about me, particularly insecure. So therefore I had to respond. Otherwise she'd be even more suspicious: she'd know I'd had someone else in the last few hours.

She raised a leg and placed her foot on my knee, hands on hips, wobbling slightly on her other leg, the classic pose, the dominant whore, except Kate was the antithesis of the whore. No reason. A girl with exactly the same looks as Kate could have been a whore, but not Kate, it was something other than looks, she was too sensitive, too wrapped up in herself, too much of a brooder, too self-aware, too self-conscious.

'So there,' she said, raising her leg even higher, pressing her silky foot into my chest and gently pushing me back on to the bed. The movement over-balanced her so that she had to let both her arms drop in order to support her as she bent over me, one knee on the bed. Her long black hair fell over her shoulders and tickled my face.

'So there,' she said again.

I stared up at her but instead of Kate all I could see was Eileen's dead face.

Kate put her hands between my legs and felt me.

'Now that I've gone to all this trouble,' she said, 'the proof of the pudding is in the eating. Let's see how much difference it really makes.'

PLENDER

The lights went out at eleven forty-five. I gave them another hour. Cold wind drifted through the branches of the trees opposite Knott's place. I shivered in sympathy and walked across the road and stood by the gate and looked at the house.

It really was very nice.

A bungalow, really, more than a house. But much more than a bungalow. New. Couldn't have been up more than three years. Long and low with one upstairs room and plenty of fashionably rough surfaces and acres of floor to ceiling double glazing. Soft lawns and neat shingle and rows of symmetrical rose bushes and plenty of nice private trellis work.

I had to admit it: the lad had done all right for himself. But he was going to do even better for me.

I opened the gate and walked up the drive. The plan of the house couldn't have been more helpful for my purposes. The garage was at the top of the sloping drive, set apart from the rest of the house. And the room where the light had been, their bedroom, was at the opposite end of the house, round the side.

I tried the handle to the sliding garage door, turning it forward and back again. Not a sound. Well oiled, like the rest of the house. I turned it back again and gave it a gentle tug. It sighed softly but nothing more. Slowly I pushed it up on its rollers. It shuddered slightly but there was hardly a rattle. I stood still for a few minutes. Nothing from the house. I took out my torch and walked into the garage. I splashed the beam on the boot and took out my machinery. A minute later it was open. The body was still there. Which was as I'd expected. I closed the lid very quietly.

I walked round to the side of the car and went to work again. When I'd finished I opened the door and released the hand brake and then I manoeuvred myself out and put my shoulder to the door jamb and began to push.

KNOTT

'You make me sick,' said my wife. 'Sick. You disgust me.'

I lay on my back and stared into the blackness.

'You're wrong,' I said.

'Shut up.'

'Wrong.'

'You don't even respect me enough to admit it.'

'It's not true.'

'Either that or you just haven't got the guts.'

'I told you. I was tired.'

'You bloody liar. You've been screwing somebody.'

'It's just that I've had a hard day.'

'Since when has screwing been hard for you?'

'It's not true.'

'You must think I'm a bloody fool. Actually that's the worst part: you still think I'm the stupid little fool you screwed into marrying you.'

'Leave it,' I said. 'For Christ's sake.'

'God, I really was a stupid little bitch. All starry-eyed at having my first lover. Imagining that it was going to be like that for the next eight hundred years.'

I said nothing.

'Well, I soon learned, didn't I? You were a good teacher. Practical. Start as we mean to go on sort of thing.'

I tried not to listen.

'Who was it anyway? Heather? Jean? Or was it the one with the...'

'Listen. I've told you. You're wrong.'

She swung herself round to face me in the darkness and the next thing I knew she'd brought her clenched fist down on my face with all her force, hitting me in the eye. The darkness exploded into jagged brilliance and she hit me again, this time catching me on the jaw. I managed to get hold of her by her wrist and she struggled for a while until she went limp at the onset of the inevitable tears. I relaxed my grip and scrambled my fingers about on the surface of the bedside table and found a cigarette, then the table lighter. I clicked on the flame and the walls leapt forward briefly and then disappeared.

Kate's sobbing finally subsided. There was silence for a while and then Kate flung herself out of bed and crashed through the darkness and out of the room. A few minutes later I could hear her making up the bed in the guest room. Then there was a click and some muffled rustling and then silence. I lay there for half an hour, listening, and at the end of it there was still silence. I sat up and got out of bed and went out of the room and listened at Kate's door. It was slightly ajar and I could hear her breathing. She was asleep.

I went back into my bedroom and put on some clothes and went down the corridor towards the hall. I wasn't intending to move Eileen now. It was too late. If I was seen then there could be no reasonable explanation at a later date. I had to wait till the morning.

It was just that, during the last half hour, while I'd been lying on my back in the darkness, I'd been taken with an enormous desire to go down to the garage and open the boot and look at what I'd done.

PLENDER

It took me two hours to drive round the river. When I got close to Brumby I was tempted to stay on the main road and drive into town and do a tour round and out again but instead I drove on to the narrow track that wound down the lee of the wolds towards the river and the quarry.

The Cortina lurched and shuddered down the rutted road and in front of me across the river I could see the vast complex of the city pegged out in the night by countless street lights. One of those lights was the light at the end of Peter Knott's street and I wondered what he was doing, was he lying in bed sweating, waiting for the daylight to come, waiting for the moment when he could decently leave the house and get on with his plan, or had he been unable to wait, had he panicked and already rushed down to the garage, propelled by fear and sickness? I smiled. That would be nothing to the fear and sickness he'd feel when he opened the garage door.

I reached the entrance to the quarry and swung the car into the leafy entrance and crawled it along the narrow track. Elderberry branches snapped at the windscreen and scrabbled on the roof. I came to the end of the track and switched off the engine.

In front of me was the great white moonlit expanse of the quarry, its screes and hillocks undulating away into the darkness. I knew every slope, every hollow, every track. We'd come here almost every weekend when we were kids. The perfect playground, for the games we played. I looked upwards, slightly to the left, trying to make out the wood at the quarry's rim. We used to play in there too.

Warm autumn sunshine flashed through the trees. Peter and I slowly crackled our way through the wood, not saying anything, just dawdling the morning away. I was quiet because I was happy and I was happy because Peter and I were on our own, away from his other friends and when he was away from them he was different, sometimes he seemed even as if he really liked me a lot.

After a while we came to the fallen tree trunk where we always stopped and sat for a while.

Nothing was said. I swung my legs, trying to dislodge a peeling piece of bark. Peter seemed wrapped up in his own thoughts. Eventually he slid his hand in his lumberjacket and pulled out a small rolled-up magazine.

'Malc Horsfall in 3L gave me this,' he said, passing it to me. 'Him and Johnno bought it on the school trip to Paris.'

I unrolled it and looked at the cover. It was called Paris Minuit. *On the cover was a drawing of a woman bending over and looking over her shoulder. She was wearing a big hat and you could see up her skirt to her underwear. She was wearing black stockings and high heeled shoes. I opened the book and thumbed through it. There were photographs of women in their underwear, most of them in similar positions to the woman on the cover, lots of them wearing hats and long black gloves, one even had a fur coat on. There were some jokes about women in their underwear as well. There was one where one girl was stretched out on the grass looking all puffed out with her knickers round her ankles and another girl who was dressed like a man standing next to a tree trunk carving a heart with an arrow through it and initials at the top and the bottom, below a number of other, similar hearts. There were stories, which* judging from the accompanying drawings seemed to be about French gangsters beating up their girlfriends. I'd never seen anything like it before.

As I progressed through the book I began to feel hot and excited but with Peter sitting next to me I felt embarrassed at my feelings, in case I showed him how I felt. So when I'd finished I pushed the book back at him as though it hadn't had any effect at all.

'What do you think of it?' said Peter.

'S'all right,' I said.

'Didn't it give you the Horn?'

I shrugged.

'Did me,' said Peter, unbuttoning his trousers. 'Look.'

I looked and blushed and sort of smiled.

'Let's see yours, then,' he said.

'Naw,' I said, as though it was unimportant.

'Didn't you get one, then?'

'Yes.'

'Bet you didn't. Bet you can't get one yet.'

'I can.'

'Bet you can't fetch.'

I didn't say anything.

'I can,' said Peter. 'I can shoot three feet. Even Glegger in 4M can't shoot that far.'

'How do you know?'

'How do I know?' he said scornfully. 'They have a Wanking Club behind the pavilion, fourth formers. Haven't you seen them?'

I shook my head.

'Every dinner-time,' he said. 'They have competitions. Sometimes Beryl Marshbanks and Janet Smith do it for them.'

I was shocked and I was excited. Beryl Marshbanks and Janet Smith.

'I'm off to do it now,' said Peter. 'Are you?'

I shrugged again and shifted my position on the log.

'You can't, can you?'

'Yes.'

'Show us, then.'

I had no choice. I unbuttoned my trousers. He looked at me. I was still soft.

'Go on, then.'

I began to do it. Peter sniggered.

'Is that how you do it?'

I blushed even more deeply and I began to feel sick.

'No wonder you can't fetch,' he said. 'Look. Watch me.'

I watched him and then started again.

'You're useless,' he said.

He leant over and pushed my hand away and took hold of me and began to do it. I didn't dare try and stop him in case he told his friends I was useless.

Then a feeling started that I'd never had before. As he kept doing it we slid off the log, down on to the crisp leaves. He put his arm round my shoulders and our heads banged together. The feeling grew and grew and then when I thought it couldn't get any better it did. And then it was over, but nothing happened to show Peter that it was over.

Immediately I felt sicker and dirtier than I'd ever felt in my life.

'Now you've got to do it to me,' he said.

KNOTT

I stood by the garage door and grasped the handle. A cloud passed from the face of the moon and suddenly my shadow appeared on the garage door and the night was almost as clear as day. Then I knew I wasn't going to be able to turn the handle.

I swung round and lurched away from the garage, down the gravel drive towards the gate, moaning and crying as I went. The faint wind rushed into my ears and flung my noise and my tears out behind me. When I reached the gate I grasped the handles and sank to my knees and pressed my wet face against the woodwork.

Later, when I'd finished, I began to feel a new fear.

The thing that brought it on was my realisation that the wind had dropped completely. There was dead silence. Nothing was moving. All the clouds had gone from the sky and the moon, black shadows of the trees were rigid and still. I turned my head and looked towards the house, the night was bright enough to reflect the trees in the windows.

The fear that came on me now was the fear of Eileen. Rather, fear of my mind, what it might conjure up in its present state. Whether reality or hallucination, it didn't matter which: even a mind's-eye apparition would be enough to make any temporary madness become my final mental condition.

Slowly I forced myself up from the gravel. I turned round to face the house and opened my eyes as wide as possible so no flickering eyelash could cause confusion. I began to walk towards the house, keeping to the centre of the drive, keeping my eyes off the garage, avoiding any glance to right or left. When I got to the hallway's glass facing, my reflected shape caused me to stop and stare at myself as if I were some shambling doppelganger.

I went into the house and the shadow disappeared.

PLENDER

I bumped the Cortina to the right and drove towards the limestone chute and the old engine houses. The narrow-gauge lines were still as they used to be, lazily curving away into the quarry basin, and there were still some panniers, long since prised off their wheelbases and overturned, lying face down on the quarry floor.

I stopped the car and got out and walked round to the boot, lifted out the body and took it over to one of the panniers that lay behind the engine house, where the shade fell all day long.

The pannier stood at the bottom of the limestone chute on the artificial scree made by years of tipping. I bent down and dug away a few stones at the base of the upturned pannier and put my hands under the lip and began to lift. It was even heavier than I'd thought it would be, but that was fine, the heavier the better. I gave a final heave and the pannier tottered over on to its side. Then I went to work on the surface of the stones that had been underneath the pannier until I'd pulled enough away to form a shallow trench. When I'd done that I picked up the body and laid it down in the trench and put the stones back until the body was covered. Then I walked round the pannier and lifted again until I'd pushed and levered it up on to its lip. I gave a final heave and the pannier toppled over back to its original position, sealing off the trench and the body. There was a slight whump as the air rushed out from under the pannier as it hit the stones.

KNOTT

Sunlight wafted on to my face. I opened my eyes. I turned my head and wondered where my wife was. I looked at my watch. It was quarter past seven. Then I remembered.

Amazingly I'd slept.

I closed my eyes again and tried to shut out the reality but it wouldn't go. I had the same suicidal desperation that is usually caused by a champagne hangover. I didn't want to move ever again.

But somehow I jerked myself out of bed and dressed and went out of the bedroom and down the corridor and across the hall and out of the house.

The day was bright and sunny but behind the trees heavy grey clouds were beginning to build up and fill the sky. I hurried across the gravel to the garage, trying not to think so that what I was going to do would be easier.

I lifted the handle and slid the garage door open.

PLENDER

I sat on my bed and played the electric razor over my face and listened to the tape recorder.

The dialling tone stopped and there was the click and a pause and then Froy's voice said:

'This is Mr Brown speaking. I'm phoning to report that the operation has reached a successful conclusion.'

The man on the other end of the phone said: 'Thank you. I had no doubt that it wouldn't.'

'Thank you, sir.'

'The Movement is fortunate to have such competent operatives in its employ, an event for which you have largely been responsible.'

Froy made some more thank you noises.

'As Leader,' said the other voice, 'I shall see that you shall not go unrewarded.'

Froy was almost screaming by now. There was a pause and then Froy ventured: 'I have had Gorton's speech written for the Leeds conference.'

'Yes.'

'I must say it reads well.'

'Who wrote it?'

'Potter of the Crusader. He's going to do a companion piece the weekend after the speech in the Sunday edition. They'll give the speech big coverage and the companion piece will re-state the issues.'

'Excellent.'

'Also the Liverpool rally is in the last stages of organisation.'

'Who are we using?'

'Davies will be the main speaker. Some of our men will be there acting as leftist-anarchist agitators. The television people will be covering it so they won't be disappointed.'

'Good. Well, everything seems to be progressing satisfactorily. The old truths are being well served. In time, England will have much to thank us for.'

'Yes, sir.'

They said their goodnights and the tape went dead. I switched off my razor and got up off the bed. There was a knock on the door. I walked over and opened the door and my landlady bustled in with my breakfast tray and put it down on the table.

'Thanks, Margaret,' I said. 'Been out yet?'

In all the time I'd lived there I'd never once seen her outside of the house.

Margaret shuddered.

'I've got more sense,' she said.

'Go on,' I said. 'Looks a nice day. Fresh air'll do you good.'

'It's bitter out,' she said. 'And it's going to rain.'

'No,' I said. 'It won't rain, not today.'

'You try telling my rheumatism that,' she said, and closed the door behind her.

I picked up my phone and dialled Gurney's number.

'How did it go last night?' I said.

'Well,' said Gurney.

'Was Camille all right?'

'Fine.'

'No messing about?'

'No, she was fine.'

'Well, you know what to do now.'

'Yes.'

'When will the pictures be ready?'

'Give me a chance, Mr Plender.'

'When?'

'Sometime tomorrow, I expect.'

'Good. Listen, there's something I want you to do for me.'

'Yes, Mr Plender.'

'Is Stoney likely to be at the garage today?'

KNOTT

I sat at the breakfast table and stared at the colour supplement. The car had gone. Somebody had taken the car. Stolen it. With Eileen in the boot. What would happen when they found the body? Abandon the car? And then the police would find the car and I'd be finished.

I hadn't told Kate the car had gone. She'd want to know why I hadn't called the police. But she'd have to know sometime. What would happen then?

Kate put a cup of coffee in front of me. Her movements expressed her mood perfectly. Her mind was still on what had upset her last night.

Nicola said: 'What time are we going over to Grandfather's, Mummy?'

Kate said: 'I don't know. Sometime after lunch.'

'Will we be able to swim in the pool?'

'Don't be silly, Nicola. It's far too cold.'

'I don't care about the cold, Mummy, honestly.'

'Well I do. You'd probably catch pneumonia.'

Kevin said: 'Don't you mean pneumonia would catch her?'

'Shut up, stupid,' Nicola said.

'It's like overtaking. It should be takeover,' said Kevin.

'You're just stupid.'

'Come on, both of you, finish your breakfast,' said Kate.

'Finished,' both of them said.

'Well in that case go and get ready for church.'

They both moaned.

'No complaining,' said Kate. 'Go and get your coats.'

They climbed down from their chairs and went out of the breakfast room. Kate stayed where she was, sipping her coffee, elbows on the table, not looking at me. In a few moments she would get up and put her coat on and take the children into the garage and find that the car was gone.

I said: 'Do they have to go?'

'They were christened so it follows that occasionally they should attend church.'

'But why today?'

'Because they haven't been for over a month.'

'I thought we might all go out for a walk together.'

Kate looked at me in mock surprise.

'Oh? What brings this on? Guilt feelings about last night?'

I didn't say anything else. Kate returned to her coffee, a bitter triumphant look on her face. She took a final sip and put her cup down and went out of the kitchen. I heard her cross the hall and open the coat cupboard and heard the children rush down the corridor to meet her.

'Mummy, it's my turn to sit in the front, isn't it?' said Nicola.

'It isn't, it isn't,' said Kevin. 'She sat in the front last time, didn't she Mummy?'

'I'm sure I can't remember,' said Kate, 'but in any case there'll be no arguments today. You can both sit in the back.'

The children groaned and complained and I heard Kate usher them across the hall and out of the house. The door closed and the double-glazing shook and then there was an ear-splitting silence except for a few bird songs drifting across from the trees that surrounded the house.

The silence continued for a while. Then there was the sound of crackling gravel as Kate ran back to the house. The door was scrambled open and Kate shouted my name, hurrying across the hall, not waiting for my answer, and then she was standing in the kitchen doorway.

'Peter,' she said, as if she didn't quite believe what she was saying, 'the car's gone.'

I looked at her and said: 'The car's gone?'

'The Mercedes. It's gone.'

'The Mercedes?'

'For Christ's sake yes. The Mercedes. Come and see.'

The madness in my mind made me consider her choice of words. Come and see the car. It's gone. The old joke. There it was, gone.

I stood up and pushed my chair back and followed her like a sleepwalker, out into the bright undecided weather.

The kids were jumping around near the garage in a state of excitement.

'The car's gone, Daddy,' Nicola shouted as I approached.

Kate was standing in the space where the car should have been, demonstrating the garage's emptiness. She stared at my face, waiting for me to make some kind of comment. I looked round the garage, as if to make sure the car really wasn't there.

'Well?' said Kate.

'I don't know,' I said.

'Has it been stolen, or what?'

'It looks like it.'

'Well, what else could it be?'

I shook my head. Kate turned round slowly and looked at the emptiness.

'I don't believe it,' she said. 'Someone came here during the night and took the car. How horrible.'

She turned full circle until she was looking at me again.

'I must say it doesn't appear to be worrying you unduly,' she said.

'It's not sunk in yet,' I said.

'Well, it had better sink in pretty quickly,' she said. 'We've got to do something.'

I nodded, knowing what the something was going to be. I felt as if I was being sucked down into a quicksand.

'You'd better phone the police,' she said.

I turned away and began to walk out of the garage.

'I'll just check that it's not out in the road,' I said, playing for time and at the same time aware that it would be ultimately useless.

'Out in the road?' said Kate. 'What on earth are you talking about? Why should it be out in the road?'

'Perhaps somebody just borrowed it for a joy-ride. It sometimes happens,' I said, starting down the drive. 'You read about it in the papers all the time. Somebody steals a car and goes for a drive and brings it back to where they found it.'

Kate followed me down the drive, and the children followed her.

'You must be joking,' she said. 'They wouldn't go to the trouble of breaking into a garage just to take a car for a joy-ride. It's obviously much more serious than that.'

I opened the gate and went and stood in the middle of the road and looked up and down, but, of course, the road was empty. Kate was standing in the open gateway looking at me as if I was some figment of her imagination. I walked back towards the gate, indescribably sick and on the verge of tears.

'I mean,' said Kate as she stood back so that I could close the gate, 'if someone wanted to joy-ride it's obvious they'd choose a parked car. They wouldn't go to the trouble of –'

She stopped in mid-sentence as I whirled round and grasped her by her arms.

'All right,' I shouted. 'You're right. For fuck's sake, you're right. Now shut up. Just shut up. Shut up, shut up, shut up.'

The children froze and stared at the two of us. At first Kate didn't attempt to free herself from my grip. Then the shock on her face turned to contempt.

'Even with the children watching,' she said.

Then she shook her arms and I let go. Kate walked over to the children and knelt down and put her arms round them. Nicola looked as if she was about to cry.

'Don't be upset,' said Kate. 'It's nothing. Daddy and Mummy love each other, really.'

I ran past them on into the house. I went into my studio and closed the door behind me and sat down in my leather chair and stared at the wall, forcing myself not to think. After a while Kate came into the room.

'You bastard,' she said eventually.

I didn't look at her and I didn't say anything.

'I hope you don't forget the looks on their faces,' said Kate.

'I'm sorry,' I said, putting a hand to my own face.

'Try telling that to Nicola.'

I just stayed the way I was, my head resting in my hand. I heard Kate light a cigarette. There was silence for a long time until Kate said:

'I want to know what's wrong.'

I didn't answer.

'There is, isn't there?' she said. 'I want to know what it is.'

I shook my head.

'Why aren't you worried about the car?' she said.

Oh Christ, I was thinking, over and over. Oh Christ. Why don't you help me?

'You're not worried about the car because you're too worried about something else. Aren't you?'

I shook my head again.

'Then why haven't you phoned the police?'

My mouth began to work, trying to say the words that my brain was unable to put together.

'It's because there's something else.'

When I made no reply she said: 'Peter. I've a right to know.'

I knew exactly what she was thinking. She was thinking I'd become so involved with someone that I wanted to leave Kate and the children.

'There's nothing wrong,' I managed to say. 'Nothing.'

'Don't lie, Peter. Have the guts to tell me the truth.'

'I don't... I can't... there's nothing. Nothing.'

Kate didn't say anything for a while. Then she said, very quietly: 'All right.'

There was another long dead silence until Kate said: 'Aren't you going to phone the police?'

I was unable to make any kind of reply.

'In that case,' she said, just as quietly, 'I'd better phone them myself.'

She walked over to my desk. I lifted my head and watched her progress with a dumb fascination. Now it was all over. I may as well tell her. It was the only thing to do. As her hand touched the receiver I opened my mouth to speak.

But before she lifted the receiver the phone began to ring.

PLENDER

A woman's voice answered.

'Corella 332,' she said.

'Hello,' I said. 'Could I speak to Peter, please?'

'Who's that calling?'

'It's Brian Plender speaking.'

I heard far away mumblings, then the receiver rattled and Knott's voice said: 'Yes?'

'Hello, Peter,' I said. 'Brian here. How's the world treating you today?'

He didn't answer.

'Been down to the garage this morning?'

I didn't even expect an answer this time.

'Look,' I said. 'I'd better come clean. I don't know whether you realise this, but last night... well, before I bumped into you (if you'll pardon the expression) I'd had a couple. You know, Saturday night and all that.'

Still nothing.

'Anyway, I really felt bad about what happened. I mean, it was my fault entirely. I felt I had to do something. I kept thinking of that beautiful car all banged up because of me. So I came back.'

'Came back?' he said. I smiled to myself. The words were slurred and hollow.

'Yes. I came back. The house was... you were all in bed. So I took the car. Took the car and drove it over to my mate's place.

You know, the one I mentioned. The one with the garage. He's working on it now. No problem. A few taps with his little rubber hammer and it'll be as right as ninepence by tonight. Now I know what you're going to say: I'd got no right to do it. And you'd be right. But as I say, I'd had a couple, and all I could think of was getting the car straightened out. No problem getting it started. Trick of the trade, really. You pick up that kind of thing.'

'You took the car,' said Knott's voice.

'My mate started on it first thing. He knew it wouldn't take long as soon as he looked at it. Course it needs a new tail light but he's got a friend who's a Mercedes dealer and he's shooting one over. Help with the wiring as well, no doubt.'

'How... how far has he got with it?'

'I don't know, but he had a good look at it, opened the boot and had a shufti from the inside, and, as I say, tonight's the night.'

There was no sound from the other end of the line.

'So what I thought was,' I said, 'as I took the liberty of taking it away like that, the least I can do is to deliver one good-as-new Mercedes to your place sometime tonight.'

Still nothing. Then: 'He opened the boot?'

'Yeah, that's right. Well, he had to, sooner or later, so's he could go to work.'

I wondered if his wife was watching his face.

'Why,' I said. 'What's the matter? Did you have the family jewels stashed away in the back?'

Nothing. Then I gave it to him.

'By the way, she's a lovely piece of machinery,' I said. 'Lovely bodywork. Pity she had to get all crunched up like that. But not to worry. It'll be all smoothed out by this evening. Won't be able to find a trace on the body.'

KNOTT

I put the phone back on its cradle.

My wife said: 'Well?'

I looked at her.

'What was that all about?' she said.

I said: 'The car. Plender took the car.'

I stood up and began to wander out of the room, for no other reason than the fact that I could no longer stay where I was.

'So that's it,' said Kate. 'That's all I get to know, is it?'

I opened the door.

'He came back and took the car away,' I said. 'To get it repaired.'

'Without telling us? He just came back and walked in and out while we were in bed?'

I nodded.

'He'd been drinking,' I said. 'He was upset. He wanted to make amends.'

I walked into the lounge and over to the drinks cabinet. I poured a large scotch. Kate stood in the doorway, staring at me.

'What are you doing?' she said.

I drank the scotch and poured another.

'You do know what time it is.'

I sat down on the leather settee and took another drink.

'I hope you're not just going to let him bring it back and leave it at that,' Kate said.

I put the scotch down and lit a cigarette.

'You are, aren't you?' she said. 'You're just going to say thank you very much for taking our car away and not telling us and frightening us half to death.'

'I'll say something to him,' I said.

'I'll bet,' said Kate. 'Well, if you don't I certainly will. When is he coming? Tonight?'

'I'm meeting him at the Ferry Boat.'

'Why there?'

'I don't know,' I said. 'It was his idea.'

I finished my drink and stood up.

'I thought you were going to church,' I said.

Kate gave me a long look.

'What's the matter?' she said. 'Waiting to make a phone call?'

I didn't answer.

'Surely she won't be expecting a call this early?'

I walked over to the cabinet and poured another drink. For Christ's sake, go to church.

'It's too late for church,' said Kate. 'But not to worry. I'll take the kids down to the river. That should give you plenty of time.'

Kate walked over to the door.

'By the way,' she said, 'Millers delivered yesterday, so there's no danger of your running out.'

She closed the door behind her.

I emptied the glass and poured another.

Plender knew.

PLENDER

I dialled a number.

'Hello?' said Harry.

'Harry,' I said, 'I understand Mr Gurney brought in some work this morning.'

'That's right, Mr Plender.'

'Much of it, is there?'

'Not too much. Why?'

'Well, in that case I was wondering if I could come down and borrow your darkroom for half an hour this afternoon. I've got some stuff of my own and I'd rather like to do it myself.'

'I understand, Mr Plender.'

'About three o'clock be all right?'

'Yes, that should be okay, Mr Plender.'

'Thanks a lot, Harry,' I said. 'Thanks very much.'

'See you at three, then,' said Harry.

'At three,' I said.

KNOTT

Kate drove.

The kids sat in the back of the Hillman and I sat next to Kate in the front.

Kate said to me: 'Would you mind opening your window?'

I turned my head to look at her.

'The whisky fumes are killing me,' she said.

I didn't answer. I just rolled down the window and went back to staring at the road.

After a while Kate said: 'Daddy's sure to notice.'

Kate slowed down to take a sharp corner.

'You had to, didn't you? You just had to get like this, today of all days.'

'I'm all right,' I said.

A line of beech trees flashed towards the car. I tried to focus on them but it was no use. I was too far gone.

But at the same time I was in that particular alcoholic state in which a part of the mind, the rational, sober remainder, can detach itself from the rest of the soggy mass and observe the imprecisions of the body and mind of that grotesque character who happens to be oneself.

The part of my mind that was outside of myself was gently amused by the situation of the lolling figure it observed in the front seat of the Hillman. Mouth sagging, eyes blank with fear, fingers convulsing like a dying man's, fuddled, unable to cope with the events of the last twenty hours, and with those events yet to come, unable to shape his thoughts into any kind of logical pattern, trying desperately to organise some kind of defence against the accumulation of shocks and frights still to make their assault on his system.

But the only thought that surfaced above the treacle in his head was the one that said Plender knows.

Of course I could always go to the police. Now there was a thought. Another one. That made two. I'd had that one last night. I could go to the police. Tell them what had happened. Tell them that I was on the way to see them, to bring them Eileen, when I'd had this accident, and so instead of bringing them the body, as it was late, you know, I thought I'd better wait till the morning, as it was late, and you'll never guess what happened next…

I began to giggle. Kate made one of her end-of-tether noises.

'What's Daddy laughing at, Mummy?' Nicola said. Even she wasn't addressing herself to me.

'Just a private joke,' I said, as Kate turned the car into her father's drive.

PLENDER

When the prints had dried I laid them out on Harry's table, then I went over to where I'd hung my jacket and took out my cigarettes and lighter and lit up. I blew out the smoke and thought how easy it had been to get back into the warehouse and let myself into Knott's studio. I'd washed the glasses and emptied the ashtrays and smoothed over the bed in the cubicle and I'd had a good look round to make sure there'd been no scarves or gloves or anything like that left lying about.

Then I'd walked over to the camera set up on its tripod, and I'd noticed that on the little Habitat table next to the tripod there'd been some rolls of exposed film. I'd examined the camera and in the camera there'd been another roll of film that had been completely exposed too. In front of the camera, where it had been pointing, there'd been a large sheepskin rug, all creased up, as though it had been rolled on, a high stool and a divan, a Put-u-up kind of thing, opened out to the full. I'd also noticed that on the camera there'd been a time exposure extension.

So I'd taken the film out of the camera and picked up the other rolls of exposed film and put them all in my pocket.

After that I'd found a plastic bucket and some rags and I'd got the Fairy Liquid from the sink where Knott made his tea and coffee and I'd gone downstairs into the warehouse and cleaned up down there. Then I'd put the rags in the polythene that I kept my car tools wrapped in and that had been that.

I walked over to Harry's table and looked at the prints.

You could see the way the evening had gone from looking at them.

First, just pin-up stuff. Even looked as though it was legitimate enough for his catalogue: crutch shots in different sets of underwear. Then it got a bit more provocative, more girly magazine type of stuff without the re-touching. In most of these he'd got her to wear a gym-slip. Then there were a few covering the stages of her removing her pants and then the dirty stuff started. He'd got her to do all sorts to herself. And finally there were some with him in, the time exposure ones. He must have told her how to operate it herself, because he couldn't have done it, not tied down to the divan like that, with a pair of panties round his knees.

If I'd known Peter and Susan had started walking out together, I'd never have asked her out with me. I'd thought it was just friendship, I really had.

What had happened was this: When Peter's father had got a better job, they'd moved up on to Westfield Road. Susan Armitage lived in the big house right at the top, where the road turns into the track that leads to Worrals Farm and the old quarry. I used to bike home from school with Peter and we'd stop at the bottom of Westfield Road and sit on our bikes and talk for a bit before I'd turn off down the hill and he'd go off up Westfield Road. This was the best part of the day to me, although I always tried hard not to show it: just sitting there on our bikes, able to talk without Peter making me feel small like he did during the day in front of his A stream mates. We'd perhaps talk about what had happened in each other's classes during the day, or make arrangements to go to the pictures or to the park (although I always hoped it would be to the pictures, because only a few of his A stream mates would be there, whereas most of them would be at the park).

And then Susan had started biking home with us. She was in the A stream too, in Peter's form, and her dad had a lot of money, he owned a good few newspaper shops, one in Brumby and the rest in the outlying villages. But my mam said that if he'd gone and done his bit in the army like everybody else had he wouldn't be so well off now.

It was awkward the first time it happened, the first time she biked home with us. I'd been waiting at the bottom of the school hill, as usual, waiting for Peter to come hurtling down the hill with all his mates, waiting to tag on behind the way I usually did, waiting for them all to peel off in different directions when they got to the market place, leaving Peter on his own. And then I'd catch up with him, and we'd bike off to the bottom of Westfield Road together.

But on this day, I saw all Peter's mates go careering past, but Peter wasn't with them. So I waited, knowing that he hadn't gone, because I was always first out of the school gate so as to be sure and not to miss him. Eventually Peter appeared out of the hill's sunlight, but instead of speeding he was sauntering, dawdling, hands on brakes, flashing his front wheel from side to side as an extra brake, and with him, riding one-handed, the other hand in her blazer pocket, her gold hair blending with the streaming sun, Susan, slightly flushed with that look that girls have when they agree to a boy accompanying them, and Peter, sullen, his face concentrated and tight, his eyes never moving from his swivelling handlebars.

There were calls from the stream of children on the pavement as they made their way to the bottom of the hill to the buses.

'Now we know you,' they shouted.

Now we know you. That meant, now we know who you like because being with them proves it. Peter ignored the calls but Susan reddened even more and now she held her handlebars with both hands.

As they drifted past me I put my feet to my pedals and slowly tagged along behind them.

At the halt sign I drew level.

'Going home, Pete?' I said.

'Where do you think?' he said.

I didn't say anything to that.

We carried on through the market place and up the hill until we came to the corner of Westfield Road.

Peter slowed down and I wondered whether I ought to turn off or not but Susan kept on going, calling out 'Bye' to Peter so I stopped and we both positioned our bikes in their usual places by the kerb.

Peter said: 'Don't think I'm going out with her because I'm not.'

'I didn't think anything,' I said.

'Well, don't. My mam and her mam have started getting friends, that's all.'

I shrugged.

'Goodlooking though, isn't she?' I said.

I could have bit my tongue off.

'Not bad.' Then he looked at me. 'Why, do you want to go with her, then?'

I shook my head.

'Naw,' I said. 'Don't be daft.'

The thing was, though, that I loved her with all my heart. I'd loved her since I'd seen her walk into the classroom on the first day at school. But she'd never noticed me. Not once during the first year had we said anything to each other. Then at the end of the first year she'd gone up into the A stream with Peter. And A stream girls didn't talk to B stream boys unless they were like Kerry and Patch.

'What's daft about it?' Peter asked.

'Well, it just is.'

'Why is it?'

'It just is,' I said. 'She wouldn't go out with me, anyway.'

'Who says?'

'A streamers don't go out with B streamers.'

'Don't be daft. Tell you what, I'll ask her for you.'

'No,' I said, panic-stricken. 'No, don't do that.'

'Why not?'

I'd rather never ask than have her say no. Besides, I'd never taken a girl out before. I'd be terrified. I wouldn't know how to behave.

'I'm not bothered,' I said. 'Honest. I just thought she wasn't bad looking, that's all.'

Peter gave me a crafty look but he didn't say anything more about it.

'You won't, will you?' I said. 'I mean, ask her?

Peter gave me the look again. Then he said: 'Off to the pictures tonight?'

I nodded. And that was that.

Until the next day, waiting for Peter at the bottom of the hill. She was with him again. Which was what I'd been hoping for all day. As they sidled by I pedalled after them, this time not tagging along behind, but drawing level with them, Susan on the inside, then Peter, then me.

And this time, when we got to Westfield Road corner, Susan didn't go on.

Peter said to her: 'Riggy wasn't half mad with Zena about her homework, wasn't she?'

'She was worse than that time Rainbow put that shrew in Karen's desk,' said Susan. 'Do you remember?'

'God, aye. She sent him to the Boss,' said Peter.

'I remember that,' I said. 'He got stick, didn't he?'

'He nearly got expelled. Boss said it was cruel to the shrew,' said Peter.

'Well, it was really,' said Susan. 'It was in the desk all night.'

Peter laughed.

'It was only a shrew,' he said.

'Shrews are nice,' said Susan.

'Nice,' said Peter, snorting.

The conversation dropped. I was trying hard to find something to say, something which would mean that Susan would have to say something in reply, directly to me. Eventually I said:

'Good picture last night, eh, Pete?'

'Not bad,' he said. 'I've seen worse.'

There was a pause. Then I said:

'Have you seen it yet, Susan?'

'No,' she said. 'I don't go to pictures in the week. I go on Saturday nights with my parents.'

She looked at me so straight that I had to look away. For a moment I had a terrible feeling that Peter had told her what I'd said.

'What are you doing tomorrow morning?' Peter asked me.

Tomorrow was Saturday.

'I dunno,' I said. 'Nothing. Why?'

'Susan and me are going biking down on the river bank. Want to come?'

I could hardly believe it. A whole morning, out of school, near Susan. And Peter wanted me to go with them.

'Yeah, all right,' I said.

'Call for us,' said Peter. 'About half past nine.'

The next morning Peter and I biked up Westfield Road. Susan was waiting outside the drive that led up to her house. We all rode off down to the river bank.

We stayed down there till gone one o'clock. I'd never enjoyed a morning so much. There was a high April wind, cold and clear, and racing turpentine-coloured clouds, and the water looked fresh and crisp with the wind roaring into it and cutting it up into thousands of tiny waves. And the mood of the day seemed to blow inside us as we ran along the beach and climbed over the broken jetties. Everything seemed funny and exhilarating and the three of us were the only people to appreciate the day. And I lost all my fears as far as talking to Susan was concerned. Today there seemed to be no barriers. And Susan seemed to like me talking to her.

On the way home Susan invited us in. I knew I should have gone straight home, because on Saturdays at one o'clock it was my job to go to Carters and get the fish and chips and Mam would be waiting. But I wanted to spend as much time as I could near Susan, and terrified as I was of Mam and terrified as I was of actually going into Susan's house, I accepted.

I'd never been in a house like it. There were so many things: so many clocks, so many pictures, so many little tables, so many rugs, carpets that fitted, wallpaper that stood out in relief, an enormous gramophone, and even a television set, a huge veneer console with a ten-inch screen.

And Mrs Armitage was as well turned out and modern as her house. Permed hair, flowered dress, even wearing high heeled shoes in the house. She looked years younger than my mam, only I knew that they must be about the same age.

Susan introduced us to her mother and then took us into a room she called 'her room'. It was at the back of the house, with bookshelves and a writing desk and a big wicker basket full of her old toys, and her school things, her satchel, her hockey stick, her tennis racket, and on the writing desk, spread all over, was her weekend homework: she must have started doing it on Friday night. And on the walls there were pictures of her in the netball team and in the hockey team, and one of her and a crowd of other children in the market place, about to get into one of Rowson's coaches at the start of last year's school holiday to France, and there was a signed photograph of Dickie Valentine, and another of Anne Shelton, and on the floor there was a brand new record player with records scattered all around it.

I took it all in, every detail, so that I'd be able to imagine her at home, in this room, listening to her records and doing her homework.

Susan put some records on the record player and after a while Mrs Armitage pushed a tea trolley into the room and on the trolley there were sandwiches and biscuits and three big glasses full of milk.

Peter and I left at about half past two.

As we biked down the hill Peter said to me: 'I reckon Susan likes you, Brian.'

'Don't be so daft,' I said.

'She does,' he said. 'I can tell.'

'How?'

'I just can.'

'Did she say anything then?'

'Naw. Lassies never do.'

'Well, then.'

'It's up to you. You've got to ask her.'

'But supposing she said no.'

'That's nowt to be frightened of, is it?'

I shook my head.

'Suppose not,' I said.

'If you like,' said Peter, 'I'll do it. I'll ask her.'

'Naw, it's all right,' I said.

'You're off to ask her yourself, then?'

I didn't say anything.

'Shall I, then?'

There was no way of getting out of it now.

I nodded.

I spent the rest of the weekend in a state of sweet terror.

At break on Monday, Peter came over to me. I was standing near the Boys' Entrance, keeping off the field so that Susan wouldn't be able to see me.

'I've asked her,' he said, grinning.

I looked at him.

'She says she will.'

I couldn't believe it.

'What did she say?' I said.

'She said to meet her behind the pavilion at dinner-time and then you can fix up a date.'

'Why there?' I said.

'I dunno,' said Peter. 'But that's what she said.'

The thought crossed my mind that she didn't want to be seen walking round the field with me, the way the other courting couples did. And then I was glad it was to be behind the pavilion, because that meant that nobody would see me, nobody would call out after me.

Between break and lunchtime the agony grew. What was I going to say to her? What would she expect me to talk about? What kind of date would I have to make? Would she expect me to bike home with her after school, on our own, without Peter?

After dinner, it was the turn of our table to put the forms and tables away after the rest of those who stayed to School Dinners had been dismissed. This usually took about five minutes. It was a hated job because it meant five minutes less football on the flags or five minutes less fighting on the bank or five minutes less smoking in the Valley. But today it was a thousand times worse. Supposing Susan got there first, waited a few minutes and then left? What would I do then?

When the last form had been stacked I rushed out of the main hall and into the washrooms and stood in front of the mirror and ran my comb under the tap. Late as I was I had to make sure my hair was all right.

Outside the day was warm and overcast. I crossed the field towards the pavilion and the ground was hard and dry under my feet.

Some second-formers were chasing a tennis ball up and down the hockey pitch. There was no sign of Susan. I'd been right. She was there already, waiting, out of sight.

I climbed the slight sandy slope that led to the back of the pavilion and turned the corner. Tall bushes made the trampled space gloomy and quiet.

She wasn't there.

I shuddered as the pent-up breath rushed from my lungs. She hadn't come yet. I leant against the white boards of the pavilion. Now I had to wait and the waiting would make me even more nervous.

I fingered my Windsor knot to make sure it was just so and patted my hair at the front and made sure that my hymn book was neat in my top pocket and I re-buttoned my blazer and made sure my shirt collar was flat.

Five minutes passed.

If she doesn't come soon, I thought, maybe the usual pavilion crowd would turn up and want to know what I was doing. And if she came while they were there, that would be terrible. She might even think I'd asked them along.

I began to want to pee.

It was nerves, just like before going out to bat. I knew, because I'd been to the toilet before I'd crossed the field. I tried not to think about it, but the more I tried the worse it was. And I daren't risk having one now in case she came just as I was doing it.

Another five minutes went by.

I looked round the corner of the pavilion to see if she was coming across the field but there was no sign of her. Perhaps she'd had a puncture on her way back from her dinner. Perhaps she'd had an accident. Maybe I ought to go and wait by the gate… behind me, the bushes rustled.

I turned round and the rustling stopped. Then, almost

immediately, there was a new noise, a snorting stifled giggle. The bushes began to tremble again.

I approached the shaking leaves and peered into the green gloom. Then the bushes exploded with laughter. In the bushes there was Peter, two of Peter's friends, Johnno and Petchy, and Susan, and Susan's friend, Stephanie Toyne. They were all lying on their stomachs, facing the pavilion. They must have been there all the time.

KNOTT

'What would you like, Peter?' said Kate's father. His voice washed over me like warm water.

'Do you feel like a drink yet, Peter?' said Kate, all polite iced concern.

'A scotch and water, please,' I said, trying to keep the words separate, lifting my head slightly from the back of my chair.

Kate's father rang the bell and Kate walked over to the French windows to hide her mood from her father. Rain streamed down the window panes. Kate's father jabbed at the logs in the fireplace with the huge brass poker. Of course he knew I was drunk, but he was damned if my impoliteness was going to get in the way of his politeness, prevent him from behaving in the proper manner. And if, like him, one wasn't the real thing, then propriety was all important; it helped paper over the cracks.

And of course it had worked when I'd first met him. I'd thought he was the real thing. It had only been later when Kate had given me the real family history that I'd found out he'd started out in totally different circumstances to the ones he'd ended up in: he'd married into money, but not before he'd made a few bob of his own; in scrap, shoddies, old furniture, lead, that sort of stuff. With the money he'd made he bought a shop with a good position just behind the city centre and began selling cheap mass-produced furniture and a bit later he bought two more shops located in the town's poorer areas and ran them almost entirely on customer credit. Then he'd met Kate's mother, Dorothea. Her family had been in just about everything there was to be in: ropes, candles, trawling, clothing, anything that was going; in principle just like Kate's old man, except that Kate's old man had three shops, a yard and a warehouse, while the Millen family had an empire. When Kate's father had met Dorothea she'd just returned after having been sent to all the places in the world a girl from Dorothea's background used to be sent to, and her family had given her a dress shop to play with until she decided to accept one of the okay short-list which the family had got standing in line waiting for her.

The shop had been next door to Mark Dixon's furniture shop, a good position just behind the city centre.

Kate's father's man came into the room.

'Negus,' said Mark Dixon, 'we'd all like a drink. Wheel the trolley in, would you?'

Negus went out and Kate's father said to me: 'How's the catalogue coming?'

'Fine,' I said. 'I'm sending in all the shots on schedule.'

'No problems?'

'Only that I need another assistant and there just doesn't appear to be one to be had.'

I marvelled at myself. Clear, precise, just the right amount of vague irritation in my voice. Not being able to find another assistant was obviously the greatest of my worries, but apart from that minor problem, everything else in my world was fine, just fine. There was no dead girl, no Brian Plender, no meeting at half past seven.

Kate turned away from the window and said: 'Nicola begins at the riding school next Sunday, Daddy.'

Kate's father turned to Nicola who was sitting at a table playing snakes and ladders with Kevin.

'Wonderful,' he said. 'You'll enjoy that, Nicola. Like mother, like daughter. Will you ride with her, Kate?'

'Oh, I don't know,' she said, assuming her arm-scratching position again. 'All those youngsters would probably make me feel a bit past it.'

'Nonsense,' her father said. 'Youth is only a state of mind.'

'Quite,' said Kate.

Negus returned with the drinks trolley and Kate's father did the honours. I moved towards the French windows.

I looked out and beyond the swimming pool and the rolling lawn and the woodland until my eyes focused on the other side of the river. White against the greyness of the afternoon I could see the quarry where I played as a child.

I turned away from the window. For Christ's sake, I thought, if he doesn't offer me another drink I'm going to give myself one. What was I doing here anyway, listening to the boring old fart and his daughter conduct their mutual admiration society.

Plender knew. That's all I could think: Plender knew.

And where was Eileen now?

PLENDER

I walked into the Ferry Boat at five past seven, their first customer of the evening. I ordered a half of bitter and went over to a corner table. The rain was still sheeting down outside. I took off my trench coat and hung it on the coat-stand and sat down and took a sip of my beer. It tasted good, and then I remembered, of course, it was Masters and Drews', the stuff they used to have in the Volunteers over in Brumby, the stuff we all used to drink as lads at school, when Mrs Burnett would let us in her back bar. The first time I'd ever got drunk had been on Masters and Drews', followed up with some V.P. Rich Red Ruby. It had been before we'd gone to the fourth form Christmas party.

We all fell out of Mrs Burnett's snug.

There was Mouncey and Croft and Storey and Ghandi and Greevo and Gilliat and Peter and me.

The cold night air hit us in our faces.

'Got the V.P., Mouncey?' Greevo said.

Mouncey pulled the bottle out of his mac pocket.

'Course I have, mate.'

'Don't drop it, Mouncey,' Croft said.

'Don't be bloody silly,' said Mouncey, wrestling the stopper out of the neck. 'Here, let's have a swig now.'

'Naw,' said Ghandi, 'not here. Somebody might see us.'

'Fuck that,' said Croft. 'Give it us here.'

Mouncey had a drink and handed the bottle to Croft. Croft took his turn and then the bottle was passed round and we all had a drink. Mouncey put the bottle back in his pocket.

'Come on,' said Peter. 'Let's all link up.'

We all linked arms and swayed off the pavement into the road.

'One two, one two, one two, one two,' Peter chanted.

We all fell in step and ran along the road towards school hill. The night was still and quiet and cold stars filled the sky.

'Let's pack it in,' said Ghandi when we got to the bottom of school hill. 'There might be somebody on staff about.'

We broke up.

'Here,' said Gilliat, reeling away from us, 'do you reckon they'll know we're pissed up?'

'I don't give two monkeys,' said Greevo. 'I'm pissed, I'm pissed, I'm pissed.'

When we walked into the school hall the dancing had started. When you reached the fourth form, games like Musical Chairs and Pass the Parcel were abandoned, and in the fourth, fifth and sixth you just danced or sat around.

There were three or four pairs of girls dancing in the middle of the floor, and the rest of the girls were on one side of the hall and all the boys at the other, and at the top of the hall was the trestle table with all the food and stuff on it with two sixth form girls standing behind it waiting to pour the soft drinks. In front of the table there was Miss Hopley and Mr Price, standing there watching the girls dancing.

We all clumped over to the trestle table and got some soft drinks. Mr Price turned to look at us, looked away, then looked back again. I could tell he knew, but he just nodded vaguely. Price was all right.

We all drifted over to the wall that was on the boys' side of the hall and leant against it. Gilliat stumbled into a tubular chair but he managed to stay standing up.

I looked round for Peter. There was no sign of him.

'Where's Peter?' I asked Croft.

'Dunno. Probably spewing his ring up in lavs.'

'Hadn't we better go and have a look?'

'What for? He'll be all right.'

I waited for a few minutes and went out of the hall and into the toilets. One of them was locked.

'Peter?' I said.

There was a sound like a foot scraping on the floor.

'Are you all right?'

'Bugger off.'

Peter's voice was thick and throaty.

'Are you coming out?'

'No.'

'Price knows we've been drinking. He might come and check lavs.'

Eventually the toilet flushed and the bolt was shot and Peter staggered out and made to leave the toilets.

'Hang on,' I said. 'You can't go back in looking like that.'

I guided him into the washroom and turned on a tap and stood there while he cleaned up his jacket and his face and his shoes and combed his hair.

When he'd finished he said: 'Don't you tell them others I've spewed up.'

'No,' I said, 'I won't tell them, Peter.'

We were walking back towards the hall when we bumped into Croft and Mouncey making for the cloakroom carrying their empty paper cups.

'Come on,' Croft said to us. 'We're off to have some more Rich Red Ruby.'

We went into the small changing room, the one the sixth formers used, and locked the door behind us.

Croft passed round the bottle. While Peter was drinking Croft said: 'Susan's waiting for you in hall, Pete.'

'She can wait, then,' Peter said and took another drink.

'Hey up, Pete, are you off to dance?'

I knew Peter had been going to Mrs Clees' dancing classes on Tuesday nights with Susan, but he'd never mentioned it to anyone.

'Naw,' he said. 'Dancings for lassies.'

'Are you off to, Plender?'

I shook my head.

'We are, aren't we, Croft?'

'Yeah.'

Croft and Mouncey wrapped their arms round one another and began to dance up and down the changing room, singing in girlish voices.

'Eh,' I said. 'Shurrup. You'll have Pricey down on us.'

'Bollocks,' said Croft.

But just the same he and Mouncey stopped dancing.

The bottle went round until it was nearly empty.

'Hadn't we better save some for the others?' Mouncey said.

'That's their look-out,' said Croft, taking a pull.

I looked at Peter. Beads of sweat were standing out on his forehead and his face looked even greyer than it had when he'd come out of the toilet.

'Give us it here, Crofty,' he said.

Croft passed him the bottle. Peter took a long swig and suddenly he pulled the bottle away from his mouth and a long jet of sick spurted out, spraying all over Croft and Mouncey.

'Bloody hell, man,' said Mouncey, dancing back to the opposite end of the changing room. 'Look at me shoes, man.'

'It's gone all over me fucking trousers,' said Croft.

'Oh, bloody hell,' whispered Peter, and sank over on his side on the locker top and closed his eyes. He began to dribble on to the floor.

'Fucking bloody bastards' said Croft. 'Me mam'll leather hell out of me.'

'Come on,' said Mouncey. 'Let's go get cleaned up.'

The two of them went out and left me alone with Peter. He seemed to have gone to sleep. I looked at the mess on the floor. It had to be cleaned up before any of the staff saw it. I found a pair of football shorts in one of the lockers and went into the washroom. Mouncey and Croft were by the sink cleaning themselves up. I had to shake my head to stop them going in and out of focus. I made my way over to one of the bowls and turned on the tap and dropped the shorts in the bowl.

Croft leant against one of the other bowls.

'What do you think you're doing?' he said.

'Got to clean up,' I said. 'Before Price sees.'

'Silly fucker,' said Croft. 'Let Price find him.'

'Naw,' said Mouncey, 'come on, we ought to. Else we'll all be in it if he gets caught.'

The shorts must have blocked the plug-hole because the water began to overflow on to the floor.

'Look what you're doing, man' said Mouncey.

I stared at the water as it flowed over the side of the sink.

'Give us it here,' said Mouncey.

He took the shorts out of the bowl.

'Come on,' he said to Croft. 'Let's go clean up.'

They both stumbled out of the washroom.

'Hey, wait,' I said. 'I was off to do that.'

'So fucking what,' said Croft.

'You're too pissed up,' said Mouncey.

'No, I'm not,' I said, detaching myself from the bowl. 'Wait on.'

'Greasing bastard,' said Croft.

I followed them into the changing room. Peter was being propped up by Croft and Mouncey was busy swabbing the

144

floor. Peter seemed to be recovering again.

'Sorry about this,' he said. 'Sorry.'

'S'all right,' said Mouncey. 'I've nearly finished.'

'You're real mates,' said Peter. 'Real mates.'

KNOTT

Kate stopped the Hillman at the entrance to the car park.

'Well, it's there,' she said.

I looked at the Mercedes, standing alone and gleaming white on the black-wet tarmac.

'That's Daddy's car,' said Nicola.

Kate said: 'What time am I to expect you back?'

'I don't know,' I said.

I'd fallen asleep in the car on the way back from Kate's father's and now the only effect the drink had on me was to heighten the sick emptiness in my stomach and to make the paraphernalia of the world around me depressingly over-real.

'I'll expect you when I see you, then,' Kate said. 'I imagine you'll be spending the evening talking over old times. After you've thanked him for stealing your car at the dead of night, that is.'

I opened the car door and got out and said goodnight to the kids. Kate started to drive off as soon as I closed the door.

I stood there, looking at the Mercedes. Rain swept over it and raced across the car park. To my right I could hear the river chopping away in the blackness.

I walked over to the car.

The doors were locked. I went round to the back and looked at the boot. A part of my mind took in the fact that there was no trace of where the damage had been but the rest of my mind was looking beyond the metal to the black space where Eileen's body had lain, bent and twisted and dead.

Or still was?

A deep shudder convulsed my body. The urge to see came over me again. Independently of my mind, my hand, like a magnet, stretched out towards the handle of the boot. Cold freezing drops of rain soldered my fingers to the metal. I pressed the button. There was a click and the lid sprang upwards half an inch. Open. It was open.

Very quickly I pushed downwards and closed the lid.

I looked towards the pub. Inside the pub was Brian Plender, my old school friend.

PLENDER

The door opened and Peter Knott came in.

He stood in the doorway, looking at me. I smiled and stood up and went to meet him.

'Peter,' I said, putting my arm round his shoulder. 'How does she look, then?'

I walked him towards the bar. He seemed unable to answer.

'The car,' I said. 'What do you think? Done a good job, eh?'

Knott nodded.

'Evening, Mr Knott,' the barman said.

Knott turned his head in the direction of the voice as though he was tracking some visible object to its source.

'What'll it be, anyway?' I said.

'Usual, Mr Knott?' said the barman, putting a glass up to the whisky optic.

Knott nodded again.

'Large one,' he said.

His voice was thick and throaty.

'Large one it is,' said the barman, pressing the glass against the metal.

'And I'll have a vodka with ice and a twist of lemon,' I said. 'Just a small one.'

'Very good, sir.'

I put a pound note on the bar. The barman did the drinks. I picked up my change and raised my glass.

'Cheers,' I said.

Knott was halfway down his when I said: 'Let's go and sit down, shall we?'

He followed me over to the table. I sat down first. Knott hesitated for a moment before pulling his chair back and jerking himself down into it like a marionette.

I nodded at the unfinished half-pint on the table.

'Masters and Drews,' I said. 'Thought I'd have a half for old times' sake.' I smiled. 'Remember Mrs Burnett? The Volunteers?'

Knott stared at the half-pint glass. Then he tippled the rest of his drink back. I made signs at the barman and he brought us over two more. When he'd gone back to the bar I took out my cigarettes and gave one to Knott and as I lit us up I said:

'No, I suppose it was a bit naughty of me, really, coming back and taking the car like that, not letting you know. But you must admit, the bloke did a good job.'

Knott just kept on looking at me. I took a sip of my drink.

'And under the circumstances,' I said, 'perhaps it was as well that I did.'

'What have you done?' he said. His mouth moved like the mouth of a ventriloquist's dummy.

I smiled and looked down into my drink.

'Well,' I said, 'really, I think it's best not to go into details too much. Best for everyone concerned. The less you know the less it can hurt you sort of thing. Although,' I said, turning the smile into a bit of laugh, 'I really ought to be the one asking you what you've done, eh, mate?'

'It was... an accident,' he said. 'An accident.'

'Sure it was,' I said. 'Sure. But whatever it was, it doesn't matter any more. I've taken care of things. Your old mate Brian's seen to everything.'

'What have you done?'

I shook my head and smiled.

'Let's just say this,' I said. 'You're safe. And let's leave it at that, eh?'

'I want to know,' he said.

'No, you don't,' I said. 'You don't want to know, really.'

He galloped his drink down.

'What am I going to do?' he said.

He began to shake his head from side to side.

'I'll tell you what you're going to do,' I said, 'if you start behaving like this, that is: you're going to let the whole of East Yorkshire know what happened last night. That's what you're going to do.'

Knott looked towards the bar. The barman looked away.

'But I didn't mean it,' he said. 'It was an accident.'

'What does it matter what it was?' I said.

'But I haven't done anything.'

I smiled.

'You were just taking her home to tuck her up in bed, were you?' I said.

'I didn't know what I was doing. I was out of my mind.'

'Well, it's a good job I wasn't.'

'Now I can't...'

'Can't what?' I said. 'Go to the Law?'

He didn't answer.

I called for some more drinks.

'Look,' I said, 'I've done you a favour. You're fireproof. I wouldn't have done it if there was the slightest danger. Because if you're in the cart, I'm in the cart. So stop worrying.'

'But why did you do it?'

I spread my hands.

'Look,' I said, 'what could I do? I came back and took the car and left it round the back of my digs for the night. So before I went in I checked the doors, because you never know, and naturally I checked the boot as well. And the boot was open.'

'Open? But I'd made sure I'd locked it?'

'Can't have done, mate.'

'But I did. My wife – I tried it.'

I looked at him.

'Your wife,' I said. 'She's not...'

He shook his head.

'I had to tell her about the car. She went and had a look, that's all.'

'And she tried the boot.'

He nodded.

'Well,' I said, 'it must have been jammed. Because it opened easy enough when I got it home.'

He didn't say anything.

'Lucky it wasn't locked,' I said. 'Otherwise it might have been Cyril down at the garage opened it first instead of me.'

He drank some of his drink.

'So,' I said. 'I opened the boot.'

I looked at him for a while but he didn't look at me and he didn't say anything.

'What happened?' I said. 'That little bang we had screw things up for you?'

He took out a cigarette. I lit it for him.

'Where were you going? The river?'

He closed his eyes and nodded. I shook my head.

'You don't know how lucky you are,' I said.

'Tell me,' he said. 'What did you do?'

'What you were going to do, only better.'

'Why?'

'What else could I do? Go to the Law and tell them my old mate's been driving around with a dead girl in the back of his car? Do you think I was going to do that? Put an old mate on the spot? Or maybe I should have phoned you up and told you to come and move her yourself. And supposing I had gone to the police?

151

There's some right bastards down there these days. They might have decided to see how much mileage they could get out of me, as well as out of you. I'm not exactly a blue-eyed boy down there.'

He didn't say anything.

'Look,' I said. 'Why don't you do as I say: forget it. There's nothing to worry about.'

He looked into my face.

'What did you do with her?'

Wearily, I closed my eyes.

'I've told you. She's safe. And so are you.'

'Where?'

'Does it matter?'

'I have to know.'

'That's the last thing you have to do. What you have to do is forget all about last night and behave normally and live the way you normally live and everything will be fine.'

'How can I?' he said. 'I've killed somebody.'

His voice was hoarse and low, a controlled scream.

'I thought you said it was an accident?'

'It was. But it was my fault.'

I could see that tears were about to appear so I said: 'Nothing's your fault if nobody knows anything about it. And nobody knows anything about it.'

'You know,' he said.

'Yes, I know,' I said. 'Luckily for you.'

He moved his glass as if to drink but it was empty again. I made some more signs at the barman and got some more drinks. When the barman had gone away I lifted my glass and said: 'So, anyway, here's to us. To the Old Boys' Reunion. Remember the motto? "Keep Faith".'

Knott downed his drink in one go. I began to hum the school song, and eventually the long-forgotten words began to break through into the front of my mind.

152

'By Humber's Green Banks, away from city strife, Two words we learn that we shall carry through life, Keep Faith in all you do, these words will stand us true, On future morrows as they do, here today...'

I grinned at Knott.

'Remember?' I said. 'Old Price wrote the words and the Boss wrote the music. Remember old Price? He wasn't half mad that time Mouncey and his crowd put their own words to the song that speech day. "Get stuffed and the same to you" they sang, do you remember? They all got carpeted. Still, Price was all right, really. The only half-bloody-decent bloke in the whole place. English and History. They were the only two lessons I used to enjoy. He used to make them interesting. I remember he got us all interested in Macbeth by telling us the story as if it was like a gangster film. And he was always fair, not like those other bastards. In fact, the one thing he couldn't stand was a cheat.'

I took a drink.

'Mind you, I almost dropped you right in it with him over the Essay Prize. Do you remember? The prize for the best piece in the school magazine? It was a toss-up between me and you. I did a story about a man who lost his memory and you did that thing about the soldier ants eating up this bloke's plantation in South America. Only you'd happened to lend me the Boys' Own Paper with the same story in it a couple of months before. I suppose you must have forgotten. And then Mallett awarded you the prize. I could have dropped you right in it,' I said. 'But I didn't.'

KNOTT

I drove the Mercedes across the city. Plender looked at his watch.

'I hope you don't mind dropping me off like this,' he said. 'I really should have grabbed a cab. I mean, it's right out of your way.'

I didn't say anything. I just clutched the steering wheel and stared straight ahead beyond the raindrops on the windscreen.

'I really do feel bad about it,' he said.

'It's all right,' I said, hoping to shut him up. The words came out of me all run together, sounding like one word.

Plender began to sing again, quietly, as he looked out of the side window.

'Dull clouds may rise,
To dim the sunlit skies
Memories like birds
Will fly back homewards again
Then we shall recall
And still feel proud to say
Keep Faith in all you do,
These words will stand as true
On future morrows, as they do, here today.'

When he'd finished the words a second time, he went back to the beginning and began to whistle the tune through again.

'Whereabouts did you say?' I said.

Plender looked at his watch again.

'Well, actually,' he said, 'I wonder if you'd mind doing me a favour? I didn't realise just what the time was.'

I slowed down to approach some traffic lights.

'Thing is, I have to meet somebody. Only take a minute or two. I wonder if you'd mind waiting?'

I stopped the car at the lights.

'Where do you want to go?'

'Do you know Sammy's Point?'

I nodded. Sammy's Point was an acre or so of wasteland in the centre of the dockland, jutting out into the river near to where the Ferry berthed. It was a favourite spot for car-parked families on summer Sunday afternoons.

Neither of us said anything else. I turned right at the lights and drove through the city centre and turned down one of the cobbled streets that led to the riverside. The road opened out on to the broad forecourt in front of the Ferry Pier. A small queue of people was standing by the ticket collector's box waiting for the collector to lift the chain so that they could walk down the gangway and board the last ferry.

'I should park outside the Tivoli,' said Plender.

The Tivoli Tavern. Last stop on a Saturday night for the boozers who had to get the last boat home. I stopped the car outside and the light from the multi-coloured windows speckled the inside of the car. Plender put his hand in his coat pocket and took out a flask and unscrewed the drinking cup and filled it and offered it to me, taking his own drink directly from the neck of the flask. I took the cap from him and downed the drink in one go.

'We've had a few in there, at one time or another,' said Plender. 'Tanking up before the last boat.'

Plender took the cap away from me and refilled it and handed it back to me. I took it because I didn't want to stop drinking; I felt as if I never wanted to be sober again. To be sober would be to see too clearly the events of the last two days, and to see too clearly would be unbearable.

The ticket collector finally lifted the chain and the queue of people began to file down the gangway towards the waiting ferry. Plender looked at his watch and briefly scanned the forecourt. Two youths clattered across the cobblestones towards the gangway.

'You're quiet, Peter,' said Plender.

I stared straight ahead of me.

'Stop thinking about it,' he said.

'What do you want?' I said.

'Nothing,' he said. 'Just to be... ah, there he is. Right on time.'

A man in a raincoat was walking across the cobblestones towards Sammy's Point.

'Come on,' said Plender.

Plender got out of the car. I didn't move. Plender stopped in front of the car and looked at me. He inclined his head and turned away and began to stroll off towards Sammy's Point. Why didn't I just drive away and leave him? There was nothing he could do. Except telephone the police and tell them where the body was. And then I'd tell them what he'd done, what had happened – I wanted to be sick. What would it matter then? The police would have me. It would be me they'd lock up for half a dozen years. Christ. I would be beyond caring what happened to Plender.

I got out of the car and found myself trailing after Plender. Plender kept on walking and eventually disappeared into the darkness of Sammy's Point. Bells rang and the Ferry began to churn away from the pier. I followed Plender into the darkness and then stopped. Lank grass fell softly over my feet. As the Ferry passed by Sammy's Point before it began its outward curve towards the other side, the lights from its portholes illuminated the bulwarks at the edge of the grass. Plender was standing at

156

the edge, talking to the man, smoking, looking amiable and relaxed. The man in the raincoat passed Plender something and Plender put whatever it was in his coat pocket and then the Ferry slid away and everything was dark again. I watched the lights of the Ferry grow smaller in the darkness and I wished I was on board and seventeen again and on my way home to my mother and one of her big suppers. Tears welled up in my eyes and then I heard voices and a few seconds later Plender and the man emerged from the blackness, talking in low voices. The man in the raincoat didn't look very happy, but Plender was still relaxed and smiling his quiet smile. Then there was a movement behind me and I began to turn to see what it was but before I could do that two men brushed past me, one either side, and walked towards Plender and the man. Plender stepped back slightly, his expression not changing. One of the two men took hold of the arms of the man in the raincoat and pinned them behind his back in a wrestler's grip. The other man hit the man in the raincoat in the stomach, twice. The man in the raincoat was released and he fell to the ground, vomiting. Plender looked down at him and said:

'That's what happens if you're late. It hurts, but it only happens once. Next time there won't be anything like this: the stuff goes straight to your wife. Or even to your kid, on her way home from school. Someone walks by her and puts some pictures in her hand. That'd be nice, wouldn't it?'

The man on the ground crawled his knees up to his chest and tried to draw his breath back into his body. Plender looked at him for a moment then stepped round him and began to stroll towards me. The other two men fell in behind him, lighting up cigarettes as they walked. It had all happened as if I hadn't been there, as if I hadn't seen anything. Plender approached me as if nothing extraordinary had happened, and the two men just ignored me.

As Plender drew level with me he said to the two men: 'Come on, lads, I'll buy you a drink.'

He winked at me and I found myself falling into step with him.

'You do all kinds of business in my kind of business,' said Plender.

The forecourt was completely deserted now. A soft drizzle had begun to drift down from the sky, wafting like thin smoke past the lights of the public convenience and the Tivoli Tavern. The pier was dark and quiet and there was no sign of the ticket collector. Our footsteps echoed in the emptiness.

A part of me wanted to run to my car and leave this present too precise unreality behind me, but another part of my mind, the part that contained the reasons for my presence, made me stay, made me wait like an actor waiting for direction.

At the Tavern, one of the two men overtook Plender and myself and pushed open the door for us. Plender went in first and walked over to the bar.

Now that the Ferry had gone the Tivoli was quiet. Only a few dockland regulars were left in the bar. A small fire burned in the grate and the smell of sawdust was thick in the small room. Plender leant against the bar and faced the two men.

'What's it to be, lads?'

'Guinness and Bitter,' said one.

'Rum and Black,' said the other.

'And two large scotches,' Plender said to the landlady. Plender turned back and said to me, 'Peter, let me introduce you. This is Col and this is Terry. We work together from time to time. Lads, this is Peter. Don't worry about him. He's one of us.'

PLENDER

I sat at my desk and drafted replies to Misters Harris, Codd, and Potter of Leeds, Doncaster and Barnsley respectively.

'Dear_____

I was thrilled to receive your reply to my advertisement which I placed in last month's Friendly Magazine. I imagine (if you are at all a like soul, as I know you are) that it was almost as difficult for you to reply as it was for me to advertise, especially as I didn't want to give the impression of being the wrong kind of person. How lucky I was, therefore, to discover in you a correspondent that so obviously realises what kind of person I am. It's wonderful to know that somewhere there is someone who understands. It was only through desperation that in fact I turned to Friendly Magazine as a last resort. But I'm sure I don't have to explain, not to you.

Your letter filled me with excitement. I can hardly wait to meet you and put into practice all the wonderful things you suggested. I think your ideas for disciplining naughty girls are delightful. (Perhaps you will demonstrate them to me when we meet. From talking to my friends, I know that my own boss would have a more efficient office if he put a few of your ideas into practice!!!)

I enclose a photograph as you requested. It was taken by my

girlfriend when we were on holiday at Filey Butlin's last summer. As you can see, short skirts can be awkward when you're roller skating!

If you would like us to meet, then you can phone me at the above telephone number after seven, any evening. I shall be waiting by the phone for your call!'

When I'd done that I went through into the outer office and asked my secretary to give me the information she'd looked up concerning the new correspondents. Two of them looked promising so I filed the data in my filing cabinet and locked the drawer.

I sat down at my desk and buzzed for coffee. Outside the day was grey and wet wind buffeted the city. I sat and stared out of the window at the sky until my secretary brought in the coffee.

'Mr Gurney's on his way up,' she said. 'Shall I send him in?'

I smiled. Gurney hated not having automatic access to my office. He always had to ask my secretary if I was available.

'Yes, all right,' I said. 'And give him a cup and saucer on his way in.'

A few moments later Gurney came in.

'Good morning Mr Plender,' he said.

'Have some coffee,' I said.

Gurney poured some coffee.

'Andrea and Len set up for tomorrow night?'

'Yes Mr Plender. Their place at eight. They're meeting the clients in Peggy's.'

I took a sip of my coffee and nodded.

'Who's taking the pictures? Harry or myself?' Gurney asked.

'I don't know,' I said. 'I'll have to think about that.'

KNOTT

I got to the studio early on Monday morning. I'd forgotten about the stains on the warehouse floor. I'd woken up at half past five, almost weeping with fear and anger at myself for not remembering. And then I'd had to lie there for another hour until I was sure my wife had gone back into a deep sleep because when I'd remembered I'd sat bolt upright in bed and startled her awake.

I'd known I'd be too late. The warehouse men started at five. But I had to get there as early as possible, just to see.

I stepped through the small door and into the warehouse. The usual men gave me the usual greetings, laced with a few remarks about the hour of my appearance. I walked over to the stairs, looking for the spot and pretending not to be looking for anything. But there were no signs of any stains. Perhaps the cobbled floor was so old and porous that the blood had sunk into the stone, not leaving a trace.

But there'd been more than just blood. I walked up the stairs trying to imagine why. No trace. No marks. No hair. Nothing. It had been cleaned away. Sometimes the warehouse men hosed down the floor, but not today: the floor was bone dry.

I shuddered as the simile struck me.

I let myself into the studio, closed the door and walked through the reception area into the studio and over to the leather chair in the middle of the floor and sat down and tried to think, but the memories of Saturday night hung round the objects in the studio so then I tried not to think at all.

The objects.

I looked round the studio. It was all wrong. It wasn't as I'd left it. It had been changed. Little things. The rug had been straightened. The divan had been folded up. The glasses were gone. The film... I stared at the coffee table. The spools of film weren't there any more. God. Where were they? I rushed over to the table as if my haste would make them miraculously reappear. I got down on all fours to see if they'd rolled under anything but there was nothing. I must have put them somewhere else. The changing room? But I hadn't been in there, not afterwards. Look anyway. I ran into the changing room. The bed had been remade. I wanted to scream. I turned and hurried into the kitchen. The glasses were all washed and dried and neatly stacked on the drainer.

Now I knew I was mad.

I went back into the studio and opened the divan and lay down on it, drawing my knees up to my chest, pulling my coat tight around me.

I lay there until quarter to ten, until Dave, my assistant, arrived.

He opened the door that led from the reception area and closed it behind him and stared at me.

'What the bloody hell's up with you?' he said.

I slid my legs off the divan and stood up.

'Hangover,' I said. 'I was out with an old school friend last night.'

Dave hung his coat up and nodded in understanding.

'Male or female?' he said.

'Male,' I said.

Dave walked past the divan and threw his newspaper on to the coffee table and went into the kitchen. I sat down again and picked up the paper and glanced through it, hoping my actions would ease my behaviour back into some semblance of normality.

I heard Dave fill the kettle.

'I expect you'd like some coffee,' he called.

'Yes, I would,' I said.

Dave leant against the doorway into the kitchen while he waited for the kettle to boil. He'd been out of the local Art School just under a year and he'd affected his generation's dispassionate attitudes just like all the rest of them. To him, I was an old man.

'So it was a heavy night on the booze, then, was it?'

I nodded.

'You should try smoking,' he said. 'Leaves you fresh as a daisy next day.'

'Perhaps I should,' I said.

'Can't understand it,' he said. 'Alcohol's a killer. Poison.'

The kettle began to whistle and Dave went back into the kitchen.

The headline read: GIRL, 17, MISSING FROM FLAT.

It was at the bottom of the page, just a paragraph. The story described how Eileen's landlady had got in touch with the police on Sunday evening after Eileen hadn't returned since going out on Saturday night. Eileen was described as a secretary with Priestley and Squires, Advertising Agents.

Dave came out of the kitchen with the coffee. I folded up the paper and put it down next to me on the divan. Dave handed me my mug and picked up the paper.

'Sod all in this rag,' he said. 'Don't know why I buy it.'

Oh but there is, I wanted to say. There's a little bit in it about me. Well, not about me, actually, but about the girl I killed on Saturday night. Well, I didn't actually kill her, but it doesn't make any difference now. I'm for the chop just the same. You'll find it at the bottom of page three, the column at the end.

Dave threw the paper back on the coffee table.

'Anyway, what do you want me to do?' he said.

'What?'

'Do. Work. What's on?'

'Oh. Work. The handbag shots. They've got to be done.'

'Terrific. Still, it's better than doing prints all day long.'

He peeled off his lumberjacket. 'Want me to start setting them up?'

'Yes,' I said.

Dave went to work setting up. I sat where I was, drinking my coffee, holding on to my cup as though it was a lifebelt.

'Anybody coming in this morning?' Dave asked, unrolling the huge expanse of backing paper.

'Coming in?' I said.

'Yeah. Any of the birds.'

'No,' I said. 'We've no models booked in this morning.'

'Thank Christ. That's one thing I can do without first thing on a Monday morning, a load of twittering dolly birds. They give me a pain in the bum. What about this afternoon?'

'Two,' I said. 'Some nightwear shots to do.'

Dave laughed.

'That nightwear stuff kills me,' he said. 'I don't believe anybody wears gear like that any more. It's pure 1950s. I mean, imagine getting into bed with a bird togged up like that. It'd give you writers' cramp.'

I drank some more coffee.

'Still, I suppose it appeals to the stocking tops and dirty macintosh brigade.'

I stood up.

'I should get a move on,' I said. 'It's all got to be clear for this afternoon.'

'Who's coming, anyway?'

'Lyn and Suki.'

'Suki. Would you fucking well believe it? Suki from the Holden Road Estate. I tell you...'

The phone rang. I knew it was Plender. I went into the reception area. Angela, my receptionist, hadn't arrived yet so I sat down on her desk and picked up the phone and said: 'Peter Knott Associates?'

'Hello, Peter,' said Plender. 'How's things?'

'It's in the paper,' I said.

'Of course it's in the paper.'

'Yes, but...'

'But nothing. It doesn't say anything about you, does it? It doesn't say anything about finding her, does it?'

'No, but...'

'And it won't. So forget it, because it's going to get much worse. It'll be on the front page tomorrow. With a picture.'

'But how can you say they won't find her; how can you say they won't trace her to me?'

'I told you last night. The only way they'll trace her to you is if you keep carrying on the way you are doing.'

'But somebody's been here.'

'How do you mean?'

'Somebody's been here over the weekend. Everything's been tidied up. There's some films missing.'

'I know,' said Plender.

'What?'

'I've got the films,' he said. 'I did the tidying up.'

'But...'

'Listen, you may not be aware of this, but you were in a bit of a state on Saturday night. Panic stations all along the line. I thought you might have been a bit hasty so I looked up your studio in the phone book and had a wander round.'

'But I didn't tell you where it... where I'd been.'

He sighed.

'No, you didn't,' he said. 'I know I'm not exactly Sherlock Holmes, but then sometimes I don't have to be.'

'Why didn't you tell me last night?'

'You had enough on your mind, what with one thing and another.'

'But I've been going mad. I haven't known what to think.'

'Then don't. I'll do the thinking for you.'

I pressed my free hand against my face and screwed up my eyes tight shut.

'All right?' came Plender's voice from the receiver.

I couldn't say anything.

'Anyway,' he said, 'I wondered if I could ask you a little favour?'

The door to the studio opened and my secretary came in.

I swivelled round on the desk so that I wouldn't have to face her.

'Yes, fine,' I said, as though I was talking to a client. 'What can I do?'

PLENDER

I walked into Peggy's. It was almost seven-thirty. It was more crowded than the last time I'd been there. Peggy wasn't around at the moment but he had three barmen on to cope which was unusual for him because he was a tight-fisted old slag and that was giving him the benefit of the doubt.

I bought my drink and shouldered my way through the cashmere sweaters and the tight pants and sat down in one of the booths. On the jukebox Harpers Bizarre were sighing their way through 'Anything Goes'. And all the sherberts were creaming down their suspenders.

I drank my drink and waited.

Peggy appeared behind the bar and cast his eyes over the assembled throng. When he saw me he disappeared back where he'd come from and the next thing I knew he was sliding his big bottom into the bench seat on the other side of the booth.

'Hello, Peggy,' I said.

Peggy slipped the evening paper on to the table between us.

I looked at the paper and then I looked at Peggy.

'Look at the picture on the front,' Peggy said. 'The dolly.'

I looked at the paper again and then gave Peggy a what-am-I-supposed-to-be-looking-at look.

'She was in here Saturday night.'

'I'm surprised you remember,' I said.

'Don't shoot shit. I'm telling you, she was in here.'

'So?'

Peggy gave me a long look.

'Mr Plender,' said Peggy. 'We have a very nice relationship. You know enough about me and I know enough about you and that's why you keep using this place and that's why I keep letting you use it. So far everything's worked out. But I want you to tell me something, Mr Plender, just so's I'll know when the boys in blue troll by. Is she part of your scene or is she not? Because you were here when she was here and I don't want the law linking your little scenes with my little scenes. That's why I'm asking.'

I gave him a tired smile.

'Peggy,' I said, 'Peggy. Do me a favour, will you?'

'Because if she is, and you're not being straight with me, then I'm going to be in a lot of trouble. Some of those bitches are just dying to bust me.'

'I've told you,' I said. 'Straight up. It's nothing to do with me.'

He gave me another look.

'I hope to Christ you're giving it me straight.'

'I am, and that's a novelty in here, Peggy.'

'Because seeing her in here with that feller, and you being in here as well, well, you do see what I mean.'

'She was with a feller?'

'Of course she was with a feller,' he said. 'You don't think she'd come in here on her own, do you?'

I took a drink.

'I don't quite follow: you saw her in here with a feller, and me in here at the same time, and somehow there's a connection?'

Peggy raised his eyes to the ceiling.

'My God, it's a right little Shirley Temple we've got here,' he said. 'Butter wouldn't melt in her little mouth. Look, this feller

168

comes in here quite often with his dollies. Sometimes your friend Mr Gurney's been in when he's been in. Saturday you were in when he was in. I know you and your watching. So I'm not completely out of my tiny mind when I think maybe there's a connection.'

'Well there isn't,' I said.

'Well, sorry I spoke, I'm sure.'

I lit a cigarette.

'So you know the feller, do you?'

'Well, when I say I know him, only through coming in here. We always have a few words. He likes camping it up. Actually, I always rather fancied him. He thinks he isn't but I know damn well he is.'

'What makes you say that?'

'Experience, Mr Plender, experience.'

'Do you know his name?'

'Yes I do, his first name. Why, do you want to pinch him off me?'

I ignored the remark and said: 'So what do you think he's done? Chopped her up in little pieces and fed her to the ducks.'

'How should I know what he's done to her,' he said. 'I don't know what fellers do to girls.' He smirked at me. 'No, but seriously, you never know these days. There's all sorts of strange people weaving in and out of life's rich pattern, aren't there, Mr Plender?'

I let that one pass too.

'I must say though, I'm relieved to know it's nothing to do with you. For my sake, that is.'

'Well, it probably isn't anything anyway. They may have gone for a dirty weekend in Scarborough and decided to make it a dirty week.'

'Maybe. But if she goes missing much longer, I might do

myself a bit of good with my friendly policeman. Now I know you're not involved, that is.'

'You mean Driscoll?'

'Who else? Do you know I reckon they'd do better at recruiting if they advertised the kind of benefits that he's knocking up instead of all this palaver about basic pay.'

'How do you mean, do yourself a bit of good?'

'Gawd give us strength. Tell him. About the feller. The feller with the girl. I mean, if she goes missing over the week, somebody down there'd like to know who she was seen with last, especially if it means they don't have to move their big bottoms outside the station.'

Another number by Harpers Bizarre began on the juke box. Out of the corner of my eye I saw Andrea and Len walk into the bar. They didn't acknowledge me and I didn't acknowledge them.

'Yes,' I said. 'I suppose they would.'

'I'd smell of violets. All over.'

'So what'll you do?' I said. 'Just wait a few more days and if she doesn't turn up then tip the nod?'

'Yes,' he said. 'If she turns up, she turns up. If not, I'll offer my services as a public-spirited citizen.'

'Of course,' I said, 'the feller she was with – what did you say his name was?'

'Peter.'

'Peter – he may not know where she is either. I mean, she may have gone missing after he'd left her.'

'May have done,' Peggy said. 'For all I know she may have gone to her grannie's in Macclesfield but they'd still appreciate the gesture.'

'Even if the gesture was futile?'

'Nobody would know whether it was futile or not until they found the girl, would they?'

'No,' I said, 'you're right there, Peggy.'

I got up and Peggy slid himself out of the booth.

'Anyway,' I said, 'I've got to get a move on. Things to do.'

'I'm sure,' said Peggy.

'Good luck with the law,' I said. 'I hope it works out to everybody's satisfaction.'

I walked out of the bar considering what Peggy had said.

KNOTT

The windscreen wipers groaned. Plender drove the Cortina quite slowly, letting anybody who wanted to overtake us. He stared straight ahead of him, his mind seeming to be considering other things than getting us where we were going.

I didn't say anything: the less I said the less likely I was to be drawn out of the protective cocoon I'd wound round myself. I was forcing myself to live in a vacuum, an empty universe which waited to receive events as they came, one by one, unevaluated. Consideration and prognosis were being kept at bay because I was afraid that the coming together of the bits of mosaic would shatter any self-control I had left with the completion of the picture. I was allowing myself to be organised and directed by Plender, trying to absorb his confidence, his certainty. Even if it was the certainty of madness, I was glad of it, because his certainty was a barrier against my own madness. I had to stay with him, go along with anything he suggested because Plender alone knew, and only he could save me, whatever his motives, whatever my feelings for him.

I was sitting in the front seat, next to him, gripping my camera tightly on my lap. I turned my head slightly to look at him. His face was placid and empty of any expression. I knew that he was aware that I was looking at him but he gave no outward sign of it. When I pictured him as I'd known him at school, it wasn't as the boy I'd known then, but as the man sitting beside me now, except wearing school uniform.

Plender turned off the main road and drove through rows of pre-war council houses until we crossed another main road and came to an estate of newer semis, a recent development. Most of the gardens were still nothing more than bulldozed rubble and there were no trees or hedges or greenery of any kind, just the stark brick and uniform windows bathed in the bland healthless glow of the sodium street lights.

Plender drove the Cortina into a cul-de-sac and parked it by the kerb. He switched off the engine and leant back in his seat. Rain swept across the roof of the car.

'Well,' he said, 'here we are.'

We got out. I stood by the car and pushed my cameras into my anorak to keep them dry and opened the rear door and took my tripod off the back seat. Plender carried on walking away from the car until he reached the corner of the cul-de-sac. He stopped and looked back to see if I was following and when he saw that I was he disappeared round the corner.

When I rounded the corner Plender was walking up the path towards one of the houses. There were no lights on. He inserted a key in the lock and opened the front door. Then he walked inside and waited for me in the hall. When I'd got inside he closed the door behind me and switched on the hall light. The hall had a cheap fitted carpet that carried on up the stairway, the walls were painted white with no decorations at all.

Plender opened a door and we walked into a lounge-cum-dining-room that was carpeted in the same material. The furniture was cheap HP stuff and I noticed there were two divans.

'Not bad, is it?' said Plender.

I didn't say anything. He took my silence to mean approval.

'I got hold of this through a friend on the council,' he said. 'That's the thing about the world today: it's not what you know, it's who you know. I'd have to have waited donkey's years otherwise.'

He sat down on the arm of one of the settees and took out his cigarettes and lit up without offering me one. He was obviously pleased to show off his success, his cleverness at getting things done. He was bright-eyed, like a child.

'I know lots of people who are always ready to do me the odd favour. You get to know them in my line of business, in one way or another.'

He blew smoke out and looked at me for a moment and then looked away and stood up and began to move around the room, inspecting the furniture and the wallpaper and the few wall fittings.

'I expect you wonder just exactly what I'm up to?' he said.

I didn't say anything. I didn't want to know. All I wanted was to live in this moment of time with no reference to either past or future or to any events or concepts that needed any kind of consideration or evaluation.

'Well, it's nothing to worry about,' said Plender, having gone full circle and sat down on the settee arm again, 'but it's a bit too complicated to explain, really. At this stage, at any rate.'

I sat down in the settee opposite. We looked at each other.

'Fancy a drink?' he said.

I nodded.

Plender went over to a small cocktail cabinet and opened the lid. Tinkling music burst on the silent room. Plender poured two drinks and closed the lid and walked back across the room. He handed me my drink and sat down again and drank his drink and looked at me.

'Ever done any of this kind of stuff before?' he said.

I shook my head. He smiled.

'What do you call Saturday night, then?' he said.

I stared at him.

'Well, I had to see, didn't I?' he said. 'I mean, when I went back to your place and picked up the spools, I had an idea, just

174

from the state the studio was in. That's why I took them. Just in case my idea was right. So I developed them to see if I was right or not.'

I opened my mouth.

'Don't worry,' he said. 'I developed them myself. Christ, you don't think...'

He left the rest of the sentence unspoken.

I knew I should be feeling sick at the thought that Plender had seen what was on the photographs but my state of mind was such that the passage of thought from brain to stomach was rigidly prevented, thus precluding any translation of thought into feeling.

'That's why I knew you wouldn't mind about tonight,' he said. 'After seeing the pictures, I mean.'

I took a drink.

'Done much of that kind of thing, have you?'

I shook my head.

'I bet,' he said. He took a drink. 'I expect it's easy in your line, though, pulling the birds. Mixing with them all the time. And you always were one for the birds, weren't you? The school Casanova.'

He smiled and looked at his watch and then finished his drink and stood up.

'They should be here soon,' he said. 'Let's go and get set up.'

He walked out of the lounge. I finished my drink and got up and followed him out of the room.

'In here,' he said.

He opened another door farther down the hall. This time he let me go first, switching on the light after I'd entered the room.

It was entirely different from the last room.

On the walls there were framed photographs of Germany before the war: German leaders, rallies, soldiers; half a dozen different pictures of Hitler. There was a bookshelf and on the top of the bookshelf there was a German helmet and a toy luger.

Plender watched me look at the pictures but he didn't say anything about them. Instead he said: 'What do you think of this?'

At first I thought he meant the room but he went over to one of the pictures, a big blow up of the Olympics, and took it down from the wall. Behind there was a small window that revealed the room where we'd just been sitting.

'Not bad, is it?' Plender said. 'We can see them but they can't see us. What do you think?'

'It's very clever,' I said.

'See, if you set up your tripod here,' he said, indicating a spot near the window, 'then you'll get a good view of everything. And the beauty of it is nobody gets camera shy.'

I put up my tripod and began to fix the Rollei on the top.

'Well,' said Plender, 'I'll leave you to it, then.'

I stared at him.

'But you're staying,' I said. 'You can't go.'

'Must, me old mate,' he said. 'Got some business to do.'

'But you can't leave me here.'

'I'm not going to. I'll be back to pick you up later on, when all the festivities are over.'

Suddenly all the feeling I'd been controlling rushed out of me.

'Listen,' I said. 'Please. Don't leave me. I can't bear it on my own. When I'm on my own I'm frightened. I can't stand to be on my own, not now.'

'But it's only for a couple of hours,' Plender said, smiling. 'I've told you, I'll pick you up later.'

'Please,' I said. 'Please.'

I sank to my knees. Plender watched me, still smiling, but the smile had changed, describing something I didn't understand. After a minute or two he said:

'Here, you'd better have this.' He took his flask out of his pocket. 'But don't drink too much. I want these pictures to come out.'

I took the flask, still kneeling.

Plender walked over to the door, opened it, and paused for a moment.

'Andrea and Len'll give you a cup of tea when the others have gone,' he said.

Then he went out.

PLENDER

I sat in my car and waited for Peggy.

There were a number of places he might decide to go after he'd closed up. He might go to the Cockatoo or White's Club or he could pop over the road to the Wimpy or go to some gay party or he could just go straight on home.

All I hoped was that he hadn't got a boyfriend with him.

He came out of the bar at eleven-thirty. He was alone.

I watched him walk round to the car park at the back of the hotel. At least he wasn't going to the Wimpy. I started the engine and waited for Peggy's Mini to nose itself out of the alley and turn right in the direction of the square.

I wasn't following him for long before I realised he was going home.

He had a flat in one of the new blocks near the football ground. It was a very nice flat, so I'd heard.

He parked his Mini outside and walked over to the lift and pressed the button and waited. I drove by and parked my car on the other side of the road and watched him get into the lift. The doors closed behind him. I waited. The lift doors on the fourth floor opened and Peggy walked along the balcony until he came to his flat. Fourth door along.

I got out of my car and walked across the road.

KNOTT

The lights were still on when I got home.

I paid off the taxi and went into the house.

My wife was sitting in the lounge, dressed for bed, reading a magazine. She looked up at me as I closed the door behind me. Before she looked into my face she'd been all prepared for a confrontation based on her previous suspicions, but when she saw my expression her own expression changed to a different kind of disbelief.

'What's wrong?' she said.

I almost told her. Like the hero of Poe's story, I wanted to pour out all my guilt, describe every small detail, encouraged by the lying perversity in my brain that told me once I'd confessed everything would be all right. But for all my madness I was aware of the falseness of the idea: I knew that nothing could be improved by telling the truth.

'Wrong?' I said. 'How do you mean, wrong?'

I was getting good. The tone of my voice was just right: the wary husband, innocent, realising that he is about to be cross-questioned by a jealous wife, puts himself on guard, creates a defence with aggressiveness.

Kate stood up.

'You look terrible,' she said.

'So I look terrible,' I said, walking over to the drinks and pouring one out. 'I've been working all day. It's gone midnight. That's why I look terrible.'

Kate's concern disappeared and her own defensive mechanism took over.

'And if you've been working late,' she said, 'why wasn't I told?'

'Because I forgot,' I said, taking a drink. 'Quite a simple explanation, really.'

'You forgot.'

'Probably because I had too much to drink yesterday,' I said. 'You'll remember that I had too much to drink.'

'I don't believe you,' she said.

'You don't believe that I had too much to drink? But my love, you kept reminding me of the fact. Surely you remember that?'

'Shut up.'

'I'm sorry,' I said, 'but I didn't begin the proceedings. I'll rest my case.'

'You'll tell me where you've been.'

I sat down in an armchair.

'I have been', I said, 'at the studio. All day. All evening. Working... mucked up some prints and so I had to redo the shots and I printed them up myself this evening so that there wouldn't be another accident. That is why it is now a quarter past twelve.'

'I don't believe you.'

'Of course.'

'I think you're having an affair.'

'Yes.'

'Just like the last time.'

'Of course.'

'Peter, tell me the truth.'

'You already know the truth.'

'I want to know.'

The phone rang. I knew who it would be.

I got up out of my chair and hurried into the studio, praying that Kate wouldn't pick up the telephone in the other room.

I lifted the receiver and said: 'Yes?'

'You left, then,' said Plender.

'I had to. My wife...'

'I said I'd be back to pick you up.'

'I know, but...'

'Well then why didn't you wait?'

'I had to get home. Listen, I have to go. My wife thinks I'm having an affair. This phone call...'

'She thinks you're having an affair?' said Plender. 'Well, that's handy, so long as that's all she suspects.'

'I'll have to go.'

'When will the prints be ready?'

'The prints?'

'The pictures you took tonight.'

'I don't know. Look...'

'I'll pick them up tomorrow,' said Plender. 'About midday.'

The line went dead.

I put the phone back on its cradle. Kate came into the room.

'Who was that?' she said.

'The printer,' I said. 'The people who print the catalogue.'

Kate looked at me.

'They do work night shift, you know.'

Kate turned away and began to walk out of the room.

'They wanted to know if I was sending the negatives over for the morning shift. I should have let them know earlier. They phoned the studio and I'd gone and so they phoned here...'

Kate closed the door behind her.

PLENDER

The receptionist was just the way I imagined she'd be. Not too different to the way the other one had looked, from what I'd been able to tell. She said to me:

'Who is it to see Mr Knott?'

'Tell him it's Mr Plender,' I said. 'He's expecting me.' She flipped her appointment book open.

'There's nothing down here,' she said.

'Probably not,' I said, looking at her. She looked back at me for as long as she could and then she pressed a switch and Knott's voice crackled through the tinny intercom.

'Yes?' he said.

'There's a Mr Plender in reception,' said the girl, waiting for the glorious moment when Knott asked her if I'd got an appointment. 'He says he's expected.'

'I'll come out,' said Knott.

The girl looked at me again. She thought she'd won. She thought Knott was just coming to see who the hell I was, so that I'd be proved a liar when I'd said I'd got an appointment. She sat back and waited.

Knott opened the inner door and I crossed the reception area and without a word closed the door behind me.

We went into Knott's office. Knott turned to face me.

'I had to leave last night,' he said.

I sat down on one of his trendy chairs.

'But I said I'd be back,' I said. 'And you only left ten minutes before I got there.'

'I couldn't stay any longer,' he said. 'I told you. My wife…'

'Yes, you told me, Peter,' I said. 'And I told you: you have to do as I say. At least for the present. Otherwise you might do something that could land you in a lot of trouble. And if you're in trouble, I'm in trouble. And I don't want to land in trouble just because I did an old mate a favour.'

'I'm sorry,' he said.

'It doesn't matter this time,' I said. 'But you see what I mean, don't you?'

He nodded his head.

'Anyway,' I said, 'let's forget it. How did the pictures turn out?'

He opened a drawer in his desk and took out a stiff-backed envelope and pushed them over to me. I took the prints out and looked through them. Knott turned his back and looked out of the window.

'What are they for?' Knott said.

I tut-tutted.

'Now, Peter,' I said. 'You know I'm not going to tell you. Wouldn't be wise, would it?'

There was a silence. Then he said: 'It was horrible. That's why I left. That was the real reason. I couldn't stand it any longer.'

I put the prints in my coat pocket.

'I thought it would have been right up your street,' I said.

He didn't answer. I stood up and walked over to the door.

'I'll see you tomorrow,' I said.

He turned to face me.

'Tomorrow?'

'Tomorrow,' I said. 'For dinner. What time would you like me to be there?'

I came out of the pictures. The second house queue scanned the leaving faces to get a preview of what the picture had been like. Knott and his gang had got out before me and the ones with girls were showing off in front of their mates without girls, now the initial embarrassment was over. They'd all been up in the balcony, on the back row with the bookable double seats. I'd been downstairs in the shillings, on my own. They all had their Saturday night clobber on, and I was wearing my blazer, because my mam said what was the use of having two jackets when you could only wear one at a time.

I wandered over to the group.

'Eh up, Pete,' said Ghandi, 'it's Plender.'

Knott smiled his odd smile.

'Now then, Plender,' he said. 'What did you think to the picture?'

I'd thought it was smashing but I said: 'Not bad.'

'It was bloody terrible, man,' said Knott. 'Bloody Doris Day.' He began to sing, in a girl's voice, a silly voice, 'By the light of the silvery moon...'

Ghandi and Mouncey fell about laughing and the girls with them, Maureen Smith and Connie Sherwood, looked at me and giggled.

Knott stopped singing.

'Come on then,' he said, 'let's go up to Market Place.'

After the pictures chucked out that was where everybody went to on a Saturday night, just to hang about, waiting for the village buses to leave one by one. There was a lovers' lane round the back where the cattle market was. Schoolboys without dates would send other schoolboys as envoys to groups of schoolgirls to tell the fancied one: 'Harry Akester wants to know if you'll go for a walk with him.' There'd be giggling and maybe the chosen one would leave her group and as a country bus would swish away into a September rain she and her suitor would sort of meet, halfway

184

between their separate groups, then disappear into the wet blue dusk of lovers' lane and kiss, thrust into damp hedges or propped up against rain-slick gateposts, the blue getting deeper, similar dark figures searching for a spot like theirs.

Knott began to walk away, holding Susan's hand. His mates followed suit. I tagged on behind, knowing that the command hadn't included me, but keeping the awareness to the back of my mind.

I was walking behind Dreevo and Denise Yarwood. They were holding hands and not talking.

'Looks a good picture next week, Dreevo,' I said.

Dreevo answered me without turning round.

'It's donkey's old,' said Dreevo. 'Saw it last year in Grimsby.'

In the Market Place I stood near Knott and Susan in Deweys doorway while Dreevo and the others took their girls down lovers' lane and then saw them on to their buses. One by one the boys returned to the doorway. When they were all assembled Knott said:

'Mam says we can all go up to our house and have our supper. Want to come?'

They all said yes and began to move off along the pavement. I began to think of an excuse to cover my embarrassment at not being included, like having to go to the chip shop for my mam, but Knott said: 'Are you coming, then, man?' in a voice that suggested I was being sullen and awkward.

At Peter's house Mrs Knott opened the door to us and gave a big welcome to Susan and the other lads. When she saw me she kept up her politeness but in a way that was meant to show me that she was less pleased to see me than she was to see the others. But again I forced the knowledge to the back of my brain because Knott had included me, he could have left me behind, and besides, I'd be near to Susan for the next hour or so.

We all went into the sitting room and Mrs Knott brought in

the supper and left us to it. Everybody got talking and the other lads were showing off a bit because Susan was the only girl there and soon the talk got round to what had happened at school recently.

'Here', said Dreevo, 'wasn't Gilliat supposed to be taking Jean Moss to pictures tonight?'

'God aye,' said Ghandi 'They were walking round cricket pitch all last week.'

'I didn't see either of them,' said Knott.

Susan said: 'She didn't turn up. She was supposed to meet him off the half past bus in the Market Place.'

'Why not?' Peter asked.

'Somebody else asked her out and she decided to go with them.'

'What, and she didn't tell him?'

'Well, she couldn't, could she? She wasn't asked till last night and there was no way she could let him know.'

'Typical lassies' trick,' said Ghandi.

'I'd have done the same if I'd been her,' said Susan.

'What do you mean?' Peter asked.

'Well, not that I would, but any girl would rather go with Noel Fletcher than John Gilliat.'

'Noel Fletcher!' said Ghandi. 'That streak of gnat's pee!'

'He's a yob,' said Peter. 'Thinks he owns the place riding round on that motor bike of his.'

'All the girls think he's ever so goodlooking,' said Susan. 'He's like Dickie Valentine.'

'Dickie Valentine!' said Peter.

'He does,' said Susan. 'All the girls at school think so.'

'It's a rotten bloody trick, though,' said Ghandi, 'not turning up like that. Don't you reckon, Pete?'

Peter looked at me.

'Dunno,' he said. 'Ask Brian.'

186

Peter and Susan looked at one another and snorted, suppressing laughter.

'God aye,' said Ghandi, laughing too, 'that time behind the pavilion.'

'Naw, we shouldn't laugh,' said Peter, laughing. 'It was mean. Old Brian was waiting nearly half an hour.'

I began to go red.

'Hey up, Brian,' said Dreevo, 'are you blushing?'

I shook my head.

'Eh, no though,' said Dreevo, 'he is. He's blushing.'

'I'm not,' I said, trying to smile, to show them how much I appreciated the joke.

'It was bloody funny, though,' said Ghandi. 'We could hardly keep from laughing. We nearly gave it away, didn't we?'

'I knew you were there a long time,' I said, 'I kept it up because I knew you were there.'

'Rotten lying bugger,' said Peter. 'You never knew anything of the sort.'

'I could see you,' I said.

'Why didn't you let on, then?' said Dreevo.

'I told you. I was playing you up.'

Knott blew a raspberry.

There was a knock on the door and Peter's mother poked her head into the room. 'Peter, love,' she said. 'Can I have a word with you a minute?'

'Yes, Mam,' said Peter. He got up and went to the door. As he went, I heard through the door his mother say: 'I'm just making a drink and I wanted to know who's for tea and who's for –'

The door closed.

I got up and said: 'Just going upstairs.'

That was where the toilet was.

I closed the door behind me. The coolness of the hall made me feel a bit better but there were still beads of sweat on my forehead.

I began to climb the stairs. At the end of the hall the kitchen door was open. I could hear cups and saucers being rattled. Mrs Knott was talking to Peter.

'It's not that I mind,' she said, 'but you do spoil *yourself* sometimes. I mean, you didn't really need to ask him to come. It's not as though you're great pals. And his mother. She just loves seeing people dragged down. She was always jealous of me, you know, when we lived down the Crescent. Oh, yes. Just because your dad wore a collar and could afford a car.'

I stopped on the stairs. Peter mumbled something in reply.

'And you must think about Susan. She might not like having to mix with that sort. I know her mother wouldn't like it. I mean, you've got to better yourself, you've got to get on, and lads like Brian, well he's all right the lad is, I've nothing against him, but lads like that'll just hold you back. They're no good to you. Now Alan and Tony, look at them. Totally different. They're like you. They'll be staying on at school and going on somewhere afterwards. College. Business. Good jobs. Those are the kind of people you'll naturally be mixing with later on, when you've left the Brians of this world behind you. I was only talking to Alan's mother the other day, she's a lovely woman, saying how pleased I was that you and him had got friendly. Incidentally they've got a lovely house behind the shop. Have you ever been in?'

I heard Peter say no.

'I mean, you don't have to be mean to the lad, you don't have to make it obvious. Just avoid him, something like that. You don't have to be cruel. Just don't encourage him.'

'I don't,' said Peter.

'I know,' said Mrs Knott. 'I know it's very difficult with people like that. Your dad and I know that only too well. When you've a position to keep up, there's always people wanting to hang on to your coat-tails. You can't blame them, but the thing is they always drag you down in the end.'

'Yes, Mum,' said Peter.

'Never mind, love,' said Mrs Knott. 'Give us a hand with the trolley.'

I went into the toilet and closed the door behind me.

KNOTT

'Look, he'll be here at eight o'clock and that's all there is to it.'

'You're damned right that's all there is to it. Except for the excuses you have to make to him.'

'I told you at the weekend he was coming.'

'And I didn't tell you that it was all right with me. So you'll just have to put him off.'

I wound the telephone cable round my wrist.

'Kate, listen,' I said. 'I know how you're feeling right now.'

'Do you?' she said. 'I wonder. Anyway that's precisely why I'm not prepared to put myself out. Why should I? Why should I do anything for you?'

'You're wrong, Kate,' I said. 'Believe me. You're so wrong.'

'I remember last time your saying exactly that. The only difference being that last time I believed you.'

'I promised it wouldn't happen again and I've kept my promise.'

'I don't believe you.'

'Look, we can't talk over the phone. Let's wait till I get home.'

'There's nothing to discuss.'

'All right,' I said. 'So you don't believe me. But just do this one thing for me.'

'Why are you so keen for him to come, anyway?'

'It's just that I can't put him off. He phoned this morning to see if it was still on and naturally I said yes. Thinking, as I told you, it'd be a one-off thing and that'd be the end of it. So having said yes, fine, I can't phone him back because in any case I don't know his number.'

'I thought you couldn't bear him.'

'I can't. I just want to get it over with.'

'You could explain and take him out to dinner.'

'That wouldn't make any difference. He wants to come to the house and sooner or later he'd make sure that he did.'

'Why does he want to come to the house?'

'I've told you what he's like. He probably wants to snoop. See what we've got, how we live. Probably wants to see what you're like.'

'Me? Why?'

'Look, Kate,' I said. 'Is it on or isn't it?'

The freeze came back into her voice.

'I don't know what I'll be able to do.'

Thank God.

'Thanks,' I said. 'And about what you think…'

'I don't want to discuss it.'

'All right,' I said.

'What time did you say?'

PLENDER

I dropped into the Ferry Boat before I went round to Knott's place. I knew Froy used the pub, and it was just an idea. I got my drink and sat down at a corner table, out of the light. If Froy came in, I didn't want him to see me first.

And he did come in, about quarter of an hour later.

He wasn't wearing his business suit. Instead he was wearing a leather sports jacket, a trendy cravat, a pink shirt, beige trousers and white corduroy shoes. His Pekinese was white, too. Certainly not the same old Froy I knew and loved.

He stood at the bar and ordered a Campari and stayed at the bar to drink it.

I just stayed where I was and looked at him, knowing that eventually he would notice me.

When he saw me, he didn't show his surprise, I'll give him that. But I knew I'd got him rattled. It was the right eyebrow that gave him away.

After I'd registered with him he turned back to his drink. I got up and walked over to the bar and stood next to him. I ordered another drink and when the barman went away I said:

'Fancy meeting you here, Mr Froy.'

He turned his head a little in my direction, but only just.

'What are you doing here?' he said.

'Same as you, Mr Froy, just having a drink.'

He took a sip of his Campari.

'I must say I do like your get-up, Mr Froy. I really do. Real gear stuff, if you'll pardon the expression.'

'Are you on business?' he said. 'If so, I ought to move on.'

'Business? No. Not business. You stay where you are, Mr Froy. It's not business. I'm just visiting.'

'You have friends out here?'

'Something like that. Actually, I'm going to dinner.'

This time Froy arched both his eyebrows.

'Dinner, eh?'

I'm not the type to be invited to dinner, that's what you mean, isn't it, Mr Froy, I thought. That's what the eyebrows are for.

'Yes,' I said. 'An old school chum.'

'Which one?'

'I beg your pardon?'

'Which school?'

I told him the name of the grammar school.

'Oh, I see,' said Froy, although he'd known all along.

You bloody old bastard, I thought. Just you wait, you old woman. Just you bloody well wait.

'It's a sort of old boys' reunion,' I said.

'Really?' said Froy. 'By the way, have you seen the evening paper?'

'No,' I said. 'Why?'

'There's an item about the proprietor of Peggy's Bar. I thought you'd have seen it. He was found dead last night.'

'Oh yes?' I said.

'Yes,' he said. 'Nasty business. Hanged himself in his own flat. Used a stocking.'

'A stocking?' I said.

'Yes, well you know what these people are like. Apparently he left a note. Typed, of course. Something about him not able to carry on. Carry on – the way he was, one assumes.'

'Well, some of them do get like that in their old age,' I said, looking at Froy.

Froy took another drink.

'Well, oh well,' I said. 'Old Peggy. That place just won't be the same without him. Did you ever get in there, Mr Froy?'

'No, I didn't,' he said. 'What I was driving at… well, you wouldn't happen to know anything about the… er, the circumstances, would you, Plender?'

'The circumstances?'

'Well, I understand you use the place as a rendezvous for certain aspects of our activities. I just wondered if perhaps in one way or another…'

'It's as big a surprise to me as it is to you, Mr Froy.'

'I hope so,' said Froy. 'You know what the position is if anything should go wrong at your end.'

'Mr Froy,' I said. 'Don't worry. I know nothing.'

'I suggest, though,' he said, 'that in any case it might be better to make different arrangements in the light of what's happened. The police are bound to be around for a time and it's better not to interfere with them too much at that level.'

'Of course, Mr Froy.'

'Now, I must be off,' he said. 'Can I get you something to drink?'

KNOTT

I stood in the dressing room, shaving with my electric razor. Kate was in the bedroom, sitting in front of her dressing table making her face up.

I stared into my own eyes as I pushed the razor round my face. My pupils were like pin-pricks and my face looked more bony than it had looked for years. My mouth was turned down at the edges in a kind of manic grimace. It was at a time like this, when I had to look at myself and see what I was, that the memories of what had happened pressed on me, from the inside, bursting to get out. I wondered how much longer my frame could bear it, how much longer it would go on, when the finale would come. The finale. What did that mean? The police? Prison? What would I feel? Relief? Or would this supernormal anxiety state persist indefinitely? Perhaps Eileen would never be found. Perhaps the police would never walk up the drive to my front door. And what would that mean? A lifetime of little favours for Plender? To have him constantly on the phone to me, asking this, asking that? Which would be worse?

I stopped shaving and unplugged my razor and went through into the bedroom. Kate was still sitting at the dressing table.

I walked over to her and stood behind her.

'Kate,' I said.

I put my hands on her shoulders and squeezed. She froze under my grip. I sank down on to my knees and buried my face in her back. The smell of her body brought tears to my eyes.

'Kate,' I said. 'Kate. What am I going to do?'

She turned round on her stool and I pushed my face into her lap. She was still stiff and I realised that my present actions would only endorse her disbelief; she would take them as proof of my unfaithfulness. My inability to control myself had made matters worse. And I'd caused Kate to panic too, to make her think the non-existent affair was far more serious than she'd imagined, because suddenly the tenseness left her and was replaced by a shuddering apprehension... and she said:

'Peter. Tell me. What is it?'

Christ. What was I going to say?

'Peter, you must tell me.'

'It's just...'

'What, Peter?'

'It's just that I can't bear you not believing me. I can't bear that you think I'm lying.'

She didn't say anything.

'You must believe me,' I said. 'I'm telling the truth.'

I felt her fingers tentatively touch my hair. I began to pull her towards me, down to the floor. She didn't resist but her movements told me she was on the verge of being convinced, that she was hoping she could believe me.

Now she was on the floor with me and I rolled on top of her, pretending passion, pushing her underskirt up to her waist, pulling at her straps, feeling her between her legs.

She reacted with a terrific suddenness. She was all over me, biting, kissing, her grip on me frantically violent, her legs thrashing up and down the length of my body, her whole body spasmodically arching and relaxing in turn. She pushed me on to my back and squirmed on top of me, kissing me, mouth wide open, blinding me with her soft dark hair, pressing her knee between my legs.

I had to stop her. Plender would be here soon.

I took hold of her by the shoulders and with great difficulty pushed upwards. Her hair drifted across my face and tickled my mouth and she took hold of my wrists and jerked my hands away and pressed down on me again, pinning my arms above my head, almost suffocating me with her interminable kisses. Eventually I managed to swivel my head to one side and I said:

'Kate, we must stop. The time.'

She shook her head and began to try to kiss me again.

'Plender,' I said. 'He'll be here any minute.'

Kate stiffened again and then eventually relaxed and rolled over on to her back.

'Later,' I said, taking hold of her hand. 'When he's gone.'

Kate lay there for a minute and then abruptly she got up and straightened herself and sat down again at the dressing table. I remained where I was, lying on my back on the floor.

PLENDER

'What does a detective do?' I said, looking at Knott's wife, drawing on my cigar. 'It's funny, everybody asks that. Peter asked me the other night, didn't you, Peter?'

Knott nodded.

'Have some more brandy,' he said.

'Thanks,' I said. I looked at Knott's wife again. 'Well, what do you think he does, Kate?'

Knott poured me some more brandy, trying not to appear too drunk. His wife said: 'And me, Peter. I'll have some more too.'

She pushed a strand of dark hair off her face and picked up her glass and offered it to Knott, her elbow on the table, her other hand supporting her chin. Knott gave her some brandy and she took a sip and said: 'Darling, while you're up, give me a cigarette.'

It was all for me. I knew that. It had been all evening. She'd been giving me those big brown eyes all night. And Knott knew it too. His wife thought he was having an affair, so what could he do about it?

I stretched out in my chair and placed my hands above my head.

'Come on,' I said. 'What do you think a private detective does?'

Knott lit his wife's cigarette and she inhaled and blew smoke

198

across the table and leant back in her seat the way I was doing except that she folded her arms across her breasts and with the fingers that held her cigarette she scratched one of her arms just below the shoulder.

'What do I think a private detective does?' she said. 'You mean apart from stealing about the grounds of old friends' houses at dead of night and making off with their cars?'

'Not fair,' I said. (Gurney always used those words whenever he protested anything.) 'That wasn't business. That was in the way of being a favour. Wasn't it, Peter?'

He nodded, not looking at me.

'All right,' she said. 'Point taken. But you knew how to get into it, how to start it without the key, and how to get it out of the garage and down the drive without waking a soul. Presumably you can count those as business methods.'

'True,' I said, 'true.'

'And so what aspect of your business entails knowing how to break and enter and steal a car?'

'You're supposed to be telling me,' I said, smiling.

'Yes, I am, aren't I,' she said. 'Well, now, let's see. On television –'

'Television!'

'On television, they don't seem to do anything very much except get beaten up and leap in and out of girls' bedrooms. And of course always producing a gun at precisely the right moment. Is that the way you do your business, Brian?'

'If I did then I'd need an awful lot of money in the bank to start with. Because I'm damned sure I'd never make any.'

'So you're in it for the money?'

'What else?'

'You're not a crusader?'

'You're back on television again.'

'All right. Describe the case you're working on at the moment. You do call them cases, don't you?'

Knott said: 'Perhaps Brian doesn't really want to talk about it, darling.'

Knott's wife twisted her head right round to look at him squarely in the face.

'You mean like a doctor or a lawyer? For ethical reasons?'

'I don't know,' he said. 'That's for Brian to say.'

'I don't mind,' I said. 'It would only be wrong if I used any names.'

I took a sip of my brandy.

'Well, for instance, recently there was a man who came into my office who was being blackmailed. He was in a fairly prominent position in local government and he didn't want to go to the police.'

'I thought the police always said that if a blackmailer was turned over to them they wouldn't press any charges against whoever it was who was being blackmailed?'

'Depends what the person had done, really.'

'Is that true?'

'Well, supposing you were being blackmailed because you'd put arsenic in Peter's cornflakes. You couldn't really expect the boys in blue to cock a deaf 'un, could you?'

I looked at Knott out of the corner of my eye. He was reaching for the brandy decanter.

'I suppose not.'

'Quite.'

'And this man you're talking about...'

'Sorry,' I said. 'No details.'

'Kate,' Knott said, 'I'm sure Brian's only being polite. He doesn't really want to answer your questions.'

'That, as you said earlier,' she said, 'is for Brian to say.'

'No, really. I don't mind,' I said, smiling as she gave her husband an ever-so-sweet I-told-you-so smile. 'Anyway, this chap, as I said, didn't want to go to the Law, so he asked me to find out who it was who was bleeding him. Nothing to it. I just followed the man from where he picked up the loot, found out who he was from where he lived and did a little bit of checking up. Then I arranged a meeting, accidentally on purpose like, and let him know what I knew. And that the Law wouldn't mind knowing either. And so he laid off.'

'The blackmailer blackmailed,' said Knott's wife.

'Something like that,' I said, looking at Knott. Knott looked the colour of white fish.

'Actually,' she said, 'it must be an awful feeling being blackmailed. Just living from week to week and knowing when the money runs out you're finished. And the blackmailer. He must be really horrible, a real bully at heart.'

'Terrible,' I said.

Knott got up from the table and said: 'Why don't we all go into the lounge?'

KNOTT

It was cool and quiet in the kitchen.

I sat down at the breakfast bar and held my glass with both hands and closed my eyes. No Kate, no Plender, no chat, no questions, no guilt. Just the quietness of the kitchen.

I sat there for a full five minutes, not thinking. Then Kate came into the kitchen.

'What the hell are you doing in here?' she said.

'I felt a bit off,' I said

'Hardly surprising,' she said. 'Anyway, I'm going to make some coffee. You'd better go in there and entertain Brian.'

I threw back my head to laugh but no laughter came.

'What's the matter?' said Kate.

I shook my head and slid off the stool and went back into the lounge.

Plender was sprawled out on the settee, smoking a cigarette, his glass full of brandy.

'Feeling all right?' he said when he saw me.

'Yes,' I said. 'I felt a bit off for a few minutes but it's passed.'

'Good,' Plender said. 'Good. Glad to hear it.'

I sat down opposite him. He was really making a meal of it. Really living out his invitation to the full.

'You know,' he said, indicating the room with the hand that held his glass, 'this really is very nice. Very nice indeed. I mean, it looked nice from outside, but it's even nicer inside. The outside doesn't do it justice. I mean, you can tell from the outside how nice it's going to be, but you'd never think it'd be quite as nice as this. Is it you or the wife?'

'I beg your pardon?'

'You or the wife. The décor. The way it's done out?'

'Oh. Both of us, I suppose.'

'Well, I must say you've done a very nice job, both of you. Mind you, I admire your taste particularly.'

'Mine?'

'Yes, yours. The missus. She's a little cracker. A real darling.'

I didn't say anything.

'Yes,' he said, 'you've really done all right for yourself, Peter. And it's very nice to see it. Mind you, it was always on the cards. You always had that air about you. That you'd make good. Everybody recognised it. Even the lads at school, in the old gang. It stuck out a mile.'

I drained my glass and got up to pour myself another drink.

'I wonder what happened to them all,' Plender said. 'Are you ever in touch with any of them, Peter?'

'Who?'

'The old gang. Do you ever hear of any of them?'

'No.'

'I would have thought maybe your mother would have kept you posted.'

I shook my head.

'I wonder what happened to them all,' he said. 'I'd really like to know. Here, do you remember old Mouncey?'

I nodded.

'Do you remember that time you and him got my General Book and rubbed my history homework out?'

Kate came in with the coffee.

'What's all this?' she said, putting the tray down. 'Old times?'

Plender laughed. Kate began to pour the coffee, bending over the coffee table, her back to Plender. He was able to look right up her skirt. He knew I'd noticed, but he didn't stop.

'No, not really,' he said. 'I was just asking Peter if he remembered this particular time when him and another lad rubbed my homework out.'

'Did what?'

Kate gave Plender his coffee and sat down next to him on the settee.

'It was really very funny,' said Plender. 'I'd been in trouble with the history master for not doing my homework. I wasn't like Peter, all industrious. Anyway, old Jepson, he was the history master, said that the next time I failed to produce a full and complete piece of homework, I was for the high jump. He'd take me to the Headmaster. Well, I wasn't in his good books, either, because one or two of the staff had been on to him about the same thing, homework, and he was one of those characters who believed that if you didn't use the facilities the school provided, adopt the right attitude, all that junk, then you had no right to be there. So of course I didn't want to get kicked out, so I went home that night and did the biggest and best piece of homework I'd ever done in my life. Something about the repeal of the Corn Laws, I think it was. Anyway, as it happened, it wasn't a Best Books exercise, it was General Books only, and you could write in pencil in General Books. So when I got to school next morning there was a big crowd waiting for me at the gate because it had got around that I was for the chop if I didn't do my homework and of course everybody thought that I wouldn't have. Everybody was amazed that I had done it. Anyway, history was first period after break… you tell it, Peter. Tell Kate what you and Mouncey did.'

Kate was looking at me, her face blank of expression. I said: 'Well, there's nothing to tell really.'

'Go on, Peter,' said Kate.

I got up.

'Well, there's nothing, except, as Brian says, Mouncey and I rubbed his homework out.'

'All six pages of it,' said Plender, laughing. 'I couldn't believe my eyes. Of course, I didn't check it when I got back in from break. As you didn't hand in General Book homework, what Old Jepson usually did was to get everybody to open their books at where their homework was written down and then he'd go by each desk and have a look, and when he'd done that he'd select one or two people to read out what they'd written. Which he did in this case. So I opened my book at the place where I'd done it, and there it was, gone. I really couldn't believe it. You can't imagine the panic I was in. I scrabbled through the pages in case I'd made a mistake, and of course all that did was to make matters worse as far as Jepson was concerned. He just thought I was trying to break the ice before he got to me. And when he did get to me all I could say was, "Well, it was there before break, sir". You can imagine what happened. He hit the roof. Yanked me out of my seat by the scruff of my neck and marched me off to the Headmaster's office. God, what a laugh.'

'And what happened?'

'Well, I didn't get the chop but it wasn't far off. I just got stopped breaks and games the rest of the term.'

'Well, I think that was a horrible thing to do.'

'It was a joke,' I said.

'Not funny,' said Kate. Then to Plender. 'Didn't you try and get your own back?'

'No,' said Plender. 'After all, as Peter says, it was only a joke.'

I looked at my watch. Plender caught the meaning but he said: 'This coffee is really nice, Kate.'

'Would you like some more?'

'Wouldn't say no,' said Plender. 'Never been known to refuse.'

PLENDER

Out of the corner of my eye I saw Knott's car creep on to the playing field.

'All right,' I said, 'at ease.'

The men stood at ease and I waited for Knott to get out of the car and walk over. But he didn't. He just sat in his car and stared across at us.

'Touching toes right hand left foot twenty times then twenty times the other way,' I said to the men. 'I'll be back in a minute.'

I walked across the field to Knott's car. He didn't take his eyes off me. I walked round to the driver's side and leant over and looked in at him. He just stared up at me. I tapped on the window and he wound it down.

'What's the matter?' I said. 'Too early for you?'

He didn't answer.

'If you exercised like we do you wouldn't feel so bad first thing in a morning.'

'I want to talk to you,' he said. His voice was dry and flat.

'Oh, yes?' I said.

Again he didn't answer.

I looked at him. Then I straightened up and strolled round to the passenger side of the car and got in. Knott hadn't moved.

'So you want to talk to me,' I said. 'Then talk to me.'

'I read the paper today. About the barman.'

'What barman?'

'The one who ran the bar. The one who saw me.'

'What about him?'

'He's dead.'

'Dead?'

'It says he hanged himself.'

'Hanged himself?'

'Yes.'

I took out a cigarette.

'So he hanged himself. I don't quite see what you're getting at.'

'He was the only one who saw me. Except you.'

'Well then I would have thought all in all things seem to have worked out very much for the best.'

'You were the only one who knew he'd seen me,' he said. 'Now he's dead.'

I threw back my head and laughed.

'You killed him, didn't you?'

'Now, why,' I said, inhaling cigarette smoke, 'should I do a thing like that?'

'Because if I'm caught, you'd be frightened I'd tell them about you.'

'And so I'd go and knock somebody over just on the off-chance that they may remember your face and her face out of all the faces that were in Peggy's bar between Saturday and now.'

He didn't say anything.

I laughed again.

'Look,' I said, 'I got into this by accident. I certainly wouldn't do anything to deliberately make things worse for myself.'

'You killed him. I know it.'

Wind sped across the playing fields and rocked the car.

'Well,' I said, 'I didn't. But obviously I'm not going to change your mind.'

He shook his head.

'And so you're going to go to the police?'

He put his head in his hands and leant forward in his seat.

'God,' he said. 'I don't know. I don't know what I'm going to do. All I know is that I just can't go on. I mean, I'm going out of my mind, I really am. It's like it must be for a condemned man. Every day it gets worse. Every day I think this is the day when it says in the paper they've found her. This is the day the police start walking up the drive.' He lifted his head and looked at me. 'I mean, they're bound to, aren't they? Sooner or later. They're bound to find her and trace her to me, whatever you say or do.'

'You obviously think so,' I said. 'So what can I say?'

'So what else is there for me to do?'

I shrugged.

'Go to the police, I suppose,' I said.

He broke down.

'That's just it,' he said. 'That's just it. I can't. I haven't the bloody guts.'

'So there you are,' I said. 'Back to square one.'

He carried on sobbing with his head in his hands. I took a handkerchief from the pocket of my tracksuit and offered it to him. He took it and sat up and wiped his face.

'After you've taken the pictures,' I said, 'you ought to do a few physical jerks with us. Blow the cobwebs away. It's surprising what a bit of exercise can do.'

He shook his head.

'No,' he said. 'I'll just take the pictures and go.'

'There's only a couple to do,' I said. 'One of us exercising and one of us in a group. It won't take you long so don't dash off.'

He didn't say anything.

'Come on,' I said, opening the door. 'Let's go over.'

Knott didn't move. I leant into the car.

'You really will feel better after a few physical jerks,' I said. 'Get stuck in there with the lads and you'll feel a new man.'

Knott reached into the back of the car and scrambled his

gear together and got out. He was a little unsteady on his legs, as though he'd just got out of the car after a marathon drive. I walked round to his side of the car and picked up his case while he fumbled a camera strap round his neck.

'Right,' I said. 'Let's go and meet the lads. I call them the Team.'

KNOTT

'Well I rather liked him,' said my wife. 'In a funny way.'

I didn't say anything. I cut off a piece of my steak and put it in my mouth and went through the motions of chewing it as though I actually wanted to eat it.

'Although,' she said, '"like" isn't really the right word. Something else. In view of what you've told me about him. In the light of what he is. It's not "like" exactly.'

I took a sip of wine and tried to listen to her words one by one, as though they weren't forming sentences, so that singly they would have no meaning.

'Is it sympathy?' she said. 'Am I sorry for him? I don't know. What is it exactly?'

I knew she was looking at me while she was speaking but I was careful to avoid her eyes. At the same time I had to find something to say in reply to her: I had to behave normally, behave the way I always behaved. I knew she was trying to needle me, so I had to behave the way she expected me to behave, to react as I normally would.

'I'm surprised,' I said.

'Surprised?'

'That you like him?'

'Why?'

'I didn't think he'd be your type.'

This was what she wanted.

'What do you mean?' she said.

'What I say. I'm surprised how you took to him.'

'Yes, but I don't really understand you. Why shouldn't I take to him?'

'Well, to begin with, what you said before you met him. About the car.'

I chewed my steak and listened to myself, sounding calm and precise and normal. Why didn't I break down in front of her, the way I had done in front of Plender? Why was I strong now?

'That was before I met him. Before I really knew anything about him.'

'And what do you know now that changes your opinion?'

Kate leant back in her chair, settling to her triumph.

'You don't like it, do you?' she said.

'Don't like what?'

'You don't like me feeling sorry for Plender.'

'Why shouldn't I like that?'

'Because you think he's a little shit, the way you did at school. And you don't like my thinking differently. It's a kind of threat to you.'

'A threat?'

'Oh, come on,' she said. 'You can't bear it when anybody disagrees with you. Anybody who isn't with you is agin you. Like a child. You've always been like that.'

'I see.'

'Oh God. And now the I've-been-hurt-but-I-insist-on-being-dignified bit.'

I put my knife and fork down on my plate.

'I'm right, though,' said Kate. 'You put that poor bastard through the mangle at school and now that I say I like him it reminds you of what a rotten bastard you were, and you don't like that, and so you get all paranoid about it.'

'You're being stupid,' I said.

'I have to be, don't I? Otherwise why should I disagree with you?'

I got up from the dining table.

'I'm going in the lounge,' I said.

'Of course,' said Kate.

The phone rang as I was walking through.

It was Plender.

'Hello, mate,' he said. 'How's things?'

'Fine,' I said. 'I'm fine.'

'Feeling better than you did this morning?'

'Yes,' I said.

'Good. I was hoping you would be because I'm in a bit of a spot. You'd never credit it but I've been let down again.'

'Let down?'

'Yes. There's a client of mine I'd arranged to have met only the laddie who was supposed to meet him has gone and got himself into a spot of bother.'

'What do you want?'

'I know it's a bit of a bind but I wondered if you'd pop along and do the honours. It shouldn't take more than an hour. You'll be back home again by eleven. I'd do it myself but I'm already tied up.'

'Look,' I said, trying to sound sane and reasonable, as if it was just an ordinary favour I was being asked. 'It's very difficult...'

'All you have to do is meet him then drive him to an address I'll give you and then leave him on the doorstep.'

I could hear Kate moving about in the dining room.

'Are you sure?' I said.

'How do you mean?'

'Are you sure that's all?'

'Of course that's all.'

'Listen,' I said, 'you've got to stop phoning me here. I can't tell Kate it's you all the time or she'll wonder why.'

'And she'll wonder why if you don't tell her it's me,' he said. 'I get the picture. Not to worry. I shan't do it again, not for this kind of reason, anyway. It's just unfortunate the way it's turned out, the fact I've been let down twice since I bumped into you. Honestly, if I could get somebody else, I would. Anyway tonight you've got a built-in excuse for the wife. Why I phoned, I mean. Tell her I was thanking you both for such a delightful evening.'

'Yes,' I said.

'All right?'

'Yes.'

'Fine. So if you can be at Peggy's Bar at nine-thirty...'

I couldn't believe what he was saying.

'Where?' I said.

'Peggy's Bar. Why, what's up?'

'What are you trying to do?'

'I don't quite follow you.'

'Peggy's Bar. You know I can't go there.'

'Why not?'

I closed my eyes.

'God.' I said. 'Listen. Just listen. You know how I feel. You must know. How can I walk in there knowing what I know. Remembering Saturday. Knowing about...'

I couldn't say the name.

'You mean thinking I killed Peggy?'

I didn't say anything.

'But I didn't.'

All right, I thought. I can't explain my real reasons. You won't let me. You don't want to understand. I'll take it at your level.

'The police might not think it was suicide,' I said. 'They might be watching the place.'

'Not a chance,' he said. 'They're well satisfied. I can tell you that for nothing.'

I wanted to cry.

'But I can't go back there,' I said. 'I can't.'

'Just put it at the back of your mind,' he said. 'You'll be as right as rain.'

I couldn't find any more words.

'Peter?' he said. 'You all right?'

'Tell me who I'm to meet,' I said.

'That's the spirit,' he said. 'And I promise, this is definitely the last time.'

PLENDER

At quarter to ten I dialled Knott's number. After a little while the receiver at the other end was lifted and I heard Kate Knott's voice give their phone number.

'Hello,' I said. 'Is that Kate?'

'Yes,' she said, not recognising my voice over the phone.

'It's Brian here,' I said. 'Brian Plender. Is Peter there?'

'No,' she said. 'He's gone out for a drink.'

'Not to worry,' I said, 'it's you I ought to speak to really. I was only phoning to say thanks for last night. It was really great.'

There was a pause while she remembered what Knott had told her earlier.

'Oh,' she said. 'I see. Well, that's nice of you, Brian. I'll tell Peter you called.'

'Is anything wrong?' I said.

'No,' she said. 'Nothing. I was dozing when you phoned. I'm not properly awake yet.'

'Trust me,' I said. 'I never dreamt you'd be in bed. I'm terribly sorry.'

'No, I wasn't in bed. I just fell asleep in the chair. Please don't worry. Actually I'm glad you woke me up.'

'That's all right, then.'

I waited.

'Brian?' she said.

'Yes?'

'I know this sounds a stupid question, but... you didn't phone earlier, did you?'

'I beg your pardon?'

'You didn't phone Peter? Earlier?'

'No,' I said. 'Why?'

'It doesn't matter,' she said.

'What makes you think I phoned earlier?'

'Nothing,' she said. 'Just something Peter said.'

I pretended to let the penny drop and began to play the faithful friend doing a swift cover-up job.

'Well, I did try and get him at work this morning, as a matter of fact, but he was out and I had to leave a message. That's probably what he was talking about.'

'No,' she said, coldly, choosing not to be let off the hook. 'No, it was definitely this evening he meant. About an hour ago.'

'Well one of you must be mixed up,' I said. 'Because I'm sure it would have been this morning he was on about.'

'Peter answered the phone an hour ago. I asked him who it was and he said it was you, phoning to thank us for last night. He was most specific.'

It was going better than I'd hoped.

'Well, I wonder why on earth he should say that?' I said, letting the false innocence in my voice be thin enough to let her hear the suspicion underneath.

'Do you?' she said.

I allowed a small pause before I said:

'Look, I know this is none of my business... but somehow I seem to have dropped Peter in it. I'm terribly sorry.'

'Don't be sorry,' she said. 'It's not your fault.'

'No, I know,' I said, 'but Peter's a mate of mine. I don't know what this is about, but I now feel terrible. If I hadn't have phoned, then this wouldn't have happened.'

'It would, I'm afraid,' she said. 'Sooner or later.'

'Oh,' I said. 'Bad as that.'

She didn't answer.

'Look,' I said. 'I know this may sound... I don't know... anyway, I'd appreciate it if you didn't tell Peter. That I phoned, I mean.' I pretended to search for words. 'What I mean is, whatever happens, I don't want him thinking I was the one to drop him in the cart. I know it sounds stupid, but...'

'No, I won't tell him,' she said. 'It doesn't actually hinge on this phone call.'

'Thanks,' I said.

There was a silence. Then I said:

'I know I only met you last night, but you being Peter's wife, and me knowing him from way back... what I'm trying to say is, if there's anything you feel you want to talk over at any time, if you feel you could use some help, advice, anything like that, well, you can always give me a ring. As I say, I know last night was the first time we met, but, you know, it's up to you. If you feel you can, then just pick up the phone. I'd like to help, if you felt that I could.'

KNOTT

I walked into Peggy's Bar. It was packed. What had happened to Peggy must have been good for business. But I was glad that the bar was crowded. The less like it had been on Saturday the better. Wastes of emptiness would only make my memories worse, and they were bad enough even away from this place.

I pushed my way through to the bar and bought a drink, a large whisky, and went and stood near the third alcove along, the way I'd been told to. Except that wasn't quite right, I'd been told to sit down there, in the alcove, but all the alcoves were packed, four to a bench seat. So I stood near the third alcove along and waited for Mr Reed to appear. Businessman. Middle forties. Thin on top. Cavalry moustache. Carrying a copy of *Mayfair* magazine. He'd be expecting to meet a girl called Lesley, and Lesley's friend, Camille, Plender had said. They all expected to meet the girls in the bar, but there was always an intermediary, just to make sure.

I concentrated on the people in the bar, using them to obstruct the bar itself, so that the décor wouldn't bring back the events of Saturday night. But everywhere I looked, it was myself and Eileen that I saw, going through the motions of our date. But by now, I was coming to a kind of acceptance of my dreadful memories, so that now the dreadfulness was dull and aching in my stomach, instead of attacking my brain and stinging me with panic. It was as if my nerve ends had been cauterised so that I couldn't feel pain any more, but at the same time, if I were to put my hands in the fire, the memory of pain would pulse slowly through my body. The worst thoughts I had now concerned the future, the worst of all being when was I ever going to feel something other than guilt and fear. Would I ever be able to laugh without the memory of what had happened rising up in my throat? Would I ever wake up in the morning without my first thoughts being of Eileen's dead face? When would there be an evening without my dreading a phone call from Plender?

There was a movement near the alcove. A man paused, surprised, then moved on quickly. It was Reed, I was sure. I watched him for a moment or two. He looked back at the booth, just to make sure he hadn't made a mistake. Then he looked round the bar and I was able to have a good look at his face. He was as Plender had described him, but beneath his Gannex coat I could see the knot of a gaily coloured cravat and his trousers didn't belong to a business suit. He turned a full circle and made uneasily for the bar.

I waited for him to order his drink then I threaded my way through the tables and stood next to him at the bar. I ordered another drink for myself and pretended to be looking at people on either side of Reed, while in fact most of the time I was watching his face. He was sweating but his skin wasn't flushed; it was very pale and white, the colour of ice-cream. His eyes flicked towards the door each time someone new came into the bar, and each time he took a sip of his drink when he looked away again.

It was a strange feeling, standing next to a man who didn't know you, yet knowing exactly why he was there and what you were going to say to him, knowing that he would be off his guard when you spoke, surprised. Perhaps a little frightened.

He caught me looking at him, then looked away quickly. I saw in his glance exactly what he was thinking: I was trying to pick him up. It made me smile a grim smile. Me, of all people. In this place, of all places.

I said to him: 'Mr Reed?'

He looked at me, startled into blankness. He didn't speak.

'Mr Reed?' I said again.

He looked me up and down, drawing away from me slightly.

'Are you waiting for Lesley and Camille?'

'Who are you?' he said.

'It's all right,' I said. 'I'm here on their behalf.'

'Who are you?'

'You are Mr Reed? The Mr Reed who replied to the magazine?'

He didn't answer.

'Don't worry,' I said. 'I'm from the magazine, not the police station.'

I listened to myself talking. I sounded like a different person.

He still didn't say anything.

'The thing is,' I said, 'it's always done this way. To protect our advertisers. On both sides.'

'Why wasn't I told in the letter?'

'We don't like to make our advertisers unduly nervous. We don't like them to feel even the suggestion that a small fraction of our advertisers may not be genuine, not at that stage.'

'What about now?'

'I'm sure that within half an hour you'll be convinced that there's no need for nervousness. As will the two clients you're making contact with.'

There was relief in the way I was talking. By being business-like and calm I was able to get away from myself for a short while.

I wondered if Plender did it this way. And I wondered what he'd think of my own approach.

'Well it's very worrying when you're not expecting anything

like this,' he said, looking about him as if to make sure there were no more surprises looming close by.

'I can understand that,' I said. 'But the sooner we get on our way the better you'll feel.'

'On our way.'

'I'm just an intermediary,' I said. 'I take you to the house and then I leave you.'

'Why don't you just give me the address?'

'We think this way is better. Then neither client runs the risk of being disappointed.'

He downed his drink.

'Very well,' he said. 'Let's be on our way.'

We didn't speak during the drive. The mood I'd assumed in the bar dropped away from me the closer we got to the council house. I remembered the other night and the things that I'd photographed, things too close to my own activities for my comfort, yet far enough removed to revolt me, and to be revolted with myself by association.

I parked the car around the corner, the way Plender had done. We got out and walked around into the other road and I took Reed up the path to the front door and rang the doorbell four times the way Plender had told me to.

The door was opened by an attractive girl wearing a blonde wig. She smiled at us both.

'Mr Reed?' she said.

'That's right,' Reed said.

'I'm Lesley,' she said. 'Come in.'

Reed went in and the girl called Lesley began to close the door. I heard her telling Reed to go into the lounge and introduce himself to Camille. I turned away and began to walk down the path but the door that had never properly closed was opened wide again and light fanned out on to the ground in front of me causing me to turn round.

Lesley was standing in the doorway motioning me to go back to the house. I stood and stared at her. Her movements became more agitated so I walked back to the doorway.

'Come in,' she whispered, looking over her shoulder. When I didn't move she tugged at my sleeve and I allowed myself to be pulled into the hall. She closed the door quietly behind her and closed the lounge door and then hurried me down the hall, out of sight, near the room where I'd taken the photographs.

'Where the hell do you think you were going?' she said.

'What do you mean?'

'Keep your voice down,' she said. 'What do you think I mean?'

I shook my head.

'The pictures,' she said. 'You're supposed to take the pictures.'

'Pictures?'

'For Mr Plender. He phoned telling us to expect a different feller tonight, and that's you, isn't it?'

'But he didn't tell me.'

'Do you take pictures for Mr Plender?'

'I have done, but...'

'Well then you'd better get in there, quick. Or else Mr Plender'll be wondering why he didn't get any pictures, and that can't be good, can it?'

'But I haven't got a camera. I didn't bring anything.'

'Mr Plender brought some stuff round with him when he let us in. So get on with it. I've got to go.'

She turned away and hurried down the hall.

I just stood there, in the dead, brightly lit hall, staring at her till she disappeared into the lounge, closing the door behind her.

The silence of the hall rang in my ears.

I stood there for a few moments longer, then went into the other room.

PLENDER

I lay on my bed listening to Froy's voice rattle out of the recorder.

'I've told Plender to stop using the place,' he was saying. 'If there was any kind of a scandal some of our friends on the Force might find it difficult just to go through the motions if one of their number discovered something about us and decided to investigate.'

'Is it what it appears to be?' said the other voice.

'I think so,' said Froy. 'I've discussed it with Plender and I believe him when he says he knows nothing about it other than what everybody else knows.'

I reached out and snapped off the recorder. Then I felt for my cigarettes and lit up and lay on my back fiddling with my lighter, pressing the tits and releasing them, letting the flame alternately spurt out and cut off.

Froy, I thought.

Froy. All I needed to know was the phone number. The phone number of the person he reported to. That was all I needed to know.

There was one way it could be done. A camera with a long lens, outside, when he dialled. But there were too many factors that had to be right. The curtains had to be open. The telephone had to be facing a certain way. The man with the camera had to be around when it was certain that Froy was going to make a call. Too many factors, all having to be dead right.

I thought about Froy and I thought about Knott.

KNOTT

At first they played a kind of charades.

One scene looked as though it was meant to be taking place in a train. The girls sat on one settee and Reed sat on the one opposite, pretending to look at his paper. The girls looked at magazines or acted out looking through the imaginary window until gradually I realised that behind the newspaper Reed was exposing himself, the way he must have wanted to on his morning train, but here he could do it in safety, relish the pretended excited shocks of the two girls and extend his fantasy into complete reality. After a while the girls fell on him and tied him and began to punish him, the punishment eventually turning into sex-play, but before the sex-play went too far, the fantasy was broken up by Reed, who gave directions to the girls to begin another game. One of the settees was pushed back and a writing desk and two chairs dragged into the centre of the room. One of the girls left the room and Reed sat behind the desk on one chair and the girl called Lesley sat on the other chair in front of the desk, holding a writing pad and a biro. Reed began to dictate to her and the girl pretended to take dictation. When she'd finished she handed Reed the notebook. Reed looked at the blank page and affected irritation. The girl pretended to be upset and Reed handed back the notebook and the performance was acted out again: Reed dictated and the girl took notes and handed the book over for inspection, and Reed pretended to be even more annoyed and the girl pretended to be even more upset. A third time they acted out the charade and this time Reed pretended to lose his temper with the girl and ordered her to bend over the desk. He took a folding two foot rule from his trouser pocket and opened it out, lifted the girl's dress and began to punish her. After a little while the other girl came into the room, threw up her hands in mock horror, then proceeded to turn the tables by helping the girl called Lesley to tie Reed across the desk and use the ruler on him.

I stopped taking pictures.

I turned away and leant against the wall, my head tilted back, my eyes closed. I felt sick again. Sick because what I had been watching was like looking into a mirror and seeing myself in the execution of my own fantasies, seeing them for what they were, sordid, self-defeating, addictive to the point where satisfaction could not be reached in the fantasy itself but only by replacing the fantasy with another; a vicious circle of fantasy followed by fantasy, frustration by frustration. Because there was no end result. No climax satisfactory enough to sate an appetite longer than a few hours. No climax satisfactory enough to generate calm and security on which the mind and body could float and feed and nourish themselves. There was nothing there but the fantasy, the mind part, and thoughts were dead and withered, divorced from any bodily satisfaction. But why? The memories of past climaxes must spur the body on to relive those memories in other, different bodies, other, different situations. Or was it just desire driven by the desperation of continued anti-climax, searching each time in the hope that this time there will be a kind of satisfaction? If not, what else was there?

And also I felt sick with myself because of my feelings at that moment in time. Pathetic and depressing as the antics in the other room were, they'd still managed to have an effect on me, sexually. In spite of the situation I was in, in spite of my own self-disgust, my affinities with the scenes in the other room were stronger than my guilt and my revulsion. I was an animal. Even now, I was excited.

The door opened. I turned my head. It was the other girl, Camille. She stood in the doorway, holding a glass and a bottle of whisky.

'Hope I'm not interrupting anything,' she said, looking me up and down. I realised what my position suggested to her and I relaxed and shrugged myself away from the wall.

'Don't worry,' she said. 'It takes a lot to embarrass me.'

She poured some whisky into the glass. She looked prettier in the soft red light of the tiny room than she had looked when I'd watched her through the window.

'Thought you might fancy a drink,' she said. 'I know I could use one.'

She took a drink from the glass before she offered it to me. The lipstick she left on the rim looked black in the room's red light.

'Thank you,' I said, taking the glass and drinking. I could feel her watching me.

'I've not seen you before, have I?' she said. 'Or have I?'

She was standing very close to me. I looked into her face. Her soft perfume washed over me. I glanced through the window, wondering why she wasn't in the other room. Reed was taking his own pictures of the girl called Lesley.

'I'm not in this one,' Camille said, in a coy way. 'This is where him and Lesley make it together. Bitch. She has all the luck. It's her eyelashes that do it. They're real, you know. Still, at least with her he's not in for any unpleasant surprises.'

I didn't know what she was talking about. I drank the rest of the whisky. The girl tipped the bottle and filled the glass again. She stared at me while she poured. I tried to avoid her eyes but there was nowhere to look except through the window into the other room. The girl looked too.

'That your sort of scene, is it?' she said.

Plender. Plender had said something like that to me.

I shook my head.

'S'pose it leaves you cold,' she said, 'I mean, you doing this all the time, for a living, like.'

I didn't answer. I couldn't take my eyes off the window. Now Reed had finished taking pictures and he and the girl were lying on the settee.

'I know it leaves me cold,' said the girl. 'But then it would, wouldn't it.'

I sensed her move closer to me.

'Here,' she said softly, 'are you sure I haven't seen you somewhere before?'

I didn't answer. There was a silence. Her arm brushed against me and her fingers touched mine.

'I know,' she said. 'Yes. I knew I had. In Peggy's. Couple of times. I knew I was right.'

I turned and faced her.

'I knew it,' she said. 'I knew I was right.'

There was something about her face. Something that the expression of triumph was doing to her features. She gripped my fingers tightly.

'You naughty boy you,' she said. 'Peggy's. Well, it certainly is a small world, isn't it?'

Her face. Different. It was altered. She pressed against me.

Then I knew.

I hit out with all the force in my body. Camille screamed and fell against the tripod, smashing the camera against the wall.

'Bastard,' screamed Camille, tears spreading the mascara down his face. 'Bloody rotten bastard.'

He tried to get up.

I lashed out with my foot and caught him full on the shoulder.

He fell back again, hugging himself in agony.

I lurched out of the room and ran down the hall and flung open the front door. I heard the door into the lounge open and then the voices of the others receding away behind me as I ran.

PLENDER

I spent the first part of the morning reading the papers. There was nothing else to do and I wasn't meeting Knott until midday in the Tivoli Tavern. After Lesley had called and let me have the story about what happened I'd given Knott half an hour to get home, just to make sure that in fact he'd done just that. When I'd heard his voice at the other end of the line I'd just told him when and where I wanted to meet him and hung up. But before I'd done that I'd heard Kate's voice in the background screaming at him to tell her who it was that was calling.

My secretary brought me my coffee at ten-thirty and I was sitting there drinking it and looking out of the window when the intercom buzzed and my secretary said: 'There's a Mrs Knott in reception to see you. She says she hasn't an appointment.'

I put my cup down on my saucer. The window shuddered. I said: 'That's all right. I'll come out.'

I got up and walked round my desk and opened the door. Kate Knott was standing in reception, her back to the desk, pretending to be mildly interested in the surroundings.

'Kate,' I said.

She turned to face me. She was wearing dark glasses and underneath her make-up her skin was pale.

'How nice,' I said. 'You're the last person I expected to see.'

'I expect I am,' she said. 'Actually I was in town shopping and I thought I'd drop in on you and see how a real detective lives.'

Her voice strained to project the lightness the remark was meant to generate.

'I don't believe you,' I said, standing back to let her go through the door into my office. 'You just didn't really believe it when I said I was a detective. You came to catch me out.'

I closed the door behind me and took her coat.

'Well, I had to look up your address in the phone book,' she said. 'And there it was in the yellow pages: B. Plender, Private and Commercial Investigator.'

'Of course,' I said, 'I was forgetting you'd have to look me up.' I indicated the low upholstered chair by the picture window. 'Would you like some coffee?'

'Thank you,' she said. 'I would.'

I buzzed for fresh coffee.

'What a marvellous view,' she said.

I turned round and walked over to the window.

'Yes,' I said. 'It's almost worth the rent.'

'You can see for miles,' she said. 'Look at the curve of the river. Isn't that Grimsby I can see?'

She lifted her dark glasses from her face and I saw the faint blue of a bruise below her right eye.

'Yes,' I said. 'Nearly twenty-five miles away. And the other way, over on the right, you can see Brumby, where Peter and I used to live.'

'Oh yes,' she said.

'Do you see the church tower?'

'The church tower. I can't... yes, there it is.'

'If you look a little to the left, you'll see a couple of big fields. Can you make them out?'

'Yes, I can see them.'

'Can you see a building just above them, standing on its own?'

'Yes.'

'That's where Peter and I went to school.'

My secretary came in with the coffee and put it down on the low table by Kate Knott's chair.

I poured her coffee out and got my cup from off my desk and filled it up and sat down opposite Knott's wife.

'Well,' I said. 'I'm glad you dropped in.'

'I nearly didn't,' she said. 'I thought you might be too busy. I really ought to have phoned first.'

'No need,' I said. 'Except for one appointment, I'm free all day.'

I sat back and sipped my coffee.

'Actually,' she said, 'the real reason I came straight round without phoning first was because if I'd phoned, I probably wouldn't have followed it through.'

'How do you mean?'

She looked out of the window.

'I mean that between phoning and actually making my way here I might have lost my courage.'

'Courage?' I said. 'I'm that frightening, am I?'

She shook her head, allowing a small smile to break on her mouth.

'No,' she said. 'I didn't mean that.'

'Well, then I don't understand.'

'I don't expect you to,' she said. 'How can you when I haven't even told you why I'm here.'

I took out my cigarettes and offered her one but she didn't accept. I lit up and blew smoke out and watched her.

'I'm putting you in an awful position by coming here,' she said.

I didn't say anything.

'I mean, the fact that you're a friend of Peter's, I shouldn't have come to you.'

She picked up her coffee cup and began to turn it round in her hands.

'But you see,' she said, 'last night... you did say... if ever I needed help...'

The tears came and she put her cup down and gathered her handbag to her and began to search for a handkerchief.

'And I meant it,' I said. 'I thought you realised that.'

'I did... I mean, I do, but it's difficult for me, you must realise that. I never meant to do anything like this. It's just that I don't know what to do. I've got to a point I never thought I'd reach.'

She found her handkerchief and took off her dark glasses and dabbed at her eyes. I looked at the bruise on her face and she saw me looking and so I said:

'That happen last night?'

She nodded.

'So you told him I called, then?'

'No,' she said. 'I kept my promise. This was something else.'

'Tell me,' I said.

'I don't really... I mean even now I can't understand what made him do it. I mean I can't see what I said that was bad enough or unusual enough to make him so furious.'

She was talking almost as though I wasn't there. She even put the dark glasses back on, as if I hadn't seen what she'd been trying to hide.

'We had a row, yes. What I mean is, he got in late, and he looked terrible, as though something awful had happened, and I asked where he'd been, what had happened, and he just wouldn't speak. He knows I suspect him of having an affair, I've told him I do, but he just behaves as though I must be mad to suspect him, as though he's been behaving normally. Anyway, after he'd been in for a while, the phone rang and he jumped up to answer it, it was so obvious that he didn't want me to get to it first, so I screamed at him while he was holding the phone. I shouted at him to tell me who it was that was calling. And then he put the phone down and walked over to me and hit me. Not just on

232

the face. All over. Punching. He kept punching me until I fell over. Then he went into the bedroom with a bottle of Scotch and locked the door behind him.'

'Did he come out again?'

'He must have. I mean, he was gone this morning. He went to the studio. I phoned there, just to make sure. Although I didn't talk to him.'

I didn't say anything.

'But the point is,' she said, 'last night was no different to a dozen other nights. I mean, the kind of row it was. But there was something really wrong last night. He was like a madman. But then for a week or more he's not been himself.'

'And you're convinced he's having an affair, and it's this affair that's making him act this way?'

'I don't know.'

'I thought you said you were certain.'

'I am. I mean I was. But now I don't know. Why should an affair affect him this way? I've known him to be unfaithful before, and I know Peter. This is different.'

There was a silence.

'And you want me to find out how different?' I said.

She didn't answer at first. Then she shook her head.

'I don't know,' she said. 'I'm not sure that I want to know.'

'Supposing you did know. Supposing you found out what was going on. What would you do?'

'I'm not sure,' she said.

Another silence elapsed.

'Because you see,' I said, 'being a friend of Peter, as you point out, if I were to find out, then...'

'Yes,' she said.

I put out my cigarette in the ashtray and lit another one. I pretended to think about things for a while.

'On the other hand,' I said, 'the way you've described Peter's behaviour, it hardly seems as though just an affair alone would make him… I mean, there could be something else. Something he can't tell you. A business problem, something financial…'

She didn't say anything.

'If it was something like that,' I said, 'then perhaps I *could* help. If it was worse, more personal, more likely to affect your relationship with one another, well, I'd really rather not be the one to provide the ammunition.'

'I understand,' she said.

'At the same time,' I said, 'if I found that he wasn't having an affair, if it was something other than that, then perhaps that would help matters… it's tricky.'

She stood up.

'I know,' she said. 'I shouldn't have come. It was wrong of me.'

I stood up too.

'No,' I said, 'you were right. I meant what I said last night. I'm glad you came.'

She looked down at the floor.

'It was just… just…'

I reached out and took her hand. Then the tears came again and she let her shoulders fall forward and then I was holding her and her head was resting on my chest.

'I just wanted to know,' she said. I felt the dampness of her face on my shirt. 'One way or the other. It's just that I'm so unhappy.'

The scent of her hair was warm and soft below my face.

I smiled to myself. Then I said: 'Look, don't worry. I'll help you, Sus…'

I stopped just in time, although I knew she hadn't noticed I'd almost called her Susan.

'Just leave it for a day or two,' I said. 'Don't do anything. I'll see if I can help. Just leave it with me.'

She lifted her head and put a hand to her face and took off her glasses so that she could dry her eyes. The movement caused me to drop my arms so that I was no longer holding her, so that she was no longer leaning against me.

'I'll see what I can do,' I said. 'Just leave it with me.'

KNOTT

I had to phone Kate. I had to try and make some kind of apology for what I'd done last night, or at least the beginnings of an apology. I couldn't let things continue so badly between us. The worse things got, the more likely it was that I'd lose control and do something foolish, something irreversible. Like what I'd done the night before. God what a bloody fool I'd been to do that. But I hadn't been able to help it. What had happened… that thing… touching me, almost close enough to…

I closed my eyes and tried to black out the picture of Camille's face. And when I'd managed to do that my thoughts flew somewhere equally unbearable: the big photograph of Eileen that had been on the front page of the morning paper, under the caption of HAVE YOU SEEN THIS GIRL? It had been taken from a holiday snap, enlarged and retouched. Her hair had been different then, and the bright summer sunshine had washed away the sharpness of her features which the retoucher had tried to redefine, and those factors combined with the grain of the blow up to make the picture hardly anything like her. But in death her features had altered too, mixing up like and unlike, and that was what the picture reminded me of, the alteration that her death had caused, the way she'd changed in front of my eyes, the way she was Eileen and not Eileen; the picture was grotesque enough to have been taken in death.

I looked at my watch. It was nearly ten-thirty. Dave was

leaning against the edge of my desk, looking at the handbag transparencies.

'Well, there you are,' he said, turning slightly and dropping the transparencies on my desk. 'If you're turned on by well photographed handbags, then those handbag photographs will turn you on, even if I do say so myself.'

I picked up the transparencies and put them on the light box and snapped on the switch. It was nearly time for Dave to go out and get the buns while my receptionist made the coffee. I wanted Angela to go for the buns and for Dave to make the coffee because I wanted to talk to Kate without any fear of Angela listening in.

So I said to Dave: 'This group will have to be re-shot.'

Dave slid off the edge of the table.

'Which group?'

'This one.' I handed him the relevant shots. 'This batch with the phony alligator skin.'

Dave held them up to the light.

'What's up with them?' he said. 'They're bloody marvellous, man.'

'I don't think so,' I said. 'The texture doesn't stand out enough. Could be anything.'

'Stands out a treat,' Dave said.

'Well as you work for me and not, as yet, vice versa, then I'd appreciate it if you'd get on with it. Starting now.'

'I was going out for the buns.'

'Yes, well, we're in a hurry so tell Angela to go and get them and you can be setting up while you're waiting for the kettle to boil. And tell her to leave me a line open on my phone before she goes.'

Dave went towards the door, looking at the transparencies as he went.

'Bloody hell,' he said, closing the door behind him.

A minute later Angela rang through and told me she had my line for me. I gave her a few minutes to get out of reception then I dialled home.

There was no reply. I dialled twice more. Still no reply. She must be out shopping. Or visiting, having coffee with one of her friends. But then I realised that Kate wouldn't be able to do that, not after what I'd done to her the night before. Or just get in the car and go shopping either. I knew Kate too well to have let myself think that. Then where was she?

Perhaps last night had been too much. The final straw. Once before, a year ago, she'd walked out, threatening to leave, and she'd got as far as the gates to her father's drive before turning round and coming back home. But then I hadn't done anything as bad to her as I'd done last night.

She couldn't have left. Not now. If she'd only stay with me now, forgive last night, see this time out with me, then I'd be able to bear it. But to be on my own, now, would be unthinkable. The madness would spread through me and then there was no telling what would happen. Who else could I turn to?

Only Plender.

I dialled the number again.

PLENDER

'But you told me I only had to take him there,' said Knott. 'You said nothing about anything else.'

'I know I didn't, mate,' I said. 'I know. It was sprung on me at the last minute. I just didn't think you'd mind helping out, that's all.'

'I told you the situation on the phone,' he said. 'About my wife, I mean.'

'Oh, sure,' I said, 'but I didn't think old Peter Knott'd have any trouble pulling the wool over the old lady's eyes.'

'You promised,' he said.

'Yes, well, situations change, don't they?'

He didn't say anything.

'And I must say,' I said. 'You put me in a bit of a spot. Our Mr Reed was most irate. Mind you, when the pros and cons of the situation had been made perfectly clear, he was rather reasonable about things, but nevertheless, it wasn't the way I'd hoped that things would turn out.'

'It was that... it was Camille.'

I laughed.

'Give you a fright, did she?'

He didn't answer.

'You need another drink,' I said.

I got up and went to the bar and ordered two more drinks and took them back to the table. I pushed his drink across to him and took a drink of mine and sat back and watched him. Eventually he reached for his glass and while he was drinking I said:

'What's it like round your way?'

He stared at me.

'What's it like?' I said. 'I mean socially. Much social life, is there?'

'Some,' he said, still staring.

'What sort of thing? Parties? Dinner parties? Get togethers?'

He nodded, slowly.

'So you know one or two people around Corella Way and its environs, do you?'

He kept nodding his head, wondering what was coming next.

'Know a bloke called Froy, do you?'

He shook his head.

'Lives near you,' I said. 'Well, when I say near, in your area.'

'Why?' he said.

'I wanted to know something about him and I wondered whether you knew him.'

He kept on looking at me.

'Funnily enough, he uses the Ferry Boat from time to time.'

He began to shake his head again, the movement accelerating until it looked as if he was having a spasm. Abruptly, the movement stopped.

'No,' he said.

'What do you mean?' I said.

'Whatever you want me to do.'

I didn't say anything.

'I can't do any more,' he said. 'I can't. You don't know what's happening to me.'

'Listen,' he said. 'Just listen. I know what you've done. But I didn't ask you to do it. You may have done it for the best, but...'

'But what? Maybe I should have just let you get on with it yourself. And if I had you can bet your life that you wouldn't be sitting here discussing the finer points of whys and wherefores if I'd done just that.'

He looked down at the table.

'I'm beginning to think I made a bit of a mistake,' I said. 'It's starting to look as though I should have let you get on with it. I mean, what am I getting out of it? Not even a thank you, and that's for sure.'

I finished my drink and stood up. Knott jerked his head back and stared into my face.

'Where are you going?' he said.

'Somewhere other than here,' I said. 'Somewhere I may even feel a little bit wanted.'

I pushed my chair back and began to button up my coat. He stretched his arm out and caught hold of my sleeve.

'Wait,' he said. 'Don't go.'

I looked at him.

'You want me to stay?'

He nodded. I sat down.

'What do you want me to do?' he said.

KNOTT

I didn't go back to the studio. Instead I drove into the city centre and parked my car in the car park of the first cinema I came to and went inside. It must have been the big film that was showing when I went in, but it wouldn't have mattered if there had been nothing in front of me but a blank white screen. I just wanted a black womb to sit inside, a soft darkness that demanded nothing from me, an auditorium big enough in which to free my thoughts without sending back any echoes. As it was I stared at the screen and allowed the meaningless shadows to fill my mind. I sat there for over two hours, letting myself be absorbed into the flatness of the lives that were being projected on to the screen.

At three o'clock I left the cinema and drove home. The Hillman wasn't in the garage but I knew that wherever Kate had been all day, she would be picking up the kids from school at approximately this time. The only question was would she be bringing them home?

I went into the house and looked to see if any of Kate's and the kids' things were missing, but as far as I could tell everything seemed to be there, and none of the suitcases had been taken.

I went into the lounge and poured a drink and waited.

Eventually I heard the Hillman turn into the drive, and a little while after the front door burst open and then the kids were rushing into the room and jumping all over me.

'Daddy,' Kevin said, 'have you seen Mummy's funny eye?'

'It's all blue and purple,' said Nicola. 'She walked into the kitchen door last night. Did you see her do it?'

'No,' I said, getting up.

'It must have been a hoot,' said Kevin.

'Where's your mother?'

'In the kitchen, I expect,' said Nicola.

I left the kids in the lounge and walked through to the kitchen. Kate had started to prepare the kids' tea. She didn't look up from what she was doing.

I stood there for a few moments without speaking.

'Kate,' I said eventually.

She took no notice. I walked towards her.

'Kate,' I said, 'look...'

She stood stock still and even though she had her back to me she threw up her hands, rigid, palms outwards, as though to ward me off.

'Don't,' she said. 'I don't want you to say anything.'

'But I want to,' I said. 'I want to...'

'All I need,' said Kate, 'is a few days. Just give me that, Peter. Just a few days, so that I can think.'

'All right,' I said. 'I'll give you that. But I just wanted to say...'

'I know what you wanted to say, Peter,' she said, 'and I don't want to hear you say it. I mean that. I really do.'

I nodded my head, even though she wasn't looking at me. There was a silence.

'And now,' she said, 'please leave me alone. I have to get the children's tea ready.'

I stood there for a few minutes longer, then I turned and walked out of the kitchen.

PLENDER

A few days later I phoned Kate Knott.

'Kate,' I said. 'It's Brian Plender. I've got some news.'

There was a pause before she answered.

'I see,' she said.

'Could I come out and see you?' I said. 'I'd rather do that than discuss anything over the phone.'

'Yes,' she said. 'That would be better.'

I took my time driving over.

All the leaves on the city's trees had gone now. A cold light wind pecked at the awnings of the shops and the sky was a clear October blue. The afternoon traffic dawdled along the main roads leading out of the city and I felt relaxed and lazy as I drove towards Corella Way.

When I got to Knott's house Kate Knott was standing behind the plate glass of the hallway, staring out at me as I parked my car in the drive. She watched me all the way as I walked to the house.

I nodded and said Hello as she opened the door for me but she didn't say anything, hardly even looked at me.

I was led into the lounge.

'Would you like a drink?' she said.

'Thank you,' I said.

'I'm sorry,' she said. 'Please sit down.'

I sat down. She walked over to the drinks cabinet and opened it and then turned to me and said: 'I should have asked: would you prefer tea?'

I shook my head.

'Scotch, gin, vodka…?'

'Vodka,' I said. 'With a little tonic.'

She poured the vodka.

'Ice?'

'Please,' I said.

'I mentioned the tea,' she said as she dropped in the ice, 'because normally that's what I have about this time. But today I thought a drink might be more appropriate.'

I didn't say anything.

She poured herself a drink. Her movements were careful, precise, self-contained, each action like a brittle buffer, designed to absorb any outside pressures that might be waiting. She brought the drinks over and gave me mine and sat down opposite me. We faced each other in the same way that we'd faced each other in my office. We both drank. She set her glass down on the table and said:

'You said you had some news.'

I nodded.

'I'd like to hear it,' she said.

I searched for my cigarettes but she slid a box across the table. I took a cigarette from the box and lit up.

'It's very difficult,' I said. 'The fact that I'm Peter's friend, that I like you both…'

'You don't have to tell me anything if you don't want to,' she said. 'But then why did you phone?'

'Would you rather I hadn't?'

She shook her head.

'Remember,' I said, 'it was you that came to me.'

'Yes, I know. I'm sorry.'

I didn't say anything for a while.

'Do go on,' she said. 'I didn't mean to sound like that.'

'I know,' I said. 'But before I do, I'd like you to tell me something.'

'What?'

'I want to know what you intend doing.'

'What about?'

'About what I've got to tell you. I have to know.'

'Then it's what I expected.'

'You see you have to understand. I don't want to be responsible... I mean I don't want to feel...'

'You don't want to be responsible for the break-up of an old friend's marriage.'

I didn't say anything.

'Well, you're not, are you?' she said. 'I mean in that case the old friend's responsible. It would be his actions that were responsible for any break-up that took place. The breaking-up would be his. You're just an instrument. Without Peter there'd be nothing to tell.'

'Perhaps not,' I said. 'I just wanted you to know how I feel.'

'And for that,' she said, 'I'm responsible. God, what a bloody situation.'

'Yes,' I said.

She didn't say anything for a moment or two. I looked round the room, as though I was trying to avoid her eyes.

'Tell me what you know,' she said. 'Even though I do know already.'

I looked at my glass.

'Well,' I said reluctantly, 'you were right.'

She nodded her head.

'It is a girl,' I said.

There was a silence.

'It's serious, isn't it?' she said.

'I don't know,' I said.

'Yes, it's serious,' she said. 'For him to behave this way.'

I didn't say anything.

'Tell me about her,' she said.

'There's nothing to tell,' I said. 'I've seen them together on three separate occasions but I don't know her name.'

'I expect she's pretty.'

I didn't answer.

'She'd have to be,' she said. 'Pretty, and the younger the better.'

'She seems quite young,' I said.

'You see, it's happened before,' she said, almost as if she was talking to herself. 'At least three times. I mean, those are the times I know about. Well, only once, definitely, with real proof, I mean, the other times I just knew. I was certain, but I knew nothing. But at the same time I knew they meant nothing. Oh, they meant something to me. I felt... well, never mind. But they meant nothing to Peter. Just... what do they call it now... ego-tripping? He loves being liked. He needs to be liked, to be the centre of things, to be admired. But I expect you know all that.'

I didn't say anything.

'So that's what I'd try and remember,' she said. 'To keep me sane: that whatever was happening was happening without meaning.'

I took another cigarette from the box and lit from the stub of the one I was smoking.

'But I made a promise to myself. I always said to myself that if he ever got involved, if he put what he had with me and the kids at risk, then I'd walk out on him. Because I'd hate him for loving someone more than us. Valuing something more than his children, more than me. I'd want to take everything away from him, make him forfeit everything. Make him realise the lie by bringing him face to face with the truth by showing him what he'd chosen to risk being rid of.'

For the first time she looked directly into my face.

'You've seen them together,' she said. 'I'm right, aren't I?'

I looked away.

'They're in love, aren't they?'

I gave a tired-world-weary-slightly-painful shrug of my shoulders.

'Yes,' she said. 'I know.'

'Look,' I said, 'don't. Don't do this...'

She began to cry. I got up and walked around the table and sat on the edge of the settee, next to her.

'Listen,' I said. 'I shouldn't have told you. I should never have...'

She began to shake her head.

'No,' she said. 'No. I wanted to know. I had to know. I had to. I had to know.'

I took hold of her hand and her body tilted towards me so that the whole weight of her body was leaning against me.

'I had to know,' she kept on saying. 'I had to know.'

I slipped my arm round her shoulders.

'I had to know.'

'Kate...'

'I had to. I had to.'

Very gently I pulled her even closer to me.

'Kate, listen, I'm sorry...'

'It's not your fault,' she said, turning her face towards me. 'It's not your fault. I asked you.'

My fingers were at the nape of her neck, pressing her head slowly towards mine. Then I lifted my other hand and brushed the hair away from her forehead and then her forehead was resting against mine.

'What am I going to do?' she said.

Now was the time. I kissed her full on the mouth.

Slowly we fell against the back of the settee. I pulled away for a second to look into her face. She stared up at me. Then I

248

kissed her again and she kissed me back. I felt her arms tighten round me. I pushed my hand down on to her breast and she kissed me even more fiercely. I moved my hand lower until my fingers found the warm nylon of her legs and I squeezed her thigh over and over and I felt her arms lock behind my neck and then I moved my hand upwards and slid my fingers in the top of her tights and her body began to writhe and squirm, pressing against me, and still she wouldn't let my mouth leave hers. Now my fingers were amongst the softness of her hair, and soon –

She broke away as violently as she'd pressed against me. I fell away from her, my back touching the arm of the settee. She rolled off the settee, landing on all fours on the floor.

'Christ,' she said. 'Bloody Christ.'

Then she began to cry even more, still on all fours, but letting her torso slump so that her bottom was sticking up in the air and her head was resting on her forearms.

'Christ, Christ, Christ,' she said.

I slid off the settee and knelt next to her, slipping my arms round her waist, pressing against her body with my body until I'd caused her to roll over on to her back.

'Kate,' I said.

Suddenly her face became calm, and her eyes filled with different thoughts. She stretched her arms above her head and slowly closed her eyes. I sank down on her and kissed her again. This time she was very passive. I kissed her for a long time. Her skirt was already up round her middle so I slid my hand to her waist and began to take off her tights and her underwear. To do this I had to stop kissing her and raise myself up on my elbow. I'd got her tights down as far as her knees when, in a flat voice, she said:

'It's no use.'

I froze.

Very quickly she sat up and tugged her tights back and slid

away from me and then she was on her feet, walking away towards the window.

For a moment or two I stayed where I was, the fury burning white behind my eyes. Then I stood up too, picking my drink off the table as I rose. I drank what was left and then gripped the glass, turning it over and over in my fingers. I had to blank out what had happened, make her start believing in my rôle again.

Eventually I managed to speak.

'I'm sorry,' I said.

She was standing with her back to me, looking out of the window.

'It doesn't matter,' she said.

'It does,' I said. 'I don't know why I… I mean, I didn't intend for that to happen.'

She shrugged.

'I was to blame, too,' she said.

'I don't want you to think that was planned. It wasn't. But now you're bound to suspect… to…'

'It doesn't matter,' she said. 'I wanted a kind of revenge, that's all.'

'Revenge?'

'On Peter. When we were lying on the floor. I wanted you to have me; it would have been perfect.'

'Perfect?'

'The irony: you of all people. The way Peter feels about you… I'm sorry. I shouldn't say that. But I know you understand what I mean.'

I heard a car go by in the road. It sounded a long way away.

'But I couldn't,' she said. 'I thought I'd be able to do it. It occurred to me when you came to dinner. I knew you were attracted to me. I thought: just supposing I could. Just supposing I could go through with it. And then after he hit me, after the other morning when I came to see you, I really thought I could.

But I had to have the excuse. I had to have the proof about Peter.'

She turned away from the window.

'Only the excuse wasn't good enough,' she said. 'I'm one of those stupid people the women's magazines are always inventing. I love my husband and I can't be other than faithful. I don't know whether it's love or guilt but whatever it is, I can't alter it. In spite of what Peter might have done.'

I put my glass down on the table.

'You think I planned it,' I said. 'You think I told you what I knew hoping that...'

She smiled at me. The smile was unbearable. So full of pity, sadness, sympathy, And disbelief. But a disbelief that, to her, was unimportant: it didn't matter what my motives had been. I was insignificant. Just someone to be sorry for.

'No,' she said. 'You did what I asked you to do.'

I couldn't stay there in the room with her any longer. I walked over to the door and opened it. But before I went there was something I had to know.

'About what I told you,' I said. 'What are you going to do?'

She shook her head.

'I need time to think,' she said. 'And don't worry. Whatever I do won't involve you. I shan't tell Peter where I got my information from.'

I closed the door behind me.

I went out of the house and got in my car and drove out of the drive and along Corella Way and took the first turning left and kept on driving until I found myself on rough ground at the river's edge.

I stopped the car and got out.

The wind had turned colder now and the river was like chopped gold in the afternoon sunlight.

I stared across the river at Brumby. I could see the square tower of St. Mary's rising behind the oaks on Beck Hill. And beyond Beck Hill the sunlit line of Westfield Road, with Susan's house on the brow of the hill, and beyond it, a little to the right, nearer to the river's edge, the quarry where Eileen's body lay.

KNOTT

I went to the Ferry Boat instead of going straight home. Plender had told me that the man called Froy sometimes went there for an early evening drink.

I sat on a stool at the bar and stared out of the window at the night. Across the river I could see the lights of the main road of Brumby. I wondered what my parents were doing. Probably my father would be in the lounge, asleep, his feet resting on the stool I'd made in woodwork at the grammar school, and my mother would be sitting at the kitchen table, smoking, the washing up draining on the sink unit. Nothing would have changed. Just the same as it had been twenty years ago, and would be till one of them died. I wished that I could intrude on the scene, walk into the kitchen and sit with my mother the way I used to do when I was a boy, spend a while talking to her until it was time for the pictures.

But now I was waiting in a pub on the other side of the river, on the off chance that someone I'd never met would come into the bar, because of the fact that somewhere a girl was lying dead. Lying dead.

What had he done with her? Had he buried her? Put her somewhere under the ground, covered her with earth and left her to rot? He must have done. What else? I began to imagine what she must look like at this moment, what was happening to her clothes and her hair and her face. All because of me.

Quickly I finished my drink and slid off the stool. I had to stop thinking. I had to get home, to surroundings that had some kind of simple reality that would neutralise the vividness of my imaginings.

I drove as quickly as I could. I was home within ten minutes.

There were no lights on in the house.

At first I thought that perhaps Kate was watching TV in the dark. She sometimes did that. But then I realised that the hall light was off too, and we always kept that on so that anyone approaching the house would be able to see where they were going.

I hurried into the house but I knew what had happened even before I found the note.

The note said:

'Peter,

I have gone to my father's with the children. I need to be away from you for a while. Don't come to see us. That would only make matters worse. I'll phone you in a few days' time when I've made up my mind what to do about the situation.

Kate'

After I'd read the note a few times I sat down on the settee and looked round the room. The house rang with emptiness. The curtains to the lounge windows were open and the black night stared in at me. The furniture seemed to scream silence at me. And my eyes kept moving back to the blackness of the windows, as if I was waiting for the dead figure of a girl to appear and illuminate the night.

I scrambled the phone towards me and dialled Plender's home number.

At first I thought he must be out because there was no answer for a long time but then I heard his voice say:

'Brian Plender speaking?'

'It's Peter,' I said. 'Are you busy?'

'Peter, old mate,' he said. 'What's on your mind?'

'Are you busy?'

'Not particularly. Why?'

'I wondered if I could see you.'

'Problems?'

He'd find out sooner or later so I said: 'It's Kate. She's gone.'

There was a slight pause before he said: 'Gone? Where?'

'To her father's. She's gone to her father's for a few days.'

'So what's so terrible about that?'

'She may not come back.'

There was an even longer pause this time.

'Well,' he said, 'I feel for you, mate, I really do. I mean, she's a bit of all right, is old Kate. Sorry to see her go. But I can't quite see what I can do about it.'

'No,' I said, 'what I mean is, I'm alone.'

'And?'

'And I wanted… to be with someone.'

'So you phoned your old mate, Brian.'

'Yes,' I said.

'Nice to know you feel you can,' he said.

'Can you see me?'

'Sure. Where?'

'I don't know. I don't want to go anywhere.'

'Well, that makes things a bit difficult, then, doesn't it?'

'What I mean is, could you come over? To my place?'

'You want me to come to your place?'

'Yes. I'd like you to. We could have a drink, talk…'

'Sounds like a nice idea,' he said. 'Yes, I'll do that. What time shall I come over?'

'Can you come now?'

'Well, I don't know. I can be there by about nine, if you like.'

'Yes,' I said. 'Nine. Or earlier, if you can.'

I put the phone down and got up and drew the curtains and

switched on the television. Then I poured a drink and sat on the settee and stared at the screen until I heard Plender's car turn into the drive.

I hurried to the front door and opened it and watched him stroll towards me, into the light. He smiled at me as he got to the door.

'I'm glad you could come,' I said.

He walked past me and into the lounge without speaking.

I made him a drink and we sat down opposite each other.

'So you've got the place to yourself,' he said.

I nodded.

'Yes,' I said. 'I didn't expect anything like this.'

'Never can tell with women,' he said. 'One minute one thing, the next another. Inconsistent.'

'I don't know what I'm going to do.'

'Just carry on living. She'll be back.'

'She won't. I know it.'

'No, she'll be back. I know women. She won't want to chuck all this out of the window.'

I stood up and went to the cocktail cabinet and brought the bottles over to the table.

'I had to phone,' I said. 'I can't be on my own right now.'

'How come?'

I stared at him.

'But you must know why,' I said.

'Oh,' he said. 'Yes. Yes, see what you mean. You're... er... you're getting a bit jumpy, are you?'

I nodded.

'You should take my advice,' he said. 'Forget it. Nothing's going to happen.'

'I can't forget. I keep thinking about her. About the girl.'

Plender didn't say anything.

'Look,' I said. 'I know you've said you won't tell me, but I must know, it keeps preying on my mind. Maybe I'll feel better if I know what you did.'

Plender smiled and shook his head.

'Just tell me what you did with her. You don't have to tell me where.'

'How do you mean?'

'Is she... did you bury her?'

Plender smiled again and took a drink.

'What do you think I did with her? Just left her lying around somewhere so that somebody could trip over her?'

I buried my face in my hands.

'I don't know,' I said. 'I don't know.'

'Well, all right,' he said, 'I'll tell you. She's under the ground in a nice safe place. She'll be well on the way of all flesh by now.'

'Stop,' I said. 'Don't.'

'You asked me,' he said. 'I didn't think it would make you feel any better.'

'Just tell me everything's going to be all right,' I said. 'That's all I want to know. That everything's going to be all right.'

'I keep telling you that, don't I, mate?' he said. 'But I just seem to be wasting my breath.'

'I'm frightened,' I said. 'You must realise that.'

He nodded.

'Yes, well,' he said, 'why don't we change the subject? Take your mind off it.'

I didn't say anything.

'Tell you what,' he said. 'I was only thinking about it the other day, actually. Remember that time old Pondy caught us scrumping in his orchard?'

I nodded: a numbing sickness was spreading through my body.

'Christ,' he said. 'That was a laugh. Remember, I got caught and you and Dreevo...'

PLENDER

I woke up with the sun shining on my face. I opened my eyes and looked round the room. It looked even better by daylight. Beautiful in fact. Everything just so, everything designed and decorated to the last detail.

I swung back the sheets and put on the dressing gown Knott had lent me. Even that seemed to blend with the decor of the room.

I went into the corridor and looked in Knott's room. He was still asleep. I went into the kitchen and made some coffee and took it into the lounge and sat down on the settee where I'd been with Knott's wife.

She was going to be sorry about what had happened on that day. The Knott and Froy thing would have to be sacrificed, of course. But I could afford to wait for Froy. I couldn't wait for Kate. The memory was too recent. The only trouble was, I'd no idea where her father lived.

The lounge door opened and Knott came in, still wearing his pyjamas.

'Hail, smiling morn,' I said.

Knott didn't say anything. I indicated the coffee pot on the table.

'Just made,' I said. 'Grab a cup. You look as if you need some.'

Knott went away and came back with a cup and poured himself some coffee.

'So what's the plan for today?' I said.

'What?' Knott said.

'The plan of action,' I said. 'Is it work, or what?'

'Oh, yes. It's work. I have to go in to the studio.'

'On a Saturday?'

'Yes. We're behind.'

'Much to do?'

'Yes.'

I stretched out on the settee.

'Well,' I said, 'today's the day I take things easy. Feet up and all that kind of thing. You'll be working all day, will you?'

He nodded.

'What time will you be back?'

He looked at me.

'I was thinking,' I said, 'if you're likely to feel tonight the same way you did last night, then I may as well stick around. I've nothing to do this weekend. I mean, it's up to you.'

He looked away.

'Brian,' he said. 'Last night I...'

'Say no more,' I said, getting up. 'If you'll be all right, then there's no point in my hanging about then, is there?'

I got as far as the door before he said: 'No, I didn't mean that. I'd like you to stay. I'd feel better if you did.'

'That's more like it,' I said. 'Tell you what, when you come home tonight, why don't we make a night of it? Put our suits on, go down the town and have a few drinks. Just like old days. Do you a power of good.'

Knott didn't answer.

'What do you say?' I said.

KNOTT

I drove towards town but I wasn't thinking about the traffic. My thoughts were full of the nightmare my life had become. Waiting for the worst to happen. My wife leaving me. Strung to Plender like a puppet. Going through each day carrying the weight of what had happened, turning into a staring, crouching, joyless thing. My mind was bulging with the pressure that was inside me. When I got to the studio I began work straightaway, trying to keep my thoughts as mechanical as my actions, but at eleven-thirty, when I was taking a break and waiting for the kettle to boil, the quietness of the studio began to creep in on me, and images of what had happened there began to take shape in the silence.

I snapped off the switch of the kettle and walked into reception and put on my coat.

I had to get Kate and my kids back.

PLENDER

Steam rose from the hot water. I nudged my foot against the hot water tap and shut it off. I lay there for a while, letting the sweat and the condensation roll off me. Then I bathed myself and dried myself and stood in front of the full-length wall-wide mirror and shaved myself with Knott's electric razor.

After I'd done that I put Knott's dressing gown back on and went into the kitchen and made myself breakfast and read the paper. Then I lit a cigarette and began to search the house for something bearing Kate Knott's maiden name, like a marriage certificate, so that I would be able to look up her father's number in the phone book. I couldn't rely on the possibility of her phoning Knott, here at the house. I was almost certain she wouldn't be getting in touch with him other than by way of her lawyers. And what I had to tell her would make that certainty a fact.

So I began to search. I could take my time, enjoy it. I had all day.

KNOTT

I'd forgotten what the date was.

I stopped my car halfway up the drive that led to Mark Dixon's and looked at all the cars parked outside his house. There must have been almost a hundred, many of them with chauffeurs. I closed my eyes. His bloody birthday. Why did it have to be his bloody birthday? Every year he did this, invited all his friends and his business associates and his business rivals to this party, an affair that started at noon and usually went on till the late afternoon or early evening. There were always three or four bars specially set up throughout the house and a buffet that never ran out. Kate and I were always expected to attend, to watch him play the benign industrialist, loved and admired by all.

I swore. How could I talk to Kate now? How could I get her to listen to me? I knew Kate. She'd use the crowd to screen her, to allow her to walk away from me, secure in the knowledge that I'd never make a scene, not there.

But there was one advantage. At least I'd be able to get past the front door.

I parked my car and walked up the steps. The men on the door knew me, and we nodded to each other.

The hall was packed. I looked around for Kate but I couldn't see any sign of her. I didn't want to go too far into the house in case I ran into her father. Luckily I saw Negus, Dixon's head man, making his way towards the study, so I pushed my way through the crowd and caught up with him.

'Negus,' I said, 'where's Mrs Knott?'

'Mrs Knott?' he said, giving me a look he'd been wanting to give me for a long time. 'I'm afraid I've no idea.'

'All right,' I said. 'You've got your instructions. But I know you don't want a scene right here and now so you'd better tell me. Where is she?'

'Mrs Knott is out,' he said.

'Come on,' I said. 'I know she's here.'

'She is staying here temporarily, sir,' he said. 'But at present I know for a fact Mrs Knott happens to be out. I believe she has taken the children down to the river. I'm afraid I don't know when to expect her back.'

I gave him a long look. He wasn't lying. Kate would want to spend as little time as possible at this party, this year.

'And now, sir, if you'll excuse me?'

He walked off. Straight to tell Dixon I was here, of course. Well, sod him. I was here and I was staying until Kate got back.

I walked over to the trestle table and asked for a large scotch.

PLENDER

The letter was dated the twelfth of April, nineteen fifty-nine.

'Dear Peter,
'How can I put into words all I want to say? I was so full of different thoughts and feelings after I left you tonight, some wonderful, some frightening, all of them tugging my mind in different directions.

What happened tonight was so incredibly marvellous that I'm just incapable of describing how I feel. The words "I love you" just aren't enough. And yet I'm scared. Scared that what happened might change things between us. Not the way that I feel, but the way that you think. You might be worried in case, now that it's happened, I might be different towards you; you see, I know all of your fears.

But, my love, I'll never change towards you. I love you too much. You have to believe that. Nothing will change. Except perhaps for the better. But how can things possibly get better when they're the way they are now?

I love you
Kate'

I put this letter down on the dressing table-top, along with the others.

KNOTT

I watched Kate walk through the crowd towards me, but she didn't look at me. When she got to me, she asked the barman to give her a drink. She took a sip and then she said:

'I thought you might do this.'

'Kate,' I said. 'Let's not talk here.'

'This is the best place to talk,' she said.

'Not for what I want to say.'

'I don't want to hear what you've got to say.'

'You must listen to me,' I said, swaying into the table and rocking it a little.

'God, must you always get like this?'

The roar of the party swept into my ears.

'Kate...'

'Peter,' she said, 'I want you to listen to me. I'm going to say something to you and then I'm going to walk away. If you do anything, I've talked to my father, and he'll have you put out.'

'I've seen him already,' I said. 'He's just loving this. He's waited for this to happen since the day we got married.'

She brushed a strand of hair from her forehead.

'Peter, are you going to listen?'

I didn't say anything.

'I'm leaving you,' she said.

I looked her in the face. Everything else blurred into the background.

'What I mean is, I want a divorce. I don't want to go on living with you any more.'

I shook my head.

'No,' I said. 'You don't mean what you're saying.'

'I do mean it, Peter.'

'You can't.'

She didn't answer.

'Not now,' I said. 'You can't leave me now.'

'Why not now?' she said.

I shook my head.

'Quite,' she said, and walked away.

'Kate,' I said, but I knew she couldn't hear me. I pushed through the crowd in the direction she'd gone. She was nowhere to be seen. I got as far as the staircase. Then I gave up. What was the use? Drunk as I was, I knew she meant it. And I knew there was nothing I could say or do to change her mind. I was too sick and empty even to try.

I sat down on the stairs. Christ, what was I going to do now?

I sat there for a while, watching the party sway back and forth across my vision. I had no inclination to move, to do anything. It was as if moving would jolt my senses and rearrange my nervous system into its proper order, and allow the pain to start seeping back.

Then somebody came and sat next to me.

'Enjoying it?' said a voice.

I turned my head slightly.

'The party,' said the man. 'Enjoying the party?'

I didn't say anything.

'You're Mark's son-in-law, aren't you?'

I took a proper look at the man. Silver hair, swept back from the forehead. Leather sports jacket. Bright cravat. Just like the picture...

'My name's Froy,' he said, holding out his hand. 'I'm a close associate of Mark's.'

…Plender had given me.

Froy?

I looked into his face.

The silver hair. The eyes. The mouth, and smile on it. The grip of his hand.

I shuddered. Sickness welled up inside me.

Still he held my hand.

'We've never met before, but I've heard a lot about you.'

'Get away,' I said.

He released my hand and stared at me.

'What on earth's the matter?'

The pressure finally burst through.

I caught hold of the man by his cravat and began to shake him as hard as I could. The man's drink slipped from his fingers and suddenly the party went totally quiet and the only sound was the smashing of Froy's glass as it hit the floor. The only sound except for my screaming. I was only vaguely aware of the words that were pouring out of my mouth, words about Kate and Eileen and Plender and Peggy. Then I sensed a movement behind me so I threw Froy to the floor and jumped away from the movement and charged my way through the stunned crowd, calling Plender's name as I ran.

PLENDER

By nine o'clock I was beginning to worry a bit. I knew he'd got a lot of work on, but then he'd said he'd be home early, home in time to have a meal before we went out. I'd phoned the studio a couple of times in the last hour or so but there'd been no reply. Where the bloody hell was he? I didn't like it when I didn't know where he was. Those were the times that were most dangerous for me: the times he was most likely to do something stupid.

I lit another cigarette and went into the main bedroom and looked it over. Only someone with my experience could ever tell I'd virtually turned it upside down. But it had all been a waste of time: I'd been through every drawer and cupboard in the house and I hadn't turned up anything with Kate Knott's maiden name on it.

I went into the kitchen and made another cup of coffee.

Where the hell was Knott?

KNOTT

Dawn light drifted in through the hotel window. I lay on the bed, my back leaning on the pillows I'd propped against the wall. I'd been like that for the last seventeen or eighteen hours. I didn't want to move and at the same time I didn't want to do anything else. I'd drunk the best part of a bottle of scotch but I'd gone beyond drunkenness and even sleep wouldn't come. I'd just lain there, letting the events of the past week unfold in my brain like a flower in a time-lapse film. All the pain had gone now and all I was left with was a numb feeling of despair.

But at least I'd come to a decision.

PLENDER

At two-thirty on Sunday afternoon I left Knott's house and drove back to my digs. There was no point in me staying there any longer. I'd keep ringing the house at regular intervals until he showed up. If he showed up. But there was nothing else I could do. I just had to wait. But if he walked into the nearest police station I was well covered; my story was watertight. What I'd intended springing on Kate Knott I could spring on the police. The fact that I'd discovered that Knott had been having an affair with a girl who was now missing by finding some discovered pictures of her in his studio would go down very well. Knott's counter-charge, that I'd got rid of the body for him without even being asked to do it, would sound like so much wishful thinking. There was only the bit about taking his car that seemed the slightest bit dubious. But that would seem crazy enough just to be true. It had been good enough for Kate Knott; it would be good enough for the Boys in Blue.

But, anyway, for Christ's sake, he wasn't going to walk into any police station. When it came right down to it, he was too fond of himself to do anything like that.

On the way into my digs I picked the latest tape on Froy from the letter box and took it up to my room with me. I closed the door behind me and took my coat and my jacket off and hung them up and pulled on a thick sweater and lit the gas fire.

Then I made myself a cup of coffee and put the tape on

the machine and lay down on my bed with a cigarette and my coffee and listened to the tape.

KNOTT

I went home first, just in case he was still there. At least that's
what I told myself. His car was no longer in the drive, but I
went into the house just the same. I went into every room, and
stood quietly in each one for a while, taking in all the details
you never normally notice: the overturned bottle of scent on
Kate's dressing table, the old teddy on top of the wardrobe in
the kids' room, the old newspapers Kate kept stacked down
the side of the sink unit. I took in everything, calmly, but each
item made the weight in my stomach a little heavier; but I did
remain calm, because I knew that to be otherwise would make
the exercise meaningless. After I'd done that I went to one of the
photo albums and picked out a shot of us all, one that a sea-front
photographer had taken at Scarborough. I put it in my pocket
and started to leave the house.

I'd got as far as the hall when the phone began to ring. I stood
there for a moment, wondering whether or not to answer it. And
then I thought that it might be Plender so I went back into the
study and picked up the receiver.

It was Kate.

'Peter?' she said.

'Yes.'

There was a silence. Then she said.

'I wondered what had happened to you. If you were all
right.'

God. I thought, not now. Not now I've made my decision.

I said:

'I'm fine.'

She didn't say anything.

'I'm sorry about yesterday,' I said.

'Listen, Peter,' she said. 'I've been talking to Daddy. He knows Plender. Knows of him, I mean. So does the man you hit. They wanted to know what connection you had with him. I told them what had happened, how you met, and they seemed concerned. I couldn't make out why, quite. But Daddy wants to talk to you. He thinks it's important that you should talk to him. So do I. I think something's wrong. Because of Plender.'

'Kate...'

'Peter, I want to come back.'

I couldn't speak.

'I want to help. Whatever it is. But look, talk to Daddy first. He's here now. Then –'

I put the phone down and stood there for a long time, just listening to the silence of the house.

PLENDER

I couldn't believe what I was hearing. Even after I'd played the tape a third time.

There were the usual ringing tones, then the receiver was lifted and Froy's voice said:

'Brown speaking.'

'Have you any news?' said the voice of the leader.

'We've put a watch on his flat but as yet he hasn't turned up.'

'And his office?'

'The same.'

There was a silence. Then the leader said: 'I wish I knew exactly what's been going on.'

'So do I, sir. Whatever it is, I'm afraid we have to assume that it's dangerous to the Movement.'

'Quite. I've got as much from my daughter this afternoon as I possibly can without making her suspicious, but there's nothing much to add to what she said while you were here: they made contact a week or so ago, he's been to the house twice, once at her invitation over this divorce business, and that's it.'

'We'll find out anything else there is to know when we question him, sir.'

'Of course. But whatever it is, he's finished. This is too close to me. We'll have to get rid of him.'

'Yes,' said Froy. 'You see I can't help thinking the worst, as I've said. Blackmail's his trade, and I'm very much afraid your son-in-law may be on his books.'

'If he ever discovered the connection between my son-in-law and myself…'

'I know.'

'So what do you intend to do?'

'Nothing till tomorrow. The people to pick him up don't get back from the meeting until late tomorrow afternoon. But I'll get on to them as soon as they return.'

'Phone me as soon as you have anything.'

'I will, sir.'

Then the line went dead. I switched off the machine.

I'd already checked about the man outside.

I sat on the edge of my bed, trying to take it in, but the thoughts in my mind refused to be organised into any kind of shape. The only thing constant in my mind was the repetition of the word finished.

It was over. The whole thing. I was finished. I'd finished myself.

I stood up.

This was where I needed all my self discipline; I'd made plans to cover this kind of a situation. I had to pull myself together and accept what had happened, however sick it was making me. Otherwise I wouldn't be finished; I'd be dead. I put my holdall on the bed and then I opened the safe and took out my money and my photostats and put them in the bottom of the bag and covered them with a few clothes. I took my gun and holster out of my drawer and put the gun on the bed and began to strap on my holster.

There was a knock on the door. I didn't move.

'Mr Plender,' came Mrs Fourness's voice. 'There's somebody to see you.'

I didn't answer.

I heard her mumble something to whoever it was and then she said: 'It's a Mr Knott. Are you at home?'

I walked over to the door and opened it a couple of inches. Then I opened it properly when I saw Knott standing next to Mrs Fourness.

'I hope it's all right,' she said. 'He said it would be.'

'Yes, it's all right,' I said.

Knott came into the room and I closed the door behind him. I saw him look at the holdall and the gun.

'That's right,' I said. 'I'm leaving.'

'Leaving? Why?'

Suddenly I felt very tired.

'You'd never believe me in a million years,' I said.

'But you can't leave yet.'

'Oh,' I said. 'Why's that?'

'Because I want you to show me where Eileen is.'

I smiled.

'Sorry,' I said.

'You'll be quite safe,' he said. 'I won't involve you. I won't tell the police anything about you. I just need to know where the body is. They have to have a body. Otherwise they might not believe me.'

I looked at him. He must have gone completely out of his mind. He didn't even realise that with me out of the way he had nothing to worry about. Christ, that would be funny if I had to tell him that.

Then the phone rang. Without thinking, I picked it up. The minute I put the receiver to my ear the line went dead. They were on their way. It was too late.

Knott picked up the gun from off the bed.

'Take me,' he said. 'I have to know where she is.'

I looked at him. They were only a few minutes away. The plans I'd made were useless now. Unless...

'I must know,' he said. 'Please take me.'

They wouldn't try and take me with Knott around, that was certain. That was something I'd taught them. Not in daylight, not when they could be identified. But the quarry, that would be different; if I let them follow me it would be dark by the time we got there; they'd try then. And I'd have the advantage there; I knew every square inch of the place.

I put my jacket on and picked up my holdall.

'All right,' I said. 'I'll take you.'

KNOTT

The closer we got the more terrified I became. It was the thought of being close to something that had once been alive, something I'd once made love to, something that was now under the earth, with the earth's things moving through it... I squeezed my eyes tight shut and thrust my hand in my pocket and gripped the cold handle of Plender's gun, like a child who is frightened of the dark grips his toy pistol under the bedclothes.

After we'd been driving for almost three-quarters of an hour, the possibility of where Plender might be taking me began to dawn on me.

'Where?' I said. 'Where did you put her?'

'I'm going to show you, mate, aren't I?' he said. 'I mean, that's what I'm here for, isn't it?'

'Not... not near there.'

Plender shrugged.

'Wait and see,' he said. 'Wait and see. This is Brian Plender's magical mystery tour. The fun starts when the ride finishes.'

He began to whistle to himself.

PLENDER

They'd kept behind me all the way. I had to give them credit; they were doing a good job. Nobody else would have guessed we were being followed.

We reached the top of the hill that overlooked Brumby. Just before I turned left down the track that led to the quarry I said:

'Want to drop in for a cup of tea with your mam before we get to the scene of the crime?'

'Shut up,' he said.

I laughed.

'Now, now Brian,' I said. 'You're not in the big city now so let's have less of your big city ways.'

We got to the overhung entrance of the quarry and I crawled the car along the narrow track until it opened out into the quarry basin and then I turned right and drove towards the old engine houses.

When we got there I switched off the engine and the lights.

Knott was sitting bolt upright, stiff with fear.

'Well, here we are,' I said.

I opened my door and got out and listened. Very faintly I could hear the other car crawling along the track. I looked back at the entrance. Dusk was turning into full night now and the mouth of the entrance was hardly visible.

I walked round to the passenger side of the Cortina and banged on the roof and opened the door.

'Let's be having you, then,' I said. 'No time for shilly-shallying. We haven't got all night.'

Knott got out of the car as if he expected something to charge out of the darkness and leap on him.

'Over here,' I said, walking towards the engine house. Knott followed me, walking on eggs. I stopped in front of the upside-down panniers.

'Now then,' I said, stroking my chin. 'Let's have a little think. Which one was it? Do you know, I'm not entirely sure I can remember.'

Knott stared at the panniers.

'Under there?' he whispered.

'Er, yes, that's right,' I said. 'But which one?'

Knott took a step or two in front of me, as though drawn by a magnet.

'Here,' I said, 'you know what it reminds me of? Have you ever seen them do that trick down the market where they have three cups face down and a peanut and they cover the peanut and shift the cups around and you have to guess which cup the nut's under? This is like that, isn't it?'

Knott sank down on to his knees.

'God,' he said. 'God help me, please.'

'Well,' I said, 'you pays your money and you takes your choice.'

The other car nosed into the quarry and the noise of its engine became suddenly louder as it fanned out across the quarry floor.

Knott twisted round like a rabbit in a snare.

'What's that?' he said.

'Friends of mine,' I said.

I saw the lights cut out and I heard the doors open.

'What's going on?' said Knott. 'For Christ's sake, tell me.'

'I couldn't begin to explain,' I said. 'But now I've done what I said I'd do, I'd like my gun back.'

Knott's hand dived into his pocket and he scrambled up

from the floor, bringing the gun out as he came.

'What's happening?' he screamed. 'Tell me what's happening.'

'For Christ's sake,' I said. 'Shut up and give me the fucking gun. I've got to move while I've the chance.'

I could hear the others moving in the direction of our voices.

'No,' said Knott. 'You haven't shown me. How do I know you're not lying? How do I know why you've brought me here?'

'The gun,' I said, walking towards him. 'Give me the fucking gun.'

'I'll kill you,' he said. 'If you don't show me, I will, I'll kill you.'

Then I heard Gurney shouting through the darkness.

'Plender?' he called. 'Are you going to come to us?'

'What do you think?' I shouted back.

I turned to Knott again.

'Quick,' I said. 'While I've got a chance.'

'It'd be best if you did,' shouted Gurney. 'It's only a talk we're after.'

Knott peered into the darkness in the direction of Gurney's voice.

'Why are they here?' he said. 'Why did you bring them?'

I made a dive for Knott and the gun but he turned towards me at exactly the moment I moved and, more out of surprise than anything else, he pulled the trigger. The bullet was yards wide of me but I automatically threw myself face down on the ground. When I looked up Knott was staring at the gun in amazement.

'All right, Mr Plender,' shouted Gurney. 'That's good enough for us.'

Three powerful torch beams cut through the night. That stupid sod Gurney thought I'd hauled off a shot at him. Knott turned slowly towards the light. I got to my feet and began to race for the back of the engine house.

KNOTT

Out of the corner of my eye I saw Plender get up and start running. Then I stared at the point where the light was coming from. I couldn't grasp what was happening. I couldn't believe it. What were these people trying to do? Whatever it was, they were preventing me from doing what I'd decided to do. How dare they? What right had they? They had to be stopped. I began to walk towards them. But the torch beams weren't trained on me. Two shots burst from the darkness and there was a crash behind me and I turned and looked where the shafts of light were pointing and I could see Plender, lying on the ground, shivering as if he was very very cold.

They've killed him, I thought. He's dead. My mind was very clear about the situation: they'd killed Plender, and now I'd have to look for Eileen myself. That wasn't fair of them. They must realise how unbearable that would be for me. They shouldn't have left me all alone, to do that. I had to let them know what they'd done to me.

PLENDER

I tried to roll over on to my back because the pain in my chest was too much to allow me to stay face down, but everything I tried to move made the pain worse so finally I had to give up. All I could do was to twist my head round to look in the direction of Knott.

I heard them begin to walk towards me, to finish the job. There was no point in taking me away now.

Then I heard Knott shout out: 'Look what you've done to him.'

'Shut up,' Gurney said. 'And stay where you are.' Two of the torches were trained on Knott now, but he had his hands at his sides, and the gun was out of range of the beam. Gurney ignored him and walked towards me, holding the other torch.

'You've killed him,' screamed Knott. 'Now what am I going to do?'

Gurney had almost reached me. Any minute now the gun would go off and that would be the last sound I'd hear. Not that it would make any difference. I knew how badly I'd been hit.

I waited for the sound of the gun.

KNOTT

I watched the beam of light shorten as the black shape approached Plender. Then the figuré stopped and I heard the hammers of the gun being pulled back.

Very quickly, I raised my own gun and pulled the trigger.

The beam of light swung through the blackness as the impact of my shot caused the man to throw his arms in the air above his head. For a split second the beam was marvellously perpendicular, shooting straight up into the night sky. Then it described a slow arc downwards again and smashed on the ground and went out. Almost immediately, one of the other torches veered over to the ground where Plender and the man were lying. For a brief second the beam played on the man's head, allowing me to see that I'd shot him in the back of the neck.

Then both the other torches swung away from me and the two men on the ground, and I listened to the footsteps of the others as they crashed away towards their car.

I walked over to where Plender was and knelt down next to him. He knew I was there because I could hear him trying to say something to me, the same words over and over, but I couldn't make them out.

Then, abruptly, the words stopped.

GBH

'When I turned round from the table Arthur's trousers and underpants were round his knees. Mickey took the glass from Arthur's hand and put it back on the card table and then he picked up the short strands of rope from next to the bucket and tied Arthur's ankles to the chair legs and his hands behind the chair back. After he'd done that Mickey moved the bucket a little closer to where Arthur was, causing a few drops of water to jump over the bucket's rim and slop down on to the bare floorboards. Then Mickey taped Arthur's mouth shut with some gauze and plaster… Mickey took his gloves from his pocket and put them on, then gathered the dangling wires to him, taking hold of them not quite at their naked ends. I was suddenly conscious of Jean's perfume as she moved very quietly to stand by my side. Now the games were over.'

In the twilight world of London's gangland, a porn king with a priceless and far-reaching empire is on the run from the mob in yet another stunning Ted Lewis thriller of violence, corruption and – grievous bodily harm…

978085730293 £8.99
www.noexit.co.uk

GETTING CARTER

Ted Lewis is one of the most important writers you've never heard of. Born in Manchester in 1940, he grew up in the tough environs of post-war Humberside, attending Hull College of Arts and Crafts before heading for London. His life described a cycle of obscurity to glamour and back to obscurity, followed by death at only 42. He sampled the bright temptations of sixties London while working in advertising, TV and films and he encountered excitement and danger in Soho drinking dens, rubbing shoulders with the 'East End boys' in gangland haunts. He wrote for *Z Cars* and had some nine books published. Alas, unable to repeat the commercial success of *Get Carter*, Lewis' life fell apart, his marriage ended and he returned to Humberside and an all too early demise.

Getting Carter is a meticulously researched and riveting account of the career of a doomed genius. Long-time admirer Nick Triplow has fashioned a thorough, sympathetic and unsparing narrative. Required reading for noirists, this book will enthral and move anyone who finds irresistible the old cocktail of rags to riches to rags.

9781843448822 £12.99
www.noexit.co.uk

NO EXIT PRESS
UNCOVERING THE BEST CRIME

'A very smart, independent publisher delivering the finest literary crime fiction' – *Big Issue*

MEET NO EXIT PRESS, the independent publisher bringing you the best in crime and noir fiction. From classic detective novels, to page-turning spy thrillers and singular writing that just grabs the attention. Our books are carefully crafted by some of the world's finest writers and delivered to you by a small, but mighty, team.

In our 30 years of business, we have published award-winning fiction and non-fiction including the work of a Pulitzer Prize winner, the British Crime Book of the Year, numerous CWA Dagger Awards, a British million copy bestselling author, the winner of the Canadian Governor General's Award for Fiction and the Scotiabank Giller Prize, to name but a few. We are the home of many crime and noir legends from the USA whose work includes iconic film adaptations and TV sensations. We pride ourselves in uncovering the most exciting new or undiscovered talents. New and not so new – you know who you are!!

We are a proactive team committed to delivering the very best, both for our authors and our readers.

Want to join the conversation and find out more about what we do?

Catch us on social media or sign up to our newsletter for all the latest news from No Exit Press HQ.

f fb.me/noexitpress 🐦 @noexitpress
noexit.co.uk/newsletter